WHEN THE KINGDOM COMES

JOHN BECKETT SERIES
BOOK 2

MATTHEW HATTERSLEY

BOOM BOOM PRESS

GET 'THE BECKETT FILES'

Read the exclusive transcript of John Beckett's top secret interview prior to him joining S-Unit.

You'll also get access to my VIP Newsletter and the opportunity to read all my books for free before anyone else.

To sign up and get 'The Beckett Files' go here:

https://www.matthewhattersley.com/jb/

1

A shimmering haze blanketed Porto's red-tiled rooftops as dawn broke over the ancient city. The morning light poured into the narrow cobbled streets, illuminating the old buildings rich with history.

Famed for its port wine, Porto was the second largest city in Portugal and one of the Iberian Peninsula's major urban areas. The city's residents were famous for being warm and friendly with a strong sense of pride in their community, and it was often said that if Lisbon served as the political hub of the country, then Porto was its industrious heart. The locals, still to this day, embraced their cultural heritage of productiveness and toil. They worked hard and they played hard.

But, recently, even the most positive-minded of citizens couldn't ignore the fact that a sinister shadow now hung over their once proud city. An insidious presence that disrupted the harmonious ebb and flow and had people watching their mouths as well as their actions.

Because up on the hillside, not far from the remains of the Fortress São João Baptista da Foz, stood the home of Salvador Barbosa. Built only five years ago, but in a classical style, the sprawling mansion was an imposing sight – grand and grotesque in equal measure. Its silhouette stood in stark contrast to the simplicity of its surroundings, a garish spectacle of wealth and power, resplendent in garnet and gold. Guarded heavily, with vehicles perpetually streaming in and out of its fortified walls, the mansion was a symbol of audacity amidst Porto's humble history and tradition – a building that seemed to sneer upon the city with disdain.

In a top-floor room, Barbosa was sitting cross-legged on an immense silk cushion. He remained still, and save for the faint wheezing emanating from his left nostril on each out-breath, he made no sound. A low mahogany table lay before him, littered with the detritus of power: smartphones, a high-end tablet, a gold-plated pen set, important-looking documents. Yet, so far this morning they lay untouched. Barbosa's eyes were closed, his mind still, surrendering to the tranquillity around him.

For this was Barbosa's sacred time – his hour of silence. A period put aside for peace and quiet reflection. He was a man who appreciated ritual as much as he did power and prestige, and his morning practice was a way of dealing with the pressures of his existence whilst focusing his energy on his next move.

The walls of his suite were adorned with huge oil paintings and exotic batiks, but on one wall, facing the bed and beneath a large gold-plated crucifix, was a solitary photograph in a simple wooden frame. A young boy with wide, hopeful eyes stared out from the worn, sepia-toned print. The boy was Barbosa, age six, a figure of poverty and innocence, as yet untouched by the brutal hands of life that would sculpt him into the ruthless kingpin he was today. Born in Alentejo, a town severely affected by drought, unemployment and underdevelopment, he'd escaped its grime-laden streets as soon as he could, carving a path of fear and respect across the country as he built his empire. The photo was there as a reminder of how far he'd come. And how far he still had to go.

Today in his hour of silence Barbosa was contemplating his recent discussions with the Mexicans. Their growing impatience was evident, but he remained confident he could uphold his part of the deal. Right now he looked more like a meditating monk than a fearsome gangster, yet a vicious heart beat below the surface. If this deal went awry, if the family made him look foolish in any way, they would pay with their lives.

He forced a wide smile, allowing the endorphins to filter through his system, before a distant sound broke his concentration. Rapid footsteps echoed in the corridor outside his suite. He stiffened, his attention leaving his thoughts as he tuned towards the interruption. His staff, his henchmen, his suppliers – they were all aware of his hour of silence. They also knew the consequences that befell anyone who broke the sanctity of his morning ritual. Whoever this thundering buffoon was, they would soon learn the price of their disturbance.

The stillness was shattered further as an alarm trilled from one of the devices on the table, signalling the end of the hour. Barbosa opened his eyes. The calm was done with for another day. Now the storm was ready to roar once again. And whoever was in the corridor outside – they were damn lucky.

As Barbosa silenced the alarm and began to stretch, the footsteps drew nearer, stopping just outside the door. A tense silence followed. Whoever it was, they knew they were risking their life coming to his suite at this time. But that meant it must be important. It had better be.

"Come in then!" he called out. "It's fine!"

The heavy wooden doors creaked open to reveal Marco, one of his main security team.

"What is it?" Barbosa asked, getting to his feet.

Marco, a large man with more muscle than intellect, shifted uncomfortably under the weight of his boss's penetrating gaze.

"*Chefe*, it's… it's about Alvarez," he stammered. "It sounds as if he's been fucking us over."

Barbosa stiffened, all his attention now trained on Marco. "In what way?"

"I heard it from one of Crespo's crew. The word is Alvarez has been skimming off the top. They say he's been doing it for months. Just a little, so we'd never notice. But one of his men jumped crews and let slip to Crespo what was going on."

Barbosa gritted his teeth and walked over to the window. Standing at only five feet one and a half inches, he was over a foot smaller than most of his henchmen and never liked to stand too close to them, especially not without his bespoke elevator shoes.

"Are you sure of this?"

"Yes, *Chefe*. We have now seen proof."

Barbosa stared out the window at the city below, his green eyes chillingly focused under his heavy brows. Betrayal. It had a nasty taste, bitter on the tongue. But rather than boil over with rage, Barbosa's round face eased into a cruel, knowing grin.

"I knew it, you know. That treacherous pig." He turned around. "Marco, do we know where this pig hides?"

Marco nodded. "He doesn't know we know. Not yet."

"Perfect."

Barbosa walked over to his desk, sinking into his plush leather chair. A gleeful chuckle escaped him as an idea formed.

"The audacity of greed," he mused, shaking his head. "What a shame it has come to this."

"What would you like me to do, *Chefe*?"

Barbosa arched an eyebrow. "For now – starve the dogs."

Marco shifted and swallowed hard. He would know immediately what Barbosa meant. In keeping with his love of drama, Barbosa had, over the years, developed a series of punishments that he fondly called his 'Theatre of Cruelty' – a nod to the surrealist visionary Antonin Artaud's concept of assaulting the senses of his audience. Although, in reality, 'Theatre of The Damned' would be a better term. It was always a one-act show and the players never performed again.

"I think we'll call this one, 'Devoured For Greed'," Barbosa said. "What do you think?"

"It's good, *Chefe*," Marco responded. "Whatever you say."

Barbosa nodded, satisfied. "Yes. I like it. It fits perfectly, I think. Allow him a false sense of security for a few days whilst the hounds grow nice and hungry. Then, to the kennels. Take his wife, too. If we're going to send a message, we should make it a strong one."

His voice was harsh and unwavering as he laid out the death sentence, but inside he felt giddy with excitement. It was another masterpiece of retribution. Poetic justice for the pig's unchecked avarice.

"Greed, my dear Marco, is like a hunger that can never be satisfied," Barbosa stated. "No amount of food can quench it." He paused and let out another dark chuckle. "So, let's see if Alvarez and his wife can satisfy the hunger of our canine friends, shall we?"

Each of Barbosa's punishments worked in similar ways; the method of demise for those who wronged him tailored to the nature of the offence. He'd always been a creative thinker and he took great delight in crafting his sinister reprisals, each one more despicable than the last. It was one reason why he was fast making a name for himself as one of the cruellest and most feared men in all of Portugal.

Next stop, Spain. Next stop, the world.

"You're clear on what needs to be done?" he asked Marco.

"Of course."

"You were wise to bring this to me. I won't forget it."

Marco nodded and smiled but he looked paler than he had done when he'd first entered the room. Good. That meant he understood the high stakes in Barbosa's world, where betrayal came at a hefty price.

The sharp ring of a phone broke the atmosphere. Barbosa's lips curled into a smirk as he noted the caller ID on the screen. It was the call he'd been waiting for. Dismissing Marco with a wave of his hand, he picked up the phone.

"Speak."

"Senhor Barbosa," Eduardo's voice crackled over the line. "I have good news. The Silva family have agreed to the terms of the deal."

"Excellent." A predatory grin spread across his face, revealing a gold tooth which he caressed with his tongue as he considered this development. "And they understand what is required of them?"

"Yes."

"And what will happen as the result of any breach on their part?"

"Well... they know who they are dealing with," Eduardo replied. "What would you like me to do next?"

Barbosa leaned back, propping his feet on the desk. "Nothing for now. Return to the house. I shall contact the Mexicans myself and let them know that all parties have aligned this end and we are ready to move forward. They will be pleased. As am I."

"Very good, *Chefe*."

Barbosa ended the call, already pondering the potential of this budding alliance. What began as a day tinged with betrayal was taking a promising turn.

Navigating the contact list on his phone, he located the direct line for Elvio Castellano, head of the infamous Sangre de Dragón Cartel across the pond. After this call, there'd be no turning back. But that's how Barbosa liked to play. All in. All the time. Maximum risk.

It was the only way to do it.

Sliding his feet off the desk, and with renewed determination, he dialled the number.

2

Two days later and over three hundred kilometres south of Porto, dusk was settling over São Lourenço, one of the many towns west of Portugal and adjacent to the Straw Sea. Despite the sun making its curtain call only a short time earlier, the town had settled into a quiet lull. A handful of cars trundled lazily up the main street, whilst distant footsteps on cobblestones echoed the weary trudge of workers heading home after a long day at work. Anyone else still out was now holed up in one of the tabernas littering the streets of the ancient town, with the doors closed and the windows shut. Once, this old town had been a thriving hotbed of activity, with locals and tourists alike filling the streets and squares with laughter and chatter into the early hours, especially on a weekend. But not anymore. Now people stayed at home. They stayed indoors. They kept to themselves.

Against this muted setting, a solitary figure entered the outskirts of the town. His stride was deliberate, his silhouette dusty from travel. The worn, sun-faded backpack slung over his shoulder told the story of a traveller used to a life on the move, his belongings pared down to the bare necessities. He stopped, surveying the run-down adobe houses and boarded-up establishments, and frowned. This wasn't the São Lourenço he'd envisioned. Venturing further into the town, he encountered an elderly woman wearing black who was sweeping her front steps with an old broom.

"*Bom dia*," he greeted, his Portuguese touched with the hint of a British accent. "Can you tell me where I might find a place to stay around here?"

The woman studied him for a moment, her eyes filled with an odd mix of curiosity and unease. John Beckett stepped back, seeing himself now through the woman's eyes: unwashed and unshaven, his dirty-blond hair grown long and shaggy. He looked, for all intents and purposes, like a vagrant, and a rather uncouth one at that. He lowered his chin and smiled, maintaining eye contact as he did so. After a pause, the woman pointed towards the centre of town, then quickly averted her gaze. Regardless, Beckett nodded his thanks and set off in the direction she'd indicated, every step a reminder of the twelve hundred and thirty kilometres he'd covered to get here.

The journey from Spain had taken several weeks, with Beckett hitchhiking much of the way and staying in towns that dotted his path. He'd bypassed border control to get into the country, navigating instead the Parque Natural do Douro Internacional – an expansive wilderness that ran along the border and which was rarely patrolled due to its inhospitable terrain and size. Beckett had made the dangerous journey on foot, relying on his survival skills and blending with the environment to avoid being detected by any potential surveillance. He'd crossed the Douro River at its narrowest point using a makeshift raft under the cover of darkness. Once in Portugal, he'd continued his journey, hitching rides with passing delivery drivers and staying on the move. But this was nothing new for Beckett. His entire adult life had been lived under the radar. His fluency in local dialects, an uncanny ability to blend into the crowd, and the occasional bribe when necessary, allowed him to stay invisible to the authorities. And, more importantly, to his former colleagues.

Now he was here, in São Lourenço – a town that once held a nostalgic charm for him. He'd visited once before in his teenage years alongside his father, and their days had been filled with fishing and mountain treks. He remembered it as a vibrant, animated place, and the locals a warm and welcoming bunch.

But no more, it seemed.

As Beckett made his way towards the centre of town, his seasoned senses, sharpened by years of fieldwork, catalogued the changes. The buildings that once boasted vibrant colours were now chipped and faded. The cobblestone streets, previously charming in their antiquity, now seemed worn and neglected. Years of litter and dust lined the pavements and the few townspeople he did encounter moved around him with their heads down and their shoulders hunched. You didn't need a soldier's intuition to sense the unease hanging in the air. It was a far cry from the lively place he remembered.

But maybe this was a sign, he thought.

He'd come here hoping to rekindle echoes of days gone by, but chasing such things was often a futile endeavour. In Beckett's experience, reality rarely lived up to the memories he held about people or places. So maybe it was wiser to continue on his original quest – to chase fresh horizons, create new memories.

After all, he now had the time.

The wonders of the world had always captivated Beckett. The pyramids at Giza, Angel Falls, the cliffs of Machu Picchu and Halong Bay's shimmering waters – these were the spectacles he now longed to witness first-hand, not just in pictures. But this desire transcended mere travel whims or a clichéd bucket list. It was about finding solace in nature's grandeur and mankind's architectural feats, hoping they'd provide a welcome reprieve from a past tainted with danger and death.

After the chaos of his former life, Beckett craved beauty and culture. He enjoyed being just another face in the crowd, a traveller, revelling in the vast tapestry of experiences the world had to offer. But so far São Lourenço was standing in stark contrast to these aspirations.

It was still relatively early in the evening, but the once lively marketplace and town square were both unnervingly subdued. The bustle and chatter he remembered had been replaced by a heavy silence. It was as if the town had somehow lost its soul. The disconnect between Beckett's teenage memory of the place and the present reality was huge. He'd anticipated it wouldn't be entirely as he remembered, but the transformation was unsettling. Something bad was happening here. He could sense it.

With a sigh he retreated from the town square, steering himself towards the backstreets. He needed food and water and somewhere to rest his weary head. Up ahead, a dilapidated old hotel still had its lights on. A sign hanging outside read *Quartos Disponíveis* – rooms available. One welcome sight, at least.

Something had bleached all the colour out of this town, but it was't his job to find out what. He was done being the hero, the soldier, the secret service operative. These days he was a simple man with simple needs. A soft bed. An uneventful night in a quiet town. Tomorrow he would head north, leave São Lourenço and its secrets behind. But for now he had a night of rest to look forward to. And seeing as he was dead on his feet, he'd gladly make the most of it.

3

Emilio Silva was a man moulded by ambition and hardened by time. His face, though scarred by age and years of relentless toil, bore a ruthless charm. Piercing hazel eyes framed by deep-set lines sat beneath a thick brow, their intense gaze often unsettling those who met him. His bottle-black hair, once a thick mane, was now thinning and patchy; even bald in some places, which gave him the look of a cancer patient. But this only added to the man's unsettling appearance. Which was good. Because to Emilio, appearances were everything.

His private estate, to the west of São Lourenço, consisted of three large single-storey houses and two outbuildings. What some townsfolk in hushed whispers called O Reino, or, The kingdom. Immense gates barred the entrance, guarding the meticulously landscaped grounds, whilst a winding driveway led up to the main mansion-house that stood in the centre of the property.

This grand white residence, an emblem of modernity and dominance, was a fitting signifier of the meteoric rise to power of its owner, who this evening was in his study, sitting behind a large leather-topped desk, deep in contemplation. This room, lined with rich mahogany panels and black marble tiles, was the nerve centre of the Silva empire, the air thick with the scent of Cuban cigars and fine brandy. An extensive collection of big game heads looked down from the walls, their lifeless eyes as cold and predatory as the man who'd taken their lives.

Lost in his musings, Silva's hand drifted once more to his head. Winding a tuft of hair around his fingers, he yanked it free from his scalp with a sharp tug. It made his eyes water, but the sharp sting was a sensation he relished. It made him feel alive.

The doctors had a name for it – trichotillomania; a compulsive urge to pull out your own hair. Some of the medical websites Silva had explored described it as an anxiety disorder – although his doctors were wise not to do so to his face – but it certainly affected him most when he was stressed or excited. The fact that the condition had manifested again recently made sense. Silva had never been more stressed or excited in his life.

A noise in the hallway snapped him from his thoughts and he sat upright at a knock on the door. Clearing his throat, he called out, "Enter."

The door groaned as it opened and his eldest son, Raul, entered the room.

"There you are," Silva growled. "I thought I told you to get here an hour ago."

Raul didn't flinch, despite his father's scalding tone. "I was busy with something at home. Antonia needed to be… Never mind. It is sorted. I'm here now."

Raul, along with his younger brother Rodrigo, acted as their father's right-hand men. Both sons were tough and ruthless, but whereas Rodrigo was driven by malice and arrogance, Raul was intense and intelligent.

"You have news for me?" the elder Silva asked, gesturing for Raul to sit in the chair opposite.

Raul did as he was instructed. He was wearing dark trousers and a white shirt unbuttoned to the navel. "Everything is on schedule," he said. "Transportation for the shipment is paid for and will be delivered soon. We still have to complete the order, but I'm confident we'll be ready to move in the next few days."

Excitement and apprehension sent a shiver down Silva's back, and his restless fingers betrayed him once more as they danced across his scalp. "And you're sure we'll be ready?" he asked, selecting a tuft of hair and beginning to wind. "We have to meet our obligations to the letter. You know this."

"I do," Raul replied. "We'll be ready on time."

"Good. But what's the hold up?"

Raul shifted in his seat. "You must understand, Father, we have to be careful. The locals fear us and the police are paid off, but everyone has a limit to what they will turn a blind eye to."

Silva tugged at his hair. It was a large tuft and brought a tear to his eye as he yanked it free. He understood his son's caution, and that the sourcing of the product was somewhat… delicate and time-sensitive, but the delay only added to his stress levels. Victory was so tantalisingly close. This deal, being brokered by Salvador Barbosa between the Silva family and the Sangre de Dragón Cartel, would finally propel the Silva organisation into the big time. The Mexicans' payment, an impending consignment of narcotics and weaponry, to be made via Barbosa, would allow them to expand their influence on neighbouring towns, creating a new era of control in the region. What they'd done in São Lourenço could be replicated in every township across southern Portugal. Their strategy was tactical and insidious. Initial moves were inconspicuous, from the lending of minor financial loans to covert police bribes.

Then, when the stage was set, when it was too late for anyone to act against you, you took it all.

But dealing with such ruthless entities as the Barbosa Syndicate and a Mexican cartel came with its own burden of tension. If the Silvas didn't complete their side of the deal soon, Emilio would have no hair left at all.

"Don't worry, Father," Raul assured him. "Everything will be fine. We still have a few days before the deadline. I'm confident we'll be ready."

Silva leaned forward, directing a bejewelled finger at his son. "Remember, Raul: failure isn't an option. We either rise or we fall. There is no middle ground."

"I know. Trust me." Raul's tone was firm, his face mirroring his father's resolve. "We can do this. We will be on time."

It gave Silva some comfort to know his son understood the risks as well as he did. If they faltered, it wouldn't just be a bruise to their reputation; it would be the end of their lives.

"Go now," Silva ordered. "Report back when you have some good news for me."

Raul nodded and left the room, leaving Silva alone with his thoughts. His hand rose once more to his scalp but he forced himself to stop. Anticipation knotted his stomach. He was on a dangerous path, but one that would lead to a better life if he could only hold his nerve. One wrong move and everything he'd built would be reduced to ash. But if he succeeded, he would ascend to the heights of power he'd always craved.

The challenge was steep, the stakes high, but he was Emilio Silva. The most feared man in São Lourenço. Soon to be the most feared man in Lisbon, in Faro, in the whole of southern Portugal. He had five days to make it work. But he could do this. He had to.

4

The bed in Beckett's cramped hotel room was too firm, the pillow too flat, and the stillness of the night too stifling against his restless soul. He'd felt exhausted as he'd checked in, but he'd now gone past the point of tiredness and was just wired. Groaning, he propped himself up in bed, his mind buzzing with too many conflicting thoughts.

Tilting his wrist into the moonlight streaming in through the room's only window, he checked his watch. It was only a cheap piece, bought off a market stall in Santarém a few days earlier, but it had kept good time so far. He had another watch in his bag, a silver Rolex that once belonged to his father, but the strap was broken and he had yet to get around to fixing it. It was the only item he had that linked him to his past life; to his family, even.

The cheap watch told him it was a few minutes after eleven. Not even that late. He lay back and closed his eyes, assessing whether he might succumb to sleep, but the restless energy vibrating in his system told him it would be elusive for the time being.

"Oh, sod it!" he muttered, throwing off the sheets and swinging his legs out of bed.

He rose, tugged on the shirt and jeans he'd been wearing for the past few days and slipped on his well-worn boots. Now the decision had been made, the idea of a late-night stroll appealed to him. Perhaps he could clear his mind, or at the very least find some food. All he'd consumed that day was a can of cold beans and a piece of Broa cornbread – not exactly a gourmet meal. With key in hand, he exited his room and headed out through the empty lobby into the cool night air.

After dark, São Lourenço was a different place again. Its winding streets were now bathed in an eerie silence compounded by the shuttered windows and locked doors. The only illumination came from dim, stuttering streetlamps that cast long shadows across the uneven cobbles.

Beckett's footsteps echoed around the old buildings, sending the curtains twitching in the windows above. The town was a ghost of its past, and he knew all too well how that felt. As he walked, a flood of nostalgia swept over him. São Lourenço was a shadow of the lively, bustling town he remembered from his youth, but he suspected his disappointment had less to do with the town's demise and more to do with his yearning for the young man he'd been back then. That bright-eyed teenager was full of dreams and passions. Unbroken and unbeaten by life and death.

Hell.

Now he needed a stiff drink as well as some food.

He headed for the town centre, hoping to see a taberna or restaurant with its lights still on, but here, too, all he encountered were locked doors and blackened windows. His stomach grumbled, voicing its dismay alongside deeper feelings of disbelief and concern.

He walked on, letting his instincts guide him until he found himself in front of an old church. This he remembered well.

He and his father had spent an afternoon exploring the ancient building. His father had enjoyed it a lot more than he had, but he'd give anything to spend that time again with his old man. Shaking his head, and with a resigned smile, he turned back. He knew when he was beaten.

All tonight had on offer was the uncomfortable bed back in his hotel room. Perhaps the rhythmic hum of the ceiling fan would lull him to sleep if he gave it a chance. Then, tomorrow he'd rise early and depart São Lourenço for good. It would at least serve as a worthy reminder that it was unwise to return to something once you'd left it behind. Moving forward was the key. It was the only way.

However, as he retraced his steps and turned the corner at the end of the next street, he stopped. Hearing the soft scuffle of quickened footsteps coming the other way and then laughter and jeering, he ducked down an alleyway. The merriment sounded so out of place in the silence of the night that his senses went into overdrive, his years of military training kicking in. As his eyes adjusted to the darkness, a group of figures emerged into view. He held his breath, trying to make them out.

There were four of them, a woman and three men. The woman was huddled over, her arms wrapped around her chest as she pressed onwards. She looked to be no older than twenty-five, and as she passed underneath a streetlight, Beckett caught the fear etched on her face. He could hear the men more clearly now, too. They were taunting her, asking her where she was going, telling her she should go with them, that they would have fun together.

As the woman hurried past, Beckett pressed himself against the wall of the alley, on high alert but not yet ready to show his hand. He sized up the men tailing her. They were young, likely in their mid-twenties, all broad-shouldered and tall. Their unsteady gait hinted at intoxication and Beckett was certain he could handle them if necessary. He waited, assessing the situation. They could be just fooling around, annoying but harmless, and if the young woman lived close, it might not come to anything. Yet as they passed by, one of them grabbed his friend boisterously around the neck and whispered in his ear. "Just grab her. There's no one around and we need to do this. Now!"

An icy prickle climbed up Beckett's spine. He'd planned on staying inconspicuous, but this was a situation he couldn't ignore. Bawdy humour was one thing, but those weren't vague threats.

Stepping out from his vantage point, he stalked behind the group, stomping his boots hard against the cobbles so they'd hear. "Hey," he called out. "Stop right there! *Parar!*"

The men halted. The woman did too. As they each turned to see who was shouting, Beckett held the woman's gaze, offering her a reassuring smile. "Don't worry," he called over. "Head on home and have a good evening. It's these idiots I wanted a word with."

She hesitated for a moment, then spun around and strode off down the street. Beckett's focus shifted to the three men, now wearing expressions of bewildered annoyance. He squared his shoulders, ready.

"Oh, did I spoil your fun?" he taunted, then repeated it in perfect Portuguese, letting them know they had no upper hand in terms of covert discussions.

The men's eyes widened a fraction, Beckett's fluency affecting a ripple of surprise amongst them. But at least it drew their attention away from the woman who had reached the end of the street. A second later she disappeared around the corner and was gone. She was safe.

"Looks like we've got ourselves a hero, boys," one of the men sneered. "A foreigner who thinks he can play tough." He was dark-skinned, with cropped hair and the hint of a moustache. He also seemed the most drunk of the three.

He'd be last, Beckett noted.

The man muttered in Portuguese, calling Beckett a son of a bitch in a voice dripping with contempt, yet there was also a trace of uncertainty underneath.

Good.

He'd rattled him.

For this guy, it was already over.

Next, the tallest and broadest of the three stepped forward. "What's your problem, old man?" he snarled in a thick accent. He had the bulbous upper body of a gym bunny whose regime didn't stretch to following a strict enough training diet. You saw it all the time with the young ones. No discipline. But he looked strong and was probably the most sober of the three of them.

He'd be first.

"I just like to make sure everyone's freedom is respected," Beckett replied, holding his hands up. "I think you boys were doing a terrible job of that."

The third man, wiry with rat-like features and a personality to match, snorted. "Oh, is that what you think? You've got no clue what the fuck you've stepped into, old man. We'll make you wish you'd never got involved in our business." This was the one who mentioned grabbing the young woman. Beckett's instincts told him he was the main player.

He'd be second.

With his strategic ordering in mind, Beckett released a slow breath, his fingers curling into fists. He hadn't wanted any trouble, but it seemed to have a habit of finding him. And now it had found these obnoxious cretins as well.

He cricked his neck to one side then the other as a primal rush washed over him – a torrent of adrenaline that marked the line between order and chaos, between the hunter and the hunted.

Then it began.

Without warning, he launched himself at the gym bunny, a coiled spring of raw power. His foot shot out, connecting with the man's knee and bending it back against the joint with a sickening crunch. As the man's pained screams pierced the still night, Beckett turned his attention to Rat Boy, who had pulled out a knife and was advancing on him.

Already in motion and anticipating the first swipe, Beckett twisted away, evading the blade as it sliced the air. Within the same breath, he counter-attacked: a punch to the gut followed by a jarring uppercut. The force of the second blow snapped the man's head back and he bit the end of his tongue clean off. He staggered, blood spurting down his front before a final boot to the jaw sent him sprawling unconscious to the ground.

Three seconds had passed.

Two down.

One to go.

The men, drunk on liquor and bravado, had clearly thought Beckett to be an easy target, but had instead found themselves facing down a human wrecking ball. As the last one turned to flee, Beckett was already on the move. There was no pause, no offer of a way out. Just the relentlessness of a man who understood violence in a way these young thugs never would. Without hesitation, he barrelled into the man with a powerful shoulder charge, lifting him off his feet and slamming him into a nearby wall.

But Beckett wasn't finished. As the dazed thug staggered forward, gasping for breath, he smashed the heel of his fist into the man's jaw. The dope almost spun a full turn before his eyes rolled back into his head and he crumpled to the ground. Done.

Five seconds.

Three threats: neutralised.

As Beckett brushed himself down, Gym Bunny began to

whimper, clutching at his injured leg. Beckett knelt beside him, wagging a finger in his face. "You and your friends need to learn some manners," he told him, speaking in Portuguese. "No wonder the town's deserted, with hooligans like you roaming the streets."

The man gritted his teeth as he fought the pain. "Fuck you," he hissed. "You have no idea what you're doing or who you're dealing with. You'll be sorry."

"Is that so?" Beckett jerked forward, feigning another blow but stopping short. The man flinched and let out a high-pitched wail.

Yeah. He was done. It was over.

"Pathetic," Beckett muttered, getting to his feet. "*Patético!*"

He'd held back tonight. They were lucky. He could have done some real damage if he'd wanted to, but that would have drawn more unwanted attention. As it was, they'd got away with an old-fashioned beating rather than anything too final. With his shattered knee, Gym Bunny might never squat again, but from the looks of it he ignored leg day anyway.

Back in the stuffy confines of his hotel room, Beckett slumped onto the stiff mattress and closed his eyes. The evening's excitement still hummed in his veins but he now felt sleep closing in on him. There was nothing like an unexpected street brawl to calm one's mind.

Still, tonight had only reinforced his decision to leave. São Lourenço had seen a glimpse of the old John Beckett, not the retired traveller but the protector, the fighter, the ghost that lurked in the shadows. His history, it seemed, was never too far away.

One more night, he told himself.

One more night before he left it all behind… again.

5

Beckett was a creature of habit. His former line of work had drilled that into him. You woke early, you acted quickly, you left no trace you were ever there.

Today he woke even before dawn had broken. He jumped out of bed and splashed water on his face from the sink unit in the corner of the room. The makeshift mirror on the wall – made from a piece of warped aluminium rather than glass – reflected a distorted version of himself. He looked even more like a vagrant. Or a blond version of Jesus. Or just a man who had stopped caring about his appearance. Perhaps he'd invest in a pair of scissors and a razor when he got to where he was going next.

Yet despite his wayward appearance, Beckett was still a man of routine and discipline, and after drying his face, he dropped to the floor to complete the four sets of push-ups and sit-ups he did every morning. As he did so, he noticed his knuckles were a little grazed, a reminder of last night's altercation. Those miserable creeps didn't know what had hit them. But as he completed his first set of push-ups, driving his upper body strength to its limit rather than counting reps, something came to him. Something one of the men — or rather boys — had said to him.

You have no idea what you're doing... or who you're dealing with.

So who was he dealing with? The threat could have just been bluster, but he didn't think so. He also didn't think the creep was referring to himself and his cronies. Why would he be? Beckett had just shown them up by kicking their arses in a matter of seconds; it would be even more embarrassing for them to make out they were a threat to him.

Which implied they worked for someone else. Someone who *was* a threat. But who? And in what capacity?

No!

Don't go there.

He shook the intrigue away as he flipped himself onto his back and began his first set of sit-ups. Thinking like that tended to invite trouble to one's door and he didn't need it. He was leaving town. Today. There was nothing for him here. *Nothing.*

After his workout, he showered in the cramped cubicle in the corner of the room and dressed in the last of his clean clothes — a pair of beige canvas trousers and a white t-shirt. He packed the rest of his sparse belongings into his backpack and made his way through the hotel's dim corridors. The silence suggested midnight rather than morning. There were no other guests in sight, and the owner who'd checked him in yesterday was absent from the front desk.

Beckett glanced at his watch. It was a few minutes past seven. Still early. He was using cash to avoid traceable credit cards, but he wasn't about to leave an envelope of money lying around, nor did he feel right leaving without paying. The hotel might not have been the nicest place he'd ever stayed, but the owner seemed like an honest man and Beckett, rugged visage aside, was still a gentleman and a man of principle.

To pass the time, he would go for a walk down to the

seafront. It would clear his head and he could get some breakfast before returning to settle his bill. Decision made, he hoisted his backpack onto his shoulder and headed out.

The town was gradually coming to life, the buildings and streets bathed in the tender glow of the morning light. The air carried a medley of sounds: the distant rhythm of the ocean, the caws from seagulls overhead, and the rumbles of awnings and clinks of crockery from the tabernas and cafés opening up for the day. A rich aroma of freshly brewed coffee tempted him from a nearby establishment, but as he peeked inside, there was no one around and the chairs were still stacked on top of the tables. He made a mental note to try again on his way back.

Continuing down to the seafront, the view he came upon was breathtaking. Beckett stood for a while breathing it in – the vastness of the ocean, its surface a shimmering mirror reflecting the brilliance of the new day's sun. He closed his eyes, lost in the rhythm of the crashing waves as another memory returned – a younger Beckett, swimming and laughing in these very waters with his father. It was a moment of uninhibited joy. A time of freedom and hope. He'd been thirteen at the time, with everything in front of him. But only two years later his father's plane was shot down over Afghanistan and Beckett's life changed forever.

He glanced along the expansive esplanade. The locals were now out in force, but like those he'd seen yesterday, their shoulders seemed to sag with the weight of existence, their downtrodden expressions etched with the wear and tear of life. There was also slowness to their movements, a worn resignation that clashed with the vibrancy of the morning and Beckett's own sharp vitality.

It was possible, he supposed, that the only thing to have changed about this town was his perceptions of it - age and cynicism readjusting the view. Everything looked fresh and lively from the perspective of youth, but maturity revealed the cracks in the façade.

Returning his attention back to the ocean, he inhaled deeply, allowing the raw beauty to wash over him, a stark contrast to the lowly scene playing out around him. He felt the fresh breeze ruffle his hair, carrying with it the sharp tang of salt and the pungent aroma of seaweed. At least the shoreline was alive with activity. Down to his left, fishermen secured their first catch of the day, their boats bobbing beside the small pier whilst flocks of seagulls dipped into the briny water, hunting for breakfast.

He found a clear patch of wall and sat for a while, watching the ocean until 8:30 rolled around. He figured the hotel owner would have started his shift by now and made his way back through the winding streets, drawn to the delicious-smelling coffee shop from earlier.

As he walked, he stretched out his back, feeling the cartilage pop and crackle. It felt good. He felt good, despite the disappointment of his visit. Turning a corner, Beckett spotted a local man of about his age wrestling with metal barrels as he unloaded them from an old truck. He slowed to a stop a short distance away and watched as the man hefted a barrel towards the dim interior of a nearby taverna. He was built like a heavyweight boxer, but despite his obvious strength, the poor guy was having trouble. The veins in his muscular arms bulged as he struggled with the heavy load, and his black hair was stuck to his forehead with sweat.

There was something familiar about his struggle, something that echoed within Beckett. A fan of classical literature from a young age, the scene reminded him of Camus's philosophical essay *The Myth of Sisyphus* – where the mortal Sisyphus is condemned by the gods to roll a boulder up a hill, only to have it roll down again once he got it to the top so he'd have to start again. It was a reflection on humanity's ceaseless struggle against life's inherent absurdity, which these days Beckett could sympathise with.

Before he knew it, he was crossing the street and stepping into the man's eyeline. "*Posso ajudar?*" he asked. *Can I help?*

The man glared at him, the sweat forming into droplets on his temples. He was out of breath, but seemingly fuelled by adrenaline and determination. He looked Beckett up and down, then nodded at the truck with a grin.

Beckett took that as a yes. Approaching the truck, he grabbed the closest barrel and hoisted it onto his shoulder. The weight was considerable, but his sturdy frame and strong core easily absorbed the load. He navigated his way through the doorway and placed the barrel on the floor, taking in the interior as he did.

The taberna was dark, lit only by the sunlight filtering through the dusty windows. The faint scent of last night's alcohol lingered in the air. Six wooden tables occupied the centre of the room, whilst a sturdy bar counter, lined with a selection of draft beer pumps, extended along one wall. None of the chairs or bar stools matched, but along with the time-worn photos on the wall, it only added to the rustic charm. It was a warm, welcoming place, somewhere Beckett wished he'd happened upon the previous night when all he found was defeat and indifference.

He spotted an open door that led to a lit stockroom and rolled the barrel over, stacking it alongside the three already there. As he made his way back to the truck, he passed the man coming the other way, rolling a barrel in front of him. The man stopped as Beckett got up to him.

"*Obrigado, senhor,*" he said, his gratitude reshaping the wrinkles around his eyes into something softer, more appreciative.

"*Não o mencione,*" Beckett replied. "It gives me something to do."

The man frowned. "Ah! You're English?"

"Indeed. For my sins."

The man let out a hearty laugh and continued rolling his barrel to the stockroom. Beckett returned to the truck, and the next two barrels were moved just as quickly. Emerging from the stockroom after the last one was in place, he found the man leaning against the bar, his dark eyes wide with a mixture of wonder and respect.

"Damn, you move fast," he said, his heavy Portuguese accent twisting around the English words. "But thank you, man. I used to have a guy who helped with deliveries. Not anymore." There was a sudden glimmer of anger in his eyes. It was only a split-second thing, a blink-and-you-miss-it moment, but Beckett was trained to catch subtleties of emotion, no matter how small.

"It's a nice place you've got here," he said, assuming the man to be the owner.

"Yeah. It was. And I guess it's okay." He shrugged, forcing a smile. "I'm Armando Lopes, by the way." He held out his hand.

Beckett shook it. "Michael Day," he replied, opting for the alias he'd been using these last few months. "But call me Mike."

"Well, thanks again, Mike. That was a great help. Can I get you a drink?"

Beckett glanced at the bar, at the shining beer pumps and the rows of liquor bottles against the back wall. "Isn't it a bit early?"

Armando glanced at his watch and his mouth curled into a bitter smile. "You'd be surprised. There was a time when my place would have been full of people by 10 a.m. Laughing, joking, telling stories, drinking outside in the sun. Not so much these days."

He looked away. Beckett felt the same twinge of curiosity

that had been niggling at him since he arrived in the town, but like before he pushed it aside.

"Maybe a glass of water would be good," he said. "Or perhaps a coffee if you have some?"

Armando screwed up his face. "It'll have to be water. The machine's bust."

"That's fine." He rubbed his hands together; the grime from the barrels had left them sticky and black. "I'll just use the bathroom first."

"No problem. It's the door over there in the corner," Armando replied, moving around the other side of the bar. "One iced water coming up."

Beckett headed for the bathroom, grateful that Armando hadn't pried into what he was doing in town. These days, avoiding awkward questions was his best defence. He'd been careful up to now, to have not left any trail, but it only took one slip-up and he'd have the entire British Secret Service bearing down on him. Not to mention the CIA.

The taberna's bathroom was as charming and basic as the rest of the establishment. A mirror, tinged green with age, hung above a chipped porcelain sink. A single bulb hanging from the ceiling provided a weak light that did little to dispel the gloom. The tap groaned as Beckett twisted it on and let the cold water splash over his hands and wrists. He washed them thoroughly and then splashed water on his face, letting the cool sensation sharpen his senses.

Drying his hands on a fraying towel, he took a moment to glance at his reflection in the mirror. He wasn't looking much better. He replaced the towel and was about to exit the bathroom when he paused. The murmur of men's voices drifted through from the main area, two new voices along with Armando's. They were speaking in Portuguese, the sound a deep rumble that he couldn't make out, but he sensed hostility. Caution flared within him. Opening the door just enough to peek through it, he saw Armando and two men standing by the bar. They were all but silhouetted against the light coming in through the entrance, but he recognised them immediately as two of the men he'd left unconscious in the alleyway – Rat Boy and Moustache. Rat Boy was talking to Armando, stabbing his finger through the air in an aggressive manner whilst Moustache prowled up and down.

Were they here for him? Had they followed him here?

Their friend's warning replayed in his mind, *You have no idea what you're doing, or who you're dealing with…*

Well, maybe it was time he found out. He eased the door closed. He needed a plan, and fast.

6

Squinting through the crack in the bathroom door, Beckett observed the scene unfolding in the taberna. Rat Boy and Moustache were now leaning over the bar, clearly trying to intimidate Armando. Even without hearing what was being said, the hostility was unmistakable.

Armando, in contrast, maintained a steady defiance in his stance and there was a steeliness in his gaze Beckett hadn't noticed before. It wasn't just an act, he sensed, but if these creeps were here for him, he wasn't about to let the friendly bar owner – or his bar – become collateral damage.

Remaining out of sight, Beckett evaluated his next steps. Moustache was the taller and more muscular of the two. A swift blow to the throat then a strike to the knees would do the job. Fast and brutal. Rat Boy would see him coming, but Beckett was confident he could neutralise him as quickly as he had done the previous night.

He released a slow breath, grounding himself. On three he'd move.

One…

Two…

But as he neared action, Armando held his hands up before reaching under the counter and coming back with a stack of notes he slid across the bar to the men. Beckett narrowed his eyes at the money. It had to be at least three hundred euros. What was Armando doing?

Rat Boy snatched up the money, his demeanour instantly shifting from hostile to triumphant as he wagged his finger at Armando and laughed. He handed the cash to his pal and they left the bar without a backward glance. Beckett stayed where he was for a few more seconds before stepping out of the bathroom.

"Everything okay, Armando?" he asked, keeping his voice low and calm, not wanting to spook the man.

Armando looked up, his expression weary but composed. "Just business, *senhor*," he replied, attempting a weak smile. "Just business."

"Really? Because it looked like a rather one-sided exchange from where I was standing. Coercion, even." He held Armando's gaze until the man looked away with a sigh.

"It's a fucking nightmare." He puffed out a long breath, his lips vibrating as he did. "I don't know about you, *amigo*. But I need a proper drink. Sure you won't join me?"

Beckett hesitated, but he couldn't leave now. There was something bigger going on in São Lourenço. The question was how far was he willing to go to find out what it was.

"Go on then, you've twisted my arm," he said, slipping onto one of the bar stools. "Just a small one."

Armando reached behind him and selected a half-empty bottle of whisky. Unscrewing the cap, he poured two hefty servings into heavy-bottomed glasses. So much for a small one, Beckett thought. But it looked as if his new acquaintance needed it.

They drank in silence, the only sound the low hum of the refrigeration units under the back counter and the occasional clink of glass. Beckett knew enough to stay quiet, to give Armando the space he needed rather than bombard him with the questions that were bubbling up inside him. The haunted look in the man's eyes was not new to him. He'd encountered it too many times in his line of work.

Eventually, Armando broke the silence. "São Lourenço was once a good town. It wasn't overly prosperous, and we didn't have the same bustling tourist trade as other towns in the area, but it was a nice place to live. A decent place to bring up a family."

Beckett took a sip of his drink, savouring the hints of citrus and smoky undertones. He had a feeling he'd soon be grateful for its comforting warmth. "So what happened?"

"The Silva family happened, that's what."

"I see." Beckett swirled the whisky in his glass, its amber glow casting reflections as he considered what little information he had. "And what are we looking at, some kind of protection racket?"

"You're a sharp guy," Armando replied. "But yeah – that. And the rest."

"And if you refuse to pay?"

Armando let out a bitter, humourless chuckle. "I know how it looks. It seems strange to you that a guy like me would be scared of those young punks. But that family, man… they've got the whole town under their control. It's just not worth crossing them."

"Who are they?" Beckett leaned forward, intrigued. "*What* are they?"

Armando hesitated, taking a long drink first, his voice rough from it when he next spoke. "Just one family. They moved here about ten years ago and already had money. They built a huge estate on the other side of town consisting of three properties and also bought up a couple of hotels in the area. The main guy is called Emilio Silva – a real evil piece of shit and no mistake. The stories I've heard about him, what he's done, who he's hurt… it would make you sick. Then there are his two sons, Raul and Rodrigo, who make their father look like the Lord Jesus Christ himself in comparison. They're a bad brood, *amigo*. There is a sister, too, but you never really hear from her. I'm not sure if she's involved in the business or even knows what goes on."

"And it's heavy stuff what they're involved in?" Beckett asked.

"You could say that. They started small, just flexing their muscles – intimidation and extortion, nothing more. But in the past few years they've grown stronger, more ruthless. There are rumours they're now involved with Salvador Barbosa, one of the biggest gangsters in Portugal, with links to the cartels in Mexico." He paused, taking another deep gulp of his whisky. "It's bad shit."

Beckett's thoughts raced. He was already familiar with Barbosa, though he kept this knowledge to himself. He was formulating his next question when Armando jumped back in, pre-empting what was going through his mind. "The police used to have a handle on things," he told him. "Even though the nearest station was in the neighbouring town, they maintained a semblance of balance. But when the old chief retired four years ago, everything unravelled. His successor is clearly in Silva's pocket and the remaining officers are either too scared to do anything or equally corrupt."

Beckett puffed out his cheeks. Now the pieces started to fit together. The weariness of the townsfolk, the streets deserted after dark. The vivacious São Lourenço of his past was now under the thumb of an oppressive force. He'd seen it happen before, but usually it was in war-ravaged third-world countries, where the lowly and dispossessed were more easily crushed under the boot of a fascist tyrant.

"Why not gather a resistance?" he suggested. "Rise up against them. It's only one family."

"One family with a lot of manpower," Armando countered, his expression sombre. "But I know what you're saying and I have thought about it. But I have a wife, a business. There's a lot at stake. It's the same for everyone in the town."

A silence fell between them. Armando finished his drink and poured another, offering the bottle to Beckett who placed his hand over the top of his glass and shook his head.

"And these people are that scary?" he asked.

Armando's voice dropped, becoming a mere whisper. "They're monsters, Mike. Men have gone missing, only to turn up dead, buried to their necks in the sand. Women, too… disappeared without a trace. São Lourenço was once a wonderful town, but now it's a living hell. A place where men are too scared to speak, too scared to act."

Beckett knew the destruction unchecked power could wreak. He finished his drink but didn't rush to get up. There was a lot to consider.

"So what's your story, Mike?" Armando asked, seemingly eager to change the subject.

"Just passing through," he replied. "I came here when I was a boy and had fond memories. I can see for myself how it's changed."

"No shit? And what do you do back in England?"

Beckett shrugged. "Not much. I was a civil servant. But my father died last year and left me some inheritance. I realised life was too short to be cooped up in an office, so I quit my job and I'm using the inheritance money to travel around the world, explore places I've always wanted to visit." He'd used the same story a couple of times already, so it flowed easily enough.

"A civil servant?" Armando enquired. "Like a clerk for the government?"

"Something like that."

"Hmm. You don't strike me as someone who works in an office."

"No? What about you?" Beckett asked, redirecting the focus away from himself. "Have you always owned bars?"

"Only for the past fifteen years. Before that I was in the military."

"Ah, a soldier. You know, I did wonder."

"Yeah," Armando said. "I reckon it takes one to know one."

Beckett stiffened but held Armando's gaze. He was too versed in these sorts of interactions to let anything slip, even for a second. "I'm not a soldier."

"Sure, okay." Armando glanced at the scuffs on Beckett's knuckles. "I guess you did that filing paperwork?"

Beckett grinned. "I didn't say I was a pushover. I met a couple of guys needing a lesson in respect."

"I knew there was something about you."

"No. There's nothing about me. I'm just travelling around, trying to find myself – or whatever it is people do."

"Fair enough." Armando held his hands up. "No more questions."

Beckett sat upright. "What happened to your employee?"

"What?" Armando frowned.

"Before – you said you had a guy who helped with deliveries."

"Ah, shit, yeah. Carlos. He was a good guy. He also ran the bar for me when my wife got sick and I had to look after our son." He looked down at his hands, pressing down on the bar top with his fingers spread wide. "But Carlos had a big mouth and a short fuse. One night Rodrigo Silva was drinking in here with some of his pals. I wasn't here, so I don't know exactly what happened, but Carlos never got home after his shift that night. He was found on the beach three days later with his tongue cut out."

Beckett nodded. There was no point acting shocked or sickened by the story, because he wasn't. He'd experienced the worst of mankind many times over in his lifetime. Nothing surprised him anymore.

"I'm sorry," was all he could say. He gripped the edge of the bar, readying himself to leave when Armando shot him a look that made him hesitate. "What is it?"

"Ah, it's nothing. It's stupid. I can't even believe I was going to say it."

Beckett let go of the bar. "Say what?"

Armando shook his head, back to staring at his hands. "It's crazy – after everything we just talked about, why the hell would you – but I was going to ask if you needed a job while you were in town. If you wanted to work a few shifts for me."

"Oh… I see…"

"Forget it," Armando carried on, waving him away. "It's crazy, like I say. You probably want to get out of town as soon as possible. I don't blame you. But thanks for listening and thanks for helping me unload the truck. I appreciate it."

Beckett paused. "I like to keep moving," he said. "There's a lot of the world to see."

"Sure. It's fine." Armando looked broken suddenly. His brow furrowed. "I understand."

"What is it?" Beckett asked.

"Nothing… it's just you'd be doing me a big favour, that's all. I have to take my wife to the hospital in the next town, and if I had someone to cover, I wouldn't have to close the bar up. Times are hard, you know? But it's not your problem."

Beckett chewed on his lip. "How long are we talking?"

"Just a few shifts. One or two. The bar doesn't get that busy these days, but any money coming in is welcome."

Beckett mulled over the request. He was probably being

rash, but his gut was telling him to stay. A few more days at least. Something was tugging at him, a gnawing curiosity to see the situation for himself, to understand more about the Silva family and their reign of terror.

"You don't even know me," he told Armando.

"Perhaps not." Armando glanced once more at his bruised knuckles. "But I'm a good judge of character. You seem like a smart guy who can handle himself if the need arises. Both good traits."

"Well... about that," Beckett started. "I should tell you, the men I had an altercation with – the guys needing a lesson in respect – they were the ones collecting money from you earlier. Silva's men. They got a good look at me. If they returned and saw me here..."

Armando pulled his lips back over his teeth, weighing up this new information. "It might be a problem. Is it for you?"

"People like that don't worry me," Beckett replied. "Like I said, I already taught them a lesson once. And they had a friend with them."

"One man against three of Silva's goons," Armando said, laughing. "I like it. So yeah, fuck it. Maybe it's time we stood up to these people."

"Maybe..."

"So you'll cover for me?"

Beckett cracked a reluctant smile. "Fine. But just for the week."

"Perfect. Thank you so much, man." Armando sounded almost hopeful. "Tomorrow at five okay for your first shift?"

"Sounds good."

Armando nodded his thanks. "You're a good man, Michael Day."

"I'm not sure about that." Beckett got to his feet, already anticipating the brewing storm. If the Silvas were as bad as Armando implied, things could get volatile once they discovered the man who'd roughed up their foot soldiers was still in town.

But he could handle volatile. Hell, volatile was a state he knew like an old friend. For a man like John Beckett – it was home.

7

The sun had barely appeared over the horizon as Beckett left his hotel and ventured out for the day. He'd spoken to the hotel owner the previous evening and paid for a full week's stay in advance. Armando had offered him the vacant room above the taberna free of charge, but he'd felt uncomfortable accepting. Beckett liked to pay his own way in life and hated being beholden to anyone. Plus, if he encountered the Silva family's thugs again, living where he worked would be a bad idea.

But he felt no regret about his decision to stay in town a while longer to help Armando. When he made decisions, he made them fast and he stuck to them. He trusted his instincts and never second-guessed or questioned himself. In his line of work, uncertainty and hesitation got you killed faster than you could say *fumbled field report*. And Armando Lopes wasn't the only one who was a good judge of character. Beckett could see he was a decent man, hardworking and honest, who'd found himself caught up in a terrible situation. He felt compelled to help him out, to give him a break. Beckett had refrained from asking the man about his wife's hospital visits, but no one went to the hospital for fun.

His agreeing to help out wasn't completely altruistic, though. The stories of the Silva family and their brutal methods had piqued his interest. He'd spent the last fifteen years infiltrating and taking down organisations just like theirs, in countries all across the world. Understanding the hows and whys of those who stood to hurt others was in his DNA. It was true what they said – once a soldier, always a soldier. Armando was a shrewd guy; he'd seen it in him.

And anyway, Beckett saw the week as an opportunity. It would give him time to explore the surrounding area, the winding coastal paths and the rugged mountains that looked down on São Lourenço – still stunningly beautiful despite the malignance that had grown in the heart of the town.

This morning he had chosen to climb the second tallest peak, and was now making his way carefully up a ridge on the east side, the terrain beneath his boots rocky and tough. It was a few minutes after seven but the day was already growing warm, a slow heat that hinted at the scorching hours to come. The morning sun painted the mountains in pastel hues of orange and pink and cast long, jagged shadows across the rugged landscape. From this vantage point, the town below looked so peaceful, so pristine. Toy-sized buildings, clustered like specks of white paint, nestled against the deep blues of the Atlantic. It was hard to imagine that darkness and despair roamed its cobbled streets, but that was the same with a lot of things when viewed from a safe distance. Even the past, with its sharp edges and shadowy corners, seemed a lot less menacing in hindsight.

Because what was it they said? Comedy was just tragedy plus time. There was something in that, Beckett thought. Although, that was no consolation when you were slap bang in the middle of it.

As he climbed higher, he came across a road that wound around the side of the mountain. A proper road, too, wide enough for two cars to pass in some places. With the cliff face here so sheer, he decided to walk on the road for a while. His heart was beating fast and he was out of breath from the altitude, but the challenge, the pure exertion, was a welcome distraction. He was a man alone with his thoughts in the splendid isolation of nature, and for the first time in a while, a sense of deep calm overcame him. Up here in the clouds, away from the world, everything was beautiful and nothing hurt. Even the scars of his own past felt a little less raw.

However, as he continued around a bend, his serenity and solitude were interrupted by the sight of a car jack-knifed across the road up ahead. Despite the tarmac beneath his feet, the vehicle seemed oddly out of place in the idyllic mountain setting. Two women stood next to the vehicle, their expressions a mixture of frustration and concern. For a moment Beckett just watched, his gaze sweeping over the scene, assessing the situation. Then, rolling his shoulders back, he made his way over to them.

The women looked to be in their mid-thirties, both locals from the looks of their tanned skin and dark hair. The taller of the two wore a vibrant sundress, while the other, smaller, mousier, was dressed in loose beige trousers and a t-shirt. Their clothes, coupled with the large designer sunglasses they both wore, marked them out as being reasonably well-off. As did the sleek Mercedes-Benz Cabriolet in racing green.

"Good morning," Beckett called out, his years of fieldwork ensuring his body language and tone were casual and non-threatening. "You look to be having a bit of car trouble. Need a hand?" He opted to speak in English, assuming his tourist status would also make him seem less of a red flag in the rich women's eyes.

The one in the sundress shot him a look that could peel

paint off a wall. "Are you a mechanic?" Her English was perfect – as was her accusatory tone – but her husky accent was all Portuguese.

Beckett stopped and held his hands up. "Not by trade. But I know my way around an engine." He pointed to the Mercedes. "May I?"

The second woman whispered something inaudible to her friend, prompting a muted exchange between the two of them. The one in the sundress lowered her chin and regarded Beckett over the top of her glasses. "Do you think you can fix it?"

"I can certainly have a look."

"Fine," she said, with a nod. "Thank you."

She stepped aside, eyeing him intently as he negotiated the bonnet release mechanism and flipped the hood. As he did so, the second woman scurried away to the rear of the car, purposely avoiding his gaze. But Beckett had already clocked the dark purple bruising behind her sunglasses.

"Are you all right?" he asked her, pointing to his own eye. "That looks nasty."

But the woman remained silent. She didn't look at him.

"She's fine. We're both fine," her friend told him. "You don't want to concern yourself with our problems. I'll ring someone and they'll send a truck."

"It could take a while and it's already hot up here in the mountains," he replied. "It's only going to get hotter, by my reckoning."

"That's summer in São Lourenço." Sundress sighed. "Very hot. Very humid."

Beckett caught her eye as she fanned herself. She was a good-looking woman. Wearing a little too much make-up for his preference perhaps, but with amazing cheekbones and full lips that looked to be the product of good genes rather than surgery.

He turned his attention back to the car. It was an E-Class,

an older model but still in good condition. The morning sun gleamed off the bodywork, warming the skin on his arms and the back of his neck as he inspected the engine. It took him only a moment to spot the problem amongst the complexity of tubes, wires, and metal.

"Here we are. I'm afraid your alternator belt's given up," he declared, holding up the shredded remains to show the woman. "It might have been a fault or just wear and tear."

She sneered at the piece of rubber. "And we need this to drive?"

"Yes. I'm afraid so."

"Can you fix it?"

Beckett tilted his head to one side to take the woman in. For someone receiving help without charge, she was certainly rude. But for some reason he found her attitude oddly endearing. Surrounded by such natural serenity, she was surly to the point of being comical. Or maybe it was just the mountain air. The altitude getting to him.

"I can at least try," he said, giving her his most charming smile. Beckett was a loner at heart, not one to naturally mix well with others. But he was also highly adept at negotiation and forging connections when circumstances demanded. "I need to check in the boot – the trunk. Is that okay?"

Sundress shrugged and stuck out her bottom lip, which he took as an affirmative. Walking around to the rear of the car and popping the boot, he found an emergency tool kit in an enclosed compartment, which also contained a spare drive belt. Jackpot.

Beckett leaned his large frame over the engine. Replacing the belt was a relatively simple but cumbersome task. First, he released the tensioner, removing the damaged belt. Then, ensuring the new one aligned perfectly with the pulleys, he secured it in place by tightening the tensioner. As he worked, he could hear the women embroiled in another whispered exchange, but he zoned them out so he could finish. There was a certain peace to be found in manual labour, in solving problems like this one.

"That should do it," he told Sundress. "Would you mind getting in and seeing if she starts?"

The woman did so without comment and Beckett couldn't help noticing how gracefully she climbed into the car and swung her legs under the steering console, flashing a section of sun-kissed thigh. He looked up, seeing her companion glaring at him. Or at least, she looked to be. It was hard to tell behind the dark glasses.

With a roar, the engine burst into life. "There we go!" Beckett said, giving the engine one last inspection and then slamming the bonnet closed. "That should get you to where you need to go."

The woman eased the car over to the mountainside so it was no longer blocking the road and turned the engine off. Beckett followed, still clapping the grime from his hands. He'd need a shower as soon as he got back to the hotel, but in this heat that was a given.

"Thank you," the woman said, removing her sunglasses as he got closer. "I appreciate your help." Then she smiled and all the steeliness fell from her demeanour. Without the glasses, her cat-like eyes were bright and intelligent-looking, her large pupils as dark as her hair.

"Happy to help," Beckett replied, not taking his eyes from hers. For a moment something unspoken passed between them, a jolt of electricity that had nothing to do with the car's wiring. The ensuing pause was heavy with potential – a sensation not foreign to Beckett, but one he hadn't felt in ages.

Then the woman broke it, her voice regaining its edge. "Can we give you a lift back into town?"

Beckett's attention shifted to the woman's silent companion. She'd stiffened at the mere suggestion of giving him a ride, her eyes widening behind the sunglasses. Something about her overt nervousness unsettled him. He didn't think it was simply down to his appearance or the fact he was a stranger. He'd been nothing but charming and affable. Hell, he'd just saved them from a long walk back to town wearing not-very-sensible shoes. But, regardless, he didn't want to exacerbate her unease.

"I appreciate the offer. But I'd prefer to walk."

The woman nodded, respect flashing in her eyes. As her friend climbed into the passenger seat, she switched on the engine, and Beckett called out to her. "Perhaps we'll cross paths again? I'm in town for the week."

The woman looked back at him, a small smile playing on her lips. "Perhaps we will."

"I'm Michael, by the way. Michael Day."

"Maria..." she began, and for some reason, Beckett knew exactly what she was going to say next. It could have been her confident attitude, the expensive car, or just that these days he expected trouble to seek him out wherever it could. He stiffened as his instincts were proven correct. "Maria Silva," she concluded, pulling the car away. "I'll see you around, Michael Day."

8

Beckett slid a fresh glass of beer towards the thin-faced man on the other side of the bar, offering him a congenial nod as he did. It was the third beer Beckett had served the man since starting his first shift at Armando's taberna an hour earlier, and the guy had already made it clear he wasn't here for conversation. He grabbed the glass of amber ale and slid a handful of coins across the counter without making eye contact.

"*Aproveite*," Beckett called out regardless, as the man shuffled away.

Despite his coloured past, it was his first time working behind a bar and he was enjoying it, even if his mind was a little preoccupied. He picked up a cloth hanging over the side of the sink and began polishing a wine glass, smirking slightly at the stereotypical bartender image he presented.

The bar hummed softly with subdued conversations, underscored by the strains of a Samba tune coming from the old jukebox in the far corner. The taberna wasn't bustling, but from what Armando had said, this was as full as it got these days. It was a real pity, Beckett mused. It was a nice place These were nice people.

An old man who'd introduced himself as Humberto sat hunched at the far end of the counter, nursing his drink. He looked to be in his mid-sixties but it was hard to tell, his weathered face was a map of hard-lived years, heavy tales deepening the lines around his eyes. He wasn't much of a talker either, yet there was a sparkle in his eyes that defied his sombre demeanour. It was as if he'd seen more than his share of both good and bad but chose to keep a cheerful spirit nonetheless.

Beckett placed the wine glass down. He'd hoped being here tonight would clear his head, but he kept looping back to his encounter on the mountain road that morning.

Maria Silva.

Before Armando had left, Beckett had mentioned their meeting and had got a deep scowl and a shake of the head in response – a stern warning to stay clear of her. All he'd said was he'd helped with her car, but Armando was adamant. She might not be involved in her father's business the way her brothers were, but she was still a Silva. She was still the eldest child and only daughter of the most feared man in town.

But for Beckett, Maria's allure wasn't just skin deep. Beyond her striking appearance and enigmatic aura, he was intrigued by her very essence, particularly within the context of her family's sinister reputation. Despite studying human nature for most of his adult life, he was still fascinated and confused by people in equal measure. He'd often toyed with the old nature or nurture debate, but it never seemed so cut and dry to him. Could someone like Maria really spring from such a dark seed? And, ultimately, did it matter?

"Hey, Mike, everything okay?"

His thoughts were broken as Armando appeared carrying a tray of clean glasses still steaming from the dishwasher out back. He placed them on the counter and began to unstack them as Beckett joined him.

"I thought you'd be gone all evening."

"Yeah, me too." Armando puffed out his cheeks. "But the doctors saw us straight away. Lina was exhausted when we got back, so I put her to bed. I figured I'd come here so I'm not rattling around the place disturbing her."

"Fair enough." Beckett stepped back, eyeing his new acquaintance.

"But you've been coping okay so far?" Armando asked.

"Yes. All good. It's a decent place you've got here."

"It's a sleepy-ass place, nowadays. I'd readily give up decency for a few more customers and more money in the till."

Beckett laughed. He knew Armando didn't mean that. Or perhaps he did. But only as far as his finances went. He moved into the main space of the taberna and collected the empty glasses. Apart from Humberto and the quiet man in the corner, there were a couple of old boys playing dominos and a young couple who'd been lost in each other's eyes since they sat down, sharing whispered asides and soft kisses. They'd bought a bottle of red wine and were certainly making it last, but Beckett thought it was sweet. Maybe he was getting soft in his old age.

As he returned to the bar, he found Armando staring at a photograph pinned to a wooden post beside the shelves of spirits. The image was of a young boy with dark hair standing on the beach. He was leering into the camera with a wide, happy smile, showing off a gap where his front teeth should have been.

"Your boy?" Beckett asked, nodding at the photo.

Armando's gaze lingered on the picture. "Yes," he replied, his voice barely above a whisper. "Ricardo. He was seven at the time. He would have turned ten last week."

Beckett faltered. *Would have.*

Across the room the jukebox shuffled onto a new tune, a gentle guitar melody setting a sombre backdrop to their words.

"I'm sorry," Beckett murmured.

Armando nodded, running his finger down the edge of the photo. "Thank you. It almost tore Lina and I apart when he passed. But we're healing, slowly. One day at a time." His eyes were glassy, locked on the memories only he could see.

Beckett busied himself with cleaning another glass, allowing the silence to sit between them. It was an art form of sorts, knowing when to push, when to pull, when to simply stand still. His eyes flicked to the entrance. The door had been left ajar and a single shaft of dying sunlight sliced through the dim interior. Outside, the town was succumbing to twilight.

A phone rang, disrupting the subdued atmosphere. As Beckett turned, he observed Armando pulling a phone from his pocket, his brow creasing as he saw the name on the screen. He answered it, speaking in muffled Portuguese for a few moments. Beckett focused his attention on the glass, trying not to listen, but he couldn't help but hear Armando saying he'd be home soon and not to worry.

"Trouble?" Beckett asked, reading the tension that had crept into his posture as he pocketed the phone.

"Yes and no," Armando replied, glancing around. "My wife... Lina. She is awake. She needs me."

Beckett gestured toward the door. "Go. I can handle things here. If you're all right with me locking up later."

Armando seemed torn momentarily, but then nodded. "You're a good man, Michael Day." Retrieving a set of keys from the back counter, he handed them over. "Hold onto these for now. I've got another set. You're sure you can handle things?"

"Absolutely," Beckett reassured him. He watched Armando hasten for the door and leave without another word. Poor guy. He looked as if he was carrying the world on his shoulders.

Returning to his position behind the bar, his eyes met Humberto's observant gaze. The old man appeared to have been watching him.

"Another beer?" Beckett asked.

Humberto wrinkled his nose. "Why the hell not."

The rest of the evening passed quickly. No one left, no one arrived. Beckett was in high spirits, joking and swapping stories with Humberto and the other old-timers who had given up on their game of dominos and taken up residence at the bar. He served drinks, collected glasses, wiped down the empty tables. He even polished the brass fixtures on the bar top. Beckett's father had drummed into him from an early age that no matter what task you were involved in, you gave it your absolute focus and did it to the best of your ability. Whether you were serving beers or saving hostages, there was nothing more rewarding than a job well done.

Three hours later, the night was winding down. Beckett was about to announce last orders when the taberna door swung open, slamming into the adjacent wall with a bang. In walked two men, their swagger barely masking their evident inebriation. Beckett watched as they prowled through the room, sizing up the patrons.

The lead man was built like a brick wall – broad-shouldered, heavily muscled, with a face that had taken a few too many punches. A cruel sneer curled his bulbous lips. His friend, on the other hand, was the polar opposite. Tall, lean, with chiselled features and an almost boyish charm. His hair was slicked back, revealing a forehead that was a bit too high. His eyes were sharp and calculating, but there was an undeniable sleaziness in his gaze, especially when it landed on the young woman sitting with her boyfriend at the side of the room.

Beckett watched as the men zeroed in on the couple. The bigger of the two approached first, full of bluster and ego.

Placing his hand on the table, he leaned into the young woman, slurring a crude comment that elicited a high-pitched laugh from his friend. Beckett straightened, preparing himself as the woman shrank from the unwanted attention. The man said something else and she let out a yelp, pressing herself against her boyfriend. He shielded her as best he could, his voice shaky as he implored the men to leave them alone. But to creeps like these, such warnings only made matters worse.

Beckett was across the room in a few strides, positioning himself between the men and the couple. "I think you've overstayed your welcome, gentlemen," he said, speaking Portuguese with a steady voice. "Besides, we're about to close. So if you wouldn't mind stepping back outside, I'd appreciate it."

The slender man, hair slicked back, confronted Beckett head-on, the disdain evident in his sneer. "Who the fuck are you?" he asked. "Where's Lopes?"

"I'm in charge tonight," Beckett replied. "Mr Lopes is busy. Now if you could please—"

"Where are you from, *amigo*?"

"England," Beckett said, returning to his native tongue. "I'm English."

"Perhaps you should fuck off back there, huh, *English*? I was trying to talk to the *mulher bonita* here." He reached down and stroked the woman's face, causing her to recoil in disgust.

"All right, that's enough." Beckett stepped closer. "Leave these people alone." As he spoke he felt the air shift and his instincts kicked in.

The burly man lunged first. His punch, bolstered by the false confidence of a half-dozen too many beers was sluggish, easy to anticipate. Beckett stepped out of the way, leaving the man swiping at thin air. He was all brute force and no technique against Beckett's military-honed instincts.

Stepping back, Beckett read the cues, saw the man's weight

shift slightly to the left. Anticipating the trajectory of the right hook, he ducked low and pivoted away, grabbing the man's outstretched wrist as he did. Leveraging the man's own momentum, Beckett executed a swift lock and twist, feeling the resistance as the joint locked. He pushed it further, forcing the arm back into an impossible angle. Another swift twist, a surge of pressure, and he heard the snap of bone and cartilage. The man howled in pain as Beckett shoved him away and spun around to face the second man, who had enough bluster inside of him to still be eager for a fight. Although quicker and more nimble than his friend, Beckett's years of experience had him deflect the flurry of quick jabs with a measured calm.

"I'll kill you," he spat, eyes wild with fury.

"I'm not so sure about that," Beckett retorted, stepping back to draw him away from the young couple. "You've not laid a hand on me yet." He was hoping to rile the young thug some more. Cool, focused anger was a useful energy in a fight – but blind rage, indignation, it could easily tip the balance the other way.

Feinting left, Beckett dodged a sharp jab and grabbed the man's hand, his thumb digging into the pressure point in his wrist. The slime ball's face contorted in pain as he instinctively tried to pull back, but Beckett's grip was unrelenting.

Switching tactics, Beckett spun on his heel, yanking the creep off balance and following up with a well-aimed elbow to the solar plexus. The man doubled over, gasping for air that wouldn't come. Beckett glanced around, conscious of his environment; he could have used a table or a bar stool to his advantage, but he didn't want to damage Armando's place any more than he had to.

And he didn't need them.

His skills, his strength, they were enough. This wasn't a bar brawl, this was a controlled display of combat skills, sending a message clear and succinct – don't mess with John Beckett.

One final uppercut sent the man sprawling onto the beer-soaked floor and just like that it was over. Done with as quickly as it had begun.

Beckett spun around, his body poised for further threats. But the bar was quiet now, the customers watching him in stunned silence. His gaze softened as it settled on the couple who had been the target of the men's harassment. They were staring at him, open-mouthed but with eyes full of gratitude. Beckett gave them a curt nod before turning his attention back to the two men.

"I think it's time you boys went home to bed," he said. It wasn't a suggestion. "Now get lost."

The larger man, clutching his broken arm, let out a pained grunt as he staggered to his feet. "*Vá se foder*," he hissed as he slunk towards the door, his teeth clenched against the hurt. "*Filho da puta.*"

Beckett stood tall, undeterred by the hollow insults thrown his way. He remained still as the second man stirred and clambered to his feet, albeit with less haste. He was holding his side, and his slick features were now marred by a burgeoning bruise and a bust lip. He swayed slightly, the effects of the beating all too clear.

He glared at Beckett, a glimmer of unbroken arrogance shining through the pain. "You've made a big mistake," he spat, enunciating each word with bitter emphasis. "A BIG FUCKING MISTAKE. You're a dead man."

The threat lingered in the air as he staggered out of the door, but Beckett was unperturbed. He'd faced more severe threats than that in his life. He waited until the two men were gone and shut the door behind them.

Now, with the pair gone, the tension in the room eased. Beckett set about cleaning up the mess with calm efficiency. He returned an overturned chair to its rightful position and carried a discarded beer bottle to the bar.

"That was very impressive," Humberto said, as Beckett placed the bottle in the recycling bin. "But you might have just landed yourself in a whole heap of trouble, my friend."

"Oh? Why's that?" Beckett asked, as he began wiping down the counter. "You know those guys?"

Humberto's expression darkened. "The big one? I'm not certain. But the other," he paused, glancing at the exit and back, "that was Rodrigo Silva."

9

Armando Lopes had a tired grin on his face as he walked, the evening breeze billowing the tails of his untucked shirt. His night had been a blur of mixed emotions, of worry and then surprise and then even contentment. The way he and Lina had talked, even her tone of voice – it had stirred the dormant embers of optimism in his heart. They might have finally turned a corner, he thought, as he strode through the town. Only time would tell.

The clock tower struck midnight as he approached the taberna. He should be at home now. He should have stayed with his wife, held her close as she slept. But he was wide awake and needed to check everything was well before he could settle for the night. The new guy, Mike, seemed more than capable and had been happy to lock up, but that little bar was Armando's livelihood and their only income since Lina had stopped working. He carried with him an insatiable need to ensure everything was as it should be, even if it meant venturing outside rather than staying in the warmth and safety of his home.

The familiar scent of aged wood, sea salt and stale beer

greeted him as he pushed open the door to his establishment, half-expecting to see Mike sitting at one of the tables, sipping an after-hours drink. He wouldn't have minded that one bit, it was one of the perks of working in a bar – so he was a little taken aback to find his new employee, broom in hand, sweeping the floor.

Mike glanced up and smiled before returning to his task. Armando watched him for a moment as he methodically ran the broom across the floor, noting the man's stature, his obvious athleticism, the muscles in his forearms rippling as they moved with purpose. He'd been evasive about a military past when Armando had brought it up, but there was something about him. Something that didn't quite add up. His dirty-blond hair fell carelessly over his forehead and his jawline was shadowed with a few days' worth of stubble, but it was the look in his eyes – familiar yet elusive – that gave Armando pause. It was as if he'd already seen too much but was ready to take on the world regardless.

"Hey, man," Armando called out. "Still working hard, huh? I'm impressed."

Mike looked up. "I wanted to make sure I left it as I found it," he said, straightening. "And that's twice you've showed up unannounced. Are you checking up on me?"

"I guess I can't keep away from the place. It's not that I don't trust you…"

"No. I get it. This bar's important to you. It's good to care about these things."

Armando liked this enigmatic Englishman. Whatever he had going on, his gut told him he was a good person. "And what is it you care about, Michael Day?" he asked.

"I care about doing what's right," he replied, but there was no reading his expression. "Speaking of which…"

"What is it?" Armando frowned, surveying the room. Mike had done a good job cleaning up but now something caught his eye – a smashed glass over in the corner, the shards reflecting the light.

"We had a bit of trouble just before closing time. A couple of drunks came in and started hassling a young couple."

"O-kay." Armando studied the man's face more intently than ever. "But you handled it?"

"Let's just say I defused the situation as efficiently as I could." His gaze was fixed on the broken glass, his regret evident.

"So what is it?" Armando asked, a sinking feeling in his belly. "What's going on, Mike?"

He sighed. "It turns out one of the men was Rodrigo Silva. I'm sorry, Armando."

"Ah shit, man. You rough him up?"

He curled his lip. "It could have gone a lot worse for him. But he didn't seem very happy with me as I was showing him the door."

Armando glanced around his bar once more, a sense of unease creeping over him. This place was more than just a business. It was his life; had been ever since Ricardo had passed. His eyes landed on a bottle of whisky on the back shelf, the pull of it almost unbearable given the circumstances. But he couldn't. He wouldn't. He'd promised Lina no more drink. Not whilst…

He glanced back at Mike. "You shouldn't have done that," he said, shaking his head.

The Englishman nodded and for a moment the silence between them was heavier than hell. "I know." He leaned the broom against the side of the bar. "And I don't want to get you in any more trouble. So I think it's best if I don't come back here." He smiled, and it was all genuine. "Thanks for the opportunity."

"Who the hell are you, Mike?" Armando asked, lowering

his voice. "I know Rodrigo is a little creep, but he always has muscle with him. You haven't got a scratch on you."

"There were only two of them."

"Jesus. And you dealt with them both that easily? What's the deal, man?"

"Like I told you," Mike replied, "I'm just a guy travelling the world. And I don't like bad people getting away with things. But I appreciate it puts you in a tough spot…"

Armando puffed his cheeks out. "Yeah, I'm sorry. I can't see any other way around it. If Rodrigo comes back with more men and you're still here, it would go really bad, really quick. If you want my advice – leave town. First thing in the morning. Here." He walked around the counter and opened the till, drawing out a handful of notes. "For your work tonight."

Mike stepped back from his outstretched hand. "No. Keep it. Buy yourself a new glass. I mean it. I don't want your money."

Armando shook his head. "I can't tell if you're the most honourable man I ever met or the dumbest."

"Can't I be both?"

They both laughed the same sort of laugh. It wasn't forced, but it wasn't particularly joyful.

"The thing is," Mike continued, "yes, Rodrigo and his buddy were throwing their weight around, upsetting people, but they were easy to take down. I thought the Silvas were this big terrifying organisation. If one of the main players is just an arrogant thug, then surely a bunch of you could—"

"No!" Armando cut him off. "They get worse the further you go up the family tree. I know what you're saying, man. And I have considered it a lot. But no one around here wants a war. Least of all me."

He thought of Lina at home, of Ricardo, and his bar. But the Englishman was still staring at him, waiting for answers he wasn't sure he could provide. Letting his shoulders sag, Armando gestured to the nearest table.

"Have a seat a second, all right?" They both sat. He composed his thoughts, then said, "The thing you've got to realise about the situation is that it didn't happen overnight. This was once a good town and they were just a rich family. Emilio Silva had a couple of legitimate businesses, a car rental firm and a winery in Lisbon. He still has them, I think. Hell, he was even some help to the town in the early days, lending money to people, providing aid to struggling businesses. People let him into their lives readily. So when the tide changed, everyone took too long to realise what was going on. And by then it was too late. Slowly but surely Silva's grip on the town tightened. Then a few years ago he started to send his men around to collect what he called 'business rates'."

Mike scoffed. "A protection racket, by any other name."

"Exactly."

"And the core of the organisation is him and the two brothers? Maria's definitely not involved?"

"Like I already told you – not as far as I know. Obviously there was a mother once too, but she was already dead when they moved here. I heard she died in mysterious circumstances when the children were small. The rumour is Emilio killed her. But no one would ever say that out loud."

"How old is this guy?"

"Early sixties, maybe. He's a big guy, weird-looking. But he's clever and cunning. People tried to fight his control at first, refusing to pay, standing up to his thugs. But those who resisted started disappearing. Now everyone is terrified, so they pay up and keep their heads down. And now I hear other rumours…"

"What rumours?"

Armando rubbed at his eyes. Did he really want to say more? He stood by his assessment of Mike Day as an honourable man, but these were things he didn't want to even consider.

Still, maybe staying silent was part of the problem.

"I don't know for sure," he started, "but in the last year everything seems to have got so much worse. People have started going missing more regularly. Even those who never crossed Emilio. Men, women, sometimes children."

Mike's wide eyes searched his face. "Your son?"

"No. He was taken by illness. But losing him... I understand why people fear the Silvas, why they bow down to them." He rubbed at his face. "They're not just protecting their livelihoods, but their loved ones too. They'll do anything to protect them. Even if that means letting themselves be walked all over."

Mike leaned back and folded his arms. Armando watched him, feeling every bit the useless coward that he was.

But what could he do?

What could anyone do?

"Someone needs to stand up to these people, Armando."

He smiled. "Maybe. But who? Me? You? You're clearly a tough guy with lots of experience dealing with people like Rodrigo. But he's a small piece of the pie. I get what you're saying, but it can't be done, man. I wish it was different but it's not. So you need to get out of town. As soon as possible."

Mike considered this for a moment, then nodded and got to his feet. "Fair enough. If that's what you want." He looked down at Armando and smiled. "You take care of yourself."

"You too, Mike." He held out his hand and they shook. "Be lucky."

The Englishman looked as if he wanted to say something else but thought better of it. Instead, he pulled the set of keys out of his pocket, handed them to Armando with a brief nod and left.

Someone needs to stand up to these people...

The words echoed in Armando's head as he watched Mike disappear into the night. Rising himself, he walked to the door and placed his hand on the light switch. His bar, his town, his way of life, they were all under threat. All because he was too scared to fight back. In that moment he felt more shame than he'd felt in a long time. But it was too late for him. It was too late for everyone in São Lourenço.

He switched off the light. Lina was at home. She needed him now.

10

Emilio Silva sat at his grand kitchen table, staring at the extensive selection of shiny chrome appliances lined up against the wall. Staring, but not really seeing. Despite the cruel and brutal way he conducted his business, he often slept like a baby and should have been asleep hours ago. But it was now 1 a.m. and he was still awake.

He sat alone, his fingers incessantly raking through his sparse, slicked-back hair, weaving and yanking at the oily tufts. He had a lot on his mind. The deadline for the deal with Barbosa was growing ever closer and they were yet to fully complete their side of the bargain. If they failed... well, it wasn't worth thinking about.

The problem was, it was all the elder Silva *could* think about.

His eyes darted across the dark wood of the kitchen table worn smooth by years of clenched fists and spilled drinks. He traced his fingers over the surface. He needed a release, an outlet for the storm brewing in his soul. It was late, but maybe a visit to 'Eagle' or 'Wolf' – the code names of his two stash houses – would dissipate the storm building inside him.

But as he stood to leave, the front door swung open then slammed shut with a force that reverberated throughout the house.

"Who's there?" he called out.

Silence.

Sidestepping over to the cabinet at the side of the room, he eased open the middle drawer and lifted out the pistol he kept there. A Beretta 8000, small and compact, and fully loaded as always. He moved to the doorway and raised the pistol as heavy footsteps echoed through the house, going as far as the front room.

With a surge of adrenaline, he left his study and crossed the dark hallway. His senses were heightened, his heart hammering against his ribs. He traversed the doorway of the front room and peered around the frame, gun in hand.

"What the fuck?" He lowered the gun and stepped into the room. His youngest son, Rodrigo, was slumped on the plush leather couch, head in his hands. "What the hell are you doing making this racket?" Silva scolded. "It's the middle of the night, for Christ's sake. Have you been drinking again?"

Rodrigo lowered his hands and looked at him. His face was a mess of bruises and broken skin.

"What the fuck?" Silva's heart clenched. The sight of Rodrigo so vulnerable, so beaten, was an affront to the family name. "What happened? Who did this to you?" He placed the gun on the sideboard and marched over to his son. "Talk to me. Now." His voice was a low growl, his hands clenched into fists at his sides as he resisted the urge to slap the kid across his swollen face.

"It's nothing. I'm fine."

Silva grabbed Rodrigo by the chin and forced his head up into the light. "You don't look fine. Who did this?"

Rodrigo snagged his head away. "Some English guy working at Armando Lopes's taberna in town. Varella and I were in there talking to some girl and he jumped us. Took us both by surprise."

"He beat you and Varella? One guy?"

Rodrigo sneered. "I said he got the jump on us. He was lucky."

"Yeah?" Silva's rage flared. The audacity of an outsider in his town beating on his men, his family. The thought alone was enough to make his blood boil. "And who is this guy?"

"I don't know. I've never seen him before."

"Was he big?"

"Kind of. But don't worry about it," Rodrigo protested, wincing as he tried to sit up. "I'm going to deal with it."

Silva stared at his son. Rodrigo had always been weak-willed and now wasn't the time for the Silva name to be tarnished. Especially not with the deal looming and them about to step into the big leagues. Salvador Barbosa wouldn't stand for shit like this.

He considered punishments, but the kid had suffered enough for one night. His ego certainly had. Perhaps it would do him good to get his ass kicked, but that didn't mean Silva was any less enraged by this stranger who had raised his hand to his family. He took it personally.

He took everything personally.

"No, Rodrigo. I'll deal with it." He straightened, his imposing figure casting a shadow over his son's bruised face. "Now get cleaned up and get to bed. We'll talk about this in the morning."

Rodrigo glared at him for a moment, but if he had any riposte he quickly thought better of it. He looked at his hands, at the floor. "Yes, Father. Thank you." He got to his feet. "I'm sorry. I didn't mean to—"

"Go!" Silva snarled. "I don't want to see you again tonight." He picked up the pistol from the sideboard along with the keys to his Jeep.

"Where are you going?" Rodrigo asked.

Silva growled to himself. The kid was pushing his luck now. Who the hell did Rodrigo think he was talking to, asking him such questions? He might be his son, but that didn't mean he wouldn't rain hell down on him if he overstepped the mark. The boy wasn't impervious to his father's rage. No one was.

"To Eagle House," he said, not turning around. "I need to check a few things."

"Sure. How's it going with the shipment?"

"We're not talking about this now," Silva responded, his back still to his son. Now more than ever he needed that release, an aside from the swirling chaos in his mind. "Go to bed. I'll deal with you later."

With that, Silva left the room, the promise of revenge simmering within him. No one stood up against him and his family and lived to tell the tale. As he closed the door behind him, he felt a cold thrill rush down his arms and legs. At least now he had something to take his mind off the Barbosa deal. This English prick would rue the day he ever messed with the Silva family.

11

Up in the north of the country, Salvador Barbosa was also awake. But unlike his new business partner, this was a common occurrence for him. A choice, even. Barbosa was wired differently than most. He preferred to work in the late hours when lesser men were asleep. When he could plan his next moves undisturbed. Since his teenage years he'd only ever needed two or three hours of sleep a night and now he thrived in the still hush of the early morning. While most men were vulnerable and exposed in the dead of night, Barbosa wielded power and control.

Tonight – or rather this morning, because it was already the next day – was no exception. Barbosa prowled the floor of his grand master bedroom, his imagination running wild as he considered the implications and possibilities that would arise from his latest venture. A temple to power and wealth, his bedroom mirrored his personality: extravagant, imposing and merciless. The floor was made of polished marble, cold and unyielding beneath his bare feet as they slapped against it. Enormous windows running the length of the room framed the nocturnal panorama of Porto, his glorious city now a murky palette of inky blues and deep purples. Down towards the south of the city flowed the Douro River, serene but relentless just like him.

The crimson silk of his dressing gown, embellished with intricate golden patterns, flowed behind him as he moved over to the window. Despite – or perhaps because of – his diminutive size, Barbosa was a man of vanity, his taste for the ostentatious not reserved just for his home. His eye-catching gown, a stark contrast against the deep emerald of his silk pyjamas, made one thing clear – Salvador Barbosa was a man unafraid of flaunting himself and his supremacy. This was his world, and he was the undisputed king.

He flinched when the piercing ring of his secure line shattered the silence like a brick through glass. Even though he'd been expecting the call, his breath quickened as he walked over to the bureau to answer it. Once there he paused, like a predator poised in the calm before an attack. Then he picked up the phone.

"Señor Castellano," he said, slipping effortlessly into Spanish on answering. "I'm glad to be speaking with you. Thank you for calling."

"It's been some while since we spoke, Señor Barbosa," Elvio Castellano replied. "I trust everything is still going to plan."

It was almost 7 p.m. in Mexico and Barbosa imagined Castellano sitting behind a desk in his Mexican fortress, the phone gripped in his huge ham hock of a hand. The two men had met only once in the flesh, but that was enough for Barbosa to remember every detail of the imposing head of the Sangre de Dragón Cartel. He was huge, a sinewy ogre of a man, with a body sculpted through violence and hardship. His dark, leathery skin was a canvas of prison tattoos and twisted scars, stories of his life told in grotesque imagery. But most unnerving was his face, the left side of which was marred by a gnarled patch of scar tissue with a glass eye nestled within the disfigurement – a cold, lifeless orb that gave his stare a chilling intensity.

Barbosa swallowed. He might be the top dog in Portugal but he wasn't yet the apex predator he dreamed of being. There were bigger, nastier individuals above him. Castellano was undeniably one of them. "Yes, Señor," he replied. "Everything is still going ahead as planned. I am waiting to hear from my people down in Lisbon regarding the shipment, and once delivered to my secure harbour, I will arrange the transportation."

"You don't currently have my shipment?"

The line crackled for a moment, amplifying the tension. Barbosa knew the next few words could decide the fate of a lot of things.

"Everything is progressing smoothly," he said, ensuring his tone was calm and measured. Confidence was key, but too much could swing things the other way.

"You are certain of this?"

"The shipment will arrive on schedule," Barbosa replied, his heart pounding against his ribcage. "You have my word."

Silence enveloped the line, the void filled only with the soft buzz of the connection. Then Castellano chuckled. A low rumble that would have sent shivers down the spines of lesser men. "This is good to hear, Señor Barbosa. For your sake, let's hope you're right. Call me in two days. By then I want to hear that my shipment is on its way. Understood?"

"Yes. Of course."

"Excellent. I'll speak to you soon."

With that, the line went dead. Barbosa placed the phone down, his belly filled with the cold dread only a conversation with Elvio Castellano could induce. As confident as he was about fulfilling the cartel's needs, the lack of recent communication from Silva was unnerving. Gazing out over the city, he wondered if a little motivation might be required.

His thoughts drifted to Duarte Rocha, his old accountant who had disastrously mishandled a money laundering operation down in Madeira. As retribution, Barbosa had devised a grotesque punishment he'd dubbed 'Torn Apart By Failure'. To reflect Rocha's actions, Barbosa had him tied to four SUVs, which were then driven in opposing directions until the pathetic bastard was literally torn into four pieces. A sardonic grin played at the corners of his mouth as remembered the scene, the pop of cartilage dislocating from bone, the tearing of muscle and flesh. It was amazing to him how cleanly and easily limbs could be ripped out of their sockets with the right amount of force. It had truly been a spectacle to behold. A thing of beauty. He could almost still hear the screams as the accountant's limbless torso hit the dirt. The ruthless punishment had been one of his very best creations and also served as an excellent motivational tool for his next – and still current – accountant.

Barbosa didn't think he'd need anything so extreme presently, but complacency was not acceptable. Action was required. His operation was a complex machine that needed constant maintenance, and sometimes a bit of oiling, a bit of pressure, could make all the difference. He walked back to his desk and picked up the phone. It was shortly after 2 a.m. but his work was far from over. He had a call to make. There was no rest for the wicked.

12

Sunlight filtered through the thin curtains of Armando's bedroom as he slipped out from under the covers and pulled on the worn trousers he'd left draped over the back of the chair. Although it was a few minutes before nine, he'd been awake for much longer, unable to sleep once the dawn had arrived, bringing with it memories of the previous evening.

Putting on a clean t-shirt, he stopped at the end of the bed to watch Lina as she slept. She looked so peaceful, so unburdened. Her chestnut hair splayed across the pillow; her delicate features softened in sleep. The sight filled Armando's heart with a mixture of love and sadness. Despite the worried phone call demanding he return last night, she'd been asleep when he'd got home and he hadn't wanted to disturb her from the rest she so desperately needed. It was the same story this morning. With the care of a mother leaving a sleeping newborn, he padded down the hallway towards their small but cosy kitchen and eased the door shut behind him.

In the kitchen he set about preparing breakfast, the comforting ritual as grounding as it was necessary. He started a pot of coffee and cracked some eggs into a bowl before chopping up a piece of chorizo and adding it to a pan with a splash of oil. Once it started to spit and the oil turned bright orange, he turned off the hob and added the eggs, stirring as he did so and allowing the residual heat to cook them. His thoughts wandered back to last night. He appreciated Michael Day was only trying to protect his customers and didn't realise who he was dealing with, but he sure had complicated things. Now he had Rodrigo Silva to concern himself with. If he came looking for retribution and Mike was no longer in town, would he leave Armando and his business in peace? Not likely. Rodrigo was hot-headed and egotistical. He'd want revenge. Maybe Armando could appeal to Emilio Silva, offer him double what he normally paid, as compensation. Yet to do that was to admit he was at fault and that could make matters worse. He didn't know what to do. It was another stress he didn't need right now.

"Something smells good, my love."

He looked up to see his wife framed in the doorway. She was wearing a white robe and her hair was loose and messy, cascading over her shoulders and framing her tired but beautiful face. Beneath her weary eyes, glimpses of the spirited woman he'd fallen in love with shone through; before Ricardo had got sick and their hearts had been shattered into a million tiny pieces.

"Hey, you," he said as she entered the room. The corners of her eyes crinkled as she returned his greeting with a weak smile, her hand brushing against his chest. "Sorry, I tried to be quiet…"

"It's fine, darling," she told him, sitting at the small table beside the window and turning her head to the sunshine coming in through the glass. "I've got things I need to do this morning anyway. And how can I sleep when breakfast smells so delicious?"

"It's nothing too special, just eggs and sausage, but it's almost ready. Do you want coffee?"

"Please." She frowned as she looked him up and down. "What's wrong?"

"Nothing… Nothing more than usual." He turned his back on her, taking two cups down from the rack. "I'm just tired."

Hanging on the wall above him was his father's old crucifix and he said a silent prayer as he reached for the coffee jug, asking the Lord for help, for answers. His father was a Godly man but tough as hell. Would he have stood up to the Silvas? Probably. Definitely. Armando poured coffee into the cups, the robust aroma filling his nostrils.

"You've got something on your mind. I can tell," Lina said, as he carried the drinks over to the table. "Come on, what is it?"

"It's nothing in particular. There's just a lot going on right now. You know…"

He returned to the hob and dished up the eggs and chorizo onto two plates, all the while feeling his wife's eyes boring into the back of his head. He hated keeping things from Lina, he hardly ever did, but he didn't want to worry her. Not now.

"Here you go." He placed the food down and sat opposite her. They ate in silence for a few minutes.

"If you don't tell me what's wrong, I'm going to worry anyway."

Armando hesitated; a forkful of eggs poised at his lips. Setting the fork down, he met his wife's penetrating gaze. Her dark eyes were wide and searching.

"I didn't want to worry you," he confessed.

"Well, you are worrying me. So you might as well come clean. What is it?"

A sigh escaped him, deflating his broad shoulders. But she was right. Not knowing something was sometimes as bad as knowing. Especially if you were already on edge and suspicious. So he told her everything, the words tumbling out in a hasty jumble. He told her about the enigmatic Englishman and last night's altercation with Rodrigo Silva. He told her of his decision to let Mike go and how he was now worried about potential consequences.

Fear sparked in Lina's eyes as he spoke, but she seemed to push it aside, replacing it eventually with something closer to hope.

"You think he's hiding something, this Englishman?" she asked.

"I don't know. He reminds me of my old captain in the army. He's strong, wise, every word he says counts, and the way he looks at you when he talks is reassuring and unsettling in equal measures." He shook his head. "It's hard to explain. But yes, I think he's got an interesting past, for sure."

"But you like him? You trust him?"

Armando considered her questions. Despite not knowing much about Michael Day, he realised he did trust him. He was honourable, courageous. Sometimes you could just tell. He told his wife as much.

"Then maybe this man can help us," she said, her tone falling to a whisper. "And not just *us*, I mean the whole town. Jesus, Armando, we need someone to help us."

He sat upright. "No, it's too dangerous."

"Armando!" she cut in, her voice firm. "We aren't safe here anymore. Not with the Silva family controlling everything. You know this. They take nearly all our profits, keep us servile. What happens when there are no customers left for the bar and it has to close? What happens when there are no more profits?"

"But, how…?"

"I don't know. But we can't continue living under their shadow," she said, placing her hand on his. "Things are only going to get worse here, my darling. You know this. We've both heard the rumours. The missing people. And now more than ever we deserve happiness, safety. We can't let them take that from us."

Armando placed his hand over hers. "I don't want to risk you or me getting hurt. Not now. And what can one man do against that family?"

"From what you say, he's willing to stand up to them. And wants to. You said it yourself – he didn't have a scratch on him after the fight. He must have rattled Rodrigo. We can build on that."

Armando huffed out a deep breath. "I don't know, baby. It's a lot to consider. Plus I advised him to leave town. He might have gone already."

"If he's still here you should talk to him. Ask his advice at least. An outsider might see things we've missed. If he's as smart as you say he is… God knows we need help, my love. Before it's too late."

Lina's words stirred something inside him – a spark of defiance, of optimism even. He stared at his wife, the weight of their loss and their shared longing for peace burning in his chest. He was torn, caught between his desire to protect her and a desperate need for a change. Outside, the day was only just beginning, but at this table, within the walls of their humble home, it felt as if a full day had passed already.

"I'll think about it," he said, glancing once more at his father's crucifix. Then he finished his eggs in silence.

13

John Beckett was a man who knew what it meant to be in the wrong place at the wrong time. Having once been part of an elite, off-the-books Special Forces unit, he was no stranger to the type of tension on display as he left his hotel and walked the quiet streets of São Lourenço. There was a subtle yet palpable disturbance in the air that was hard to pinpoint but impossible to ignore. As a soldier he had confronted terrors that would leave most men paralysed with fear, but those dangers usually had a face, there was a clear target. What he picked up on in São Lourenço was different. It was like an insidious fog, hard to grasp, harder to combat. The Silva family might have had the town in a vice-like grip, but it was fear itself that poisoned the air here.

The morning light spilled across the town, illuminating the winding streets. As he walked, his piercing blue eyes scanned his surroundings with practised vigilance, every movement, every muted conversation tugging at his well-tuned instincts. He was a man trained to read his environment, to react swiftly and decisively. And today the environment suggested caution.

He didn't want to be the catalyst for more chaos in an

already beleaguered town. But given his run-in with the younger Silva last night, there was a good chance that ship had sailed. He wondered if he should stick around. Face whatever was coming head-on. Armando had been adamant he should leave São Lourenço behind, but Beckett felt indebted to him. And, truth be told, a part of him wouldn't mind another face-off with Rodrigo Silva.

As he strode through the town, the weight of the decision pressed on him. Was he truly what he told people he was – a simple traveller, committed to no one and nothing? Or was the soldier in him, the protector, still too dominant to ignore, especially when the vulnerable were at stake? More worryingly, if he couldn't answer these simple questions, how could he expect to ever move forward with his life?

Navigating the weave of streets and winding lanes, he was greeted by the sight of the main square up ahead. It was already showing signs of life as locals assembled their produce stalls and the few remaining cafés began morning preparations. The aroma of fresh bread wafted out from a nearby bakery, intertwining with the distinct scent of strong coffee. Amongst the hum of activity, Beckett zoned in on a familiar face, seated alone at a café across the other side of the square. Today she had her hair up in a high ponytail, and although she was wearing another pair of immense sunglasses that obscured most of her face, her razor-sharp cheekbones and full pout – coloured today with bright red lipstick – were distinct. It was her. The woman from the mountainside.

Maria Silva.

She seemed lost in thought, in a world of her own amidst the growing noise of the town square. Her perfectly sculpted eyebrows furrowed slightly as she sipped her coffee. However, as Beckett approached, recognition flashed across her face and the frown was replaced by an enigmatic smile. "Well, look who it is. Michael Day, the helpful Englishman."

Playing along, Beckett stopped and doffed an invisible cap, immediately wishing he hadn't. Maria giggled as he straightened and cleared his throat.

"Good morning," he said. "I assume your car made it back into town okay."

"It drove like a dream," she replied. "Thank you again."

"Don't mention it."

She sat back, flicking her ponytail over her shoulder. The morning light did nothing to diminish her mysterious aura as she removed her sunglasses and her dark, feline eyes fixed on his. "Would you like to join me?" she asked.

Beckett hesitated momentarily. After his actions the previous night, being seen with Maria Silva would only add fuel to an already out of control fire. Yet there was something about her that drew him in. She was certainly beautiful, but it was more than that – she had a captivating manner, old-school class but with a sense of mischief.

"If you don't mind." He pulled out a chair and sat, glancing around the square as he made himself comfortable. None of the people gathered here were looking over, but there was a palpable restlessness in the air, like everyone was on tenterhooks, waiting to see what happened next.

A silent exchange of smiles ensued, punctuated by Maria tilting her head to one side. "You know, my father and brothers aren't very happy with you."

Beckett maintained his composure while a myriad of thoughts whirled in his head. "Is that so?"

"Well, unless there's another blond Englishman in town. But I've not seen any so far." She narrowed her eyes at him. "You were the one who beat up my younger brother yesterday evening. Yes?"

He remained still, trying to get a read on her. Her tone was playful and the look in her eyes didn't suggest malice. "He was making a nuisance of himself with a young woman. I intervened. He and his friend didn't like it."

Maria smirked, the action devoid of any humour. "That sounds like my brother. But you shouldn't have done that. My father is angry."

"Is he really?"

She narrowed her eyes even further; her turn to try and get a read on him. "Do you know who my father is, Mr Day?"

"I've heard him mentioned."

She shook her head, a more genuine smile teasing at her lips. "Typical British sense of humour. Or are you just an idiot?"

"Do I seem like an idiot?" he asked, catching the server's attention and pointing at Maria's cup of steaming coffee and then at himself, requesting the same.

"No, you don't. But if you've heard of my father, then you should know you're in a lot of trouble."

"Is that a threat?"

"No, it's not." She leaned forward and lowered her voice. For a brief moment her stoic demeanour faltered, replaced by a wave of heavy emotion. "I am not my father or my brothers. I hardly see them. The only reason I know what happened is because Rodrigo called me this morning to tell me to stay away from you. I do not like what they do, or who they are. I never have done…" She glanced away and sighed as if trying to expel a lifetime of worries. Gathering herself, she continued. "I strongly advise you to leave São Lourenço. For your own safety."

Beckett offered a wry smile. "You know, you're not the first person to tell me that."

"I can understand it. My father runs this town and not in a way that benefits anyone but himself and his operations. He is a powerful man, but cruel. The people here do as he says. They fear him. You have no safe haven here, Michael. Look around, people are watching you. The word has spread regarding what you did to Rodrigo. That will only anger my father and brothers more. I mean it. You should go."

Beckett felt a familiar tug of internal conflict. His instincts, shaped through years of service, screamed at him to do what she suggested and escape the impending storm. There were odds involved in battle, and there was nothing shameful in walking away when the outcome wasn't expected to be favourable. That wasn't cowardice, it was logic. And yet another part of him, the part that had trained rigorously to serve as protector, recoiled at the idea of running.

"It sounds like you're afraid of them."

Maria averted her gaze. "I know what they're like, that's all."

"You mustn't concern yourself with me, Maria. I can handle myself."

She snapped her head up to glare at him. "Who the hell are you, anyway?"

"I'm no one."

"Is that so?" She regarded him with scepticism. "Actually, I don't care. I don't want to know. It's probably better if I don't."

She had no idea how true that was, Beckett thought, sitting back as a cup of coffee was set before him. He thanked the server and picked up the teaspoon from the saucer. Slowly he began to stir, allowing the froth to meld with the liquid underneath and giving Maria space to speak some more.

When thirty seconds went by and she hadn't said anything, he raised his head. "Have they ever hurt you?"

Maria hesitated and her gaze dropped. So that was an affirmative, Beckett thought. "Has who ever hurt me?" she asked.

"Any of them. Your father."

She touched her jaw, her neck, shook her head. "No."

Beckett observed her as he leaned over and took a sip of his coffee. It wasn't as hot as he'd have liked but it tasted good, strong with notes of cocoa. He hadn't intended to ask Maria these questions but something – an impulse, an instinct – had compelled him to. Maybe he was looking for an excuse to stay, to fight.

"And the woman you were with yesterday?" he ventured. "Who was she?"

Maria lowered her chin and took a measured breath. "Her name is Antonia. She is the wife of my other brother, Raul."

"I see. And what happened to her eye?"

"Ah yes, she was hoping no one would notice that."

"I notice everything."

A flicker of respect flashed across her face before being replaced with a defensive sneer. "She told me it was an accident."

"Sure. Well, if that's what she told you."

Annoyance flared in her eyes. "What the fuck do you want me to say, Michael? I have told you my family are dangerous. That you are not safe here. Whatever you are thinking, nothing good will come of it."

She finished her coffee and slid her chair back, grabbing her phone and sunglasses from the table.

"Maria, wait." Beckett held his hand out. "I'm genuinely sorry. It's just that there's talk of this formidable family who have the town gripped in fear and you don't seem like that at all. My intention wasn't to upset you."

She pulled away and got to her feet. "You didn't upset me. And I'm sorry too, I shouldn't have asked you to join me. I wanted to say thank you for yesterday and I suppose I was curious about you also. But it was a mistake."

Beckett poised himself to respond, but Maria's phone buzzed in her hand before he could. She glanced at the screen and her face drained of colour.

"I have to go," she said, donning her sunglasses. "And so do you."

Beckett watched as she walked away. The rational part of him echoed both her and Armando's advice that he should leave town. He was just one man and this wasn't his fight. Yet the trained operative in him wanted to know more about the Silva family, their tyranny, their victims. How powerful were these people? He scoffed to himself as an idea hit him. It was risky, bordering on stupid, but it was also the quickest way to answer that question.

He finished his coffee and slipped a ten euro note under the saucer before getting to his feet and weaving through the now crowded square back the way he came. Leaving São Lourenço would certainly be a wise move, but he couldn't do it. Not yet, at least. Not until he had more of an idea who he was dealing with.

A few more hours and he'd know more.

Then he'd decide.

14

The heat of the afternoon sun pressed down on the town like a stifling shroud, the cobblestones shimmering in the haze as Beckett made his way down to the seafront. He had spent several hours walking the town's busiest streets, strolling around the shops and sitting at tables outside eating establishments, making his presence known. Now, with the locals seeking respite from the sun in their homes, the streets were nearly deserted except for the occasional stray dog seeking shade. As he ventured further from the centre, and the shop fronts and tabernas gave way to residential buildings, the air was filled with the rhythmic chirp of cicadas.

At an intersection Beckett paused, wiping his hand across his forehead as he pondered which way to go. Glancing over his shoulder, he caught sight of an old man swiftly ducking into an alleyway. The nagging sensation of being watched, which had begun upon his arrival in the square earlier and continued throughout the morning, was now a certainty. Clearly he was the feature of the day – the Englishman with a death wish who had stood up to the Silvas.

As he made his way alongside the small harbour he attempted to lock eyes with the local fishermen, but hardly any of them would even look at him. Those who did so glanced away immediately, their faces etched with dread and dismay. With each harried expression and nervous exchange, he began to see exactly how much of a chokehold the family had on these people.

Now he wanted to see for himself how far its influence ran.

He was wearing his usual heavy boots and kept them on as he made his way across the dry sand, a fiery carpet under the scorching sun. He found a solitary spot under a weather-beaten parasol and sat crossed-legged in the sand, his eyes drawn to the boundless ocean. Its vastness offered both a comfort and a stark reminder of how alone he was. He closed his eyes, pulled in some deep breaths. He almost felt relaxed. He almost felt content. But this really wasn't the time.

Ten minutes went by.

Twenty.

Then half an hour.

His intuition picked up on it first. His senses, as always, attuned to the smallest of changes in atmosphere. But as he opened his eyes he saw them – two large shadows stretching out across the sandy expanse on either side of him. He remained seated. Didn't move. But now he knew. The townsfolk, fearful and under the cosh, had spread word of his location and the Silva attack dogs had come to claim their pound of flesh.

With deliberate calm he got to his feet, brushing the clinging sand from his trousers. His heart pounded but not with fear. This was pure adrenaline kicking in.

As the shadows drew longer, Beckett turned around, squinting into the afternoon sunlight at the two men who'd been sent to deal with him. They looked to be hired heavies, easily identifiable from their thuggish demeanour and over-developed muscles, built for intimidation, not ideas. One sported a tight Hawaiian shirt, its garish pattern straining over his hefty build, whilst the other, wearing jeans and a white vest, showcased an upper body almost entirely covered in tattoos.

Hawaiian Shirt sneered as he looked Beckett up and down. In his meaty hands he was clutching a rusty pipe wrench as if it were an extension of his body. The other man appeared to be unarmed but was even bigger than his partner, with hands that looked like they could crush rocks.

Beckett assessed them, mentally running through potential sequences of the imminent fight. The odds were against him, physically at least, but that only made the challenge more appealing.

"Afternoon, gentlemen," he said. "I was actually expecting you sooner. Another ten minutes and you'd have missed me. I forgot my suntan lotion and you know how us Brits have sensitive skin. Still, you're here now."

The tattooed giant made a low growling noise, baring his teeth, whilst Hawaiian shirt snorted disdainfully then spat onto the sand. Beckett kept his eyes on him. He was going to move first.

Sure enough, with a roar Hawaiian lunged, swinging the pipe wrench at Beckett's head. Seeing it coming, he dodged nimbly to the side, the wrench digging a ditch in the sand where he'd been standing a moment earlier. Without missing a beat, Beckett spun around, smashing his elbow into the thug's exposed solar plexus. The man grunted in pain, but as he faltered, the tattooed giant advanced.

Rapid calculations ran through Beckett's mind. He'd fought men like this before, big but ungainly, bulked up on misplaced bravado and most likely steroids. It wasn't about matching them blow for blow. It was about using their own weight and momentum against them. It was about outsmarting them.

As the tattooed thug lunged, Beckett closed the distance, a move the man wasn't expecting. Before he could adjust, Beckett landed a solid knee to the man's midsection followed by a swift uppercut. The blow was heavy and on target, the heel of Beckett's fist slamming into the man's jaw and causing hundreds of neurotransmitters to fire at the same time, overloading his nervous system. With his equilibrium shattered, the tattooed giant staggered back, then toppled onto the sand, unconscious.

In contrast, Hawaiian Shirt was rallying, blind rage replacing any pretence of strategy. He charged, wielding the pipe wrench over his shoulder. But as he did so, Beckett knew he had him. Such a heavy weapon would require effort to swing it forward again, an effort that would be telegraphed to him long before it happened.

He waited until the last possible second, then stepped to one side as the man bore down on him. The pipe wrench whooshed through the air, the momentum of the missed swing sending the raging thug off balance. He yelled out but Beckett was already two steps ahead. Taking advantage of the opening, he pivoted on his heel and landed a heavy roundhouse kick to the man's knee.

There was a sickening crunch and the man screamed, falling to the sand as his leg gave out from under him. He rolled into an awkward sitting position, his meaty hand clutching at his knee as he gnashed his teeth in pain. But Beckett wasn't done. Stepping forward he delivered another perfectly placed kick to the side of the man's jaw, rattling his brain in his skull and sending him crashing to the sand.

Regaining his focus, Beckett spotted the tattooed giant attempting to push himself up from the sand. Though dazed, the man clearly had some fight left in him.

Well, good.

So did Beckett.

Approaching swiftly, he pinned the man's wrist under his boot, immobilising him.

"Fuck you!" the man spat, speaking English in a thick accent. "You're a dead man."

Beckett shook his head, almost amused. Why did people say such gauche things when they were clearly getting their arses handed to them? In one fluid motion he manoeuvred behind the beast, snaking his arm around his throat and leaning into him, positioning his forearm under the guy's chin. Predictably, the man reached up for Beckett's arm, providing him the opportunity to slide his other hand behind the man's head and stabilise his grip. Now, with the leverage needed, he leaned back, restricting the blood flow to each of the man's carotid arteries. The tattooed giant struggled for a few seconds more, then went limp. Beckett released his hold, and as the unconscious thug wilted onto the sand, he turned to the first man, who was just starting to stir. A hard kick to the ribs kept him down.

Kneeling, Beckett grabbed a handful of greasy hair and tilted the man's head back, forcing him to meet his gaze. "Tell your boss I'm leaving town," Beckett said, his Portuguese clear and precise. "Tell him I don't need the trouble. But you also tell him he's damn lucky. Got that?"

Releasing his grip, Beckett let the man's head fall back onto the sand. As he rose to his feet and brushed himself down, he noticed a crowd of townsfolk watching from a distance. But they quickly averted their eyes when he acknowledged them with a brief nod, retreating to their homes or hiding behind newspapers.

Cowards.

He understood they were scared, and sympathised with their desire to protect their families and livelihoods, but countless missions across the globe had taught him that no organisation, however powerful, was invincible. The Silvas, though influential, were just one family. If enough people rose up, they'd have a chance against them. Yet the people in this town would rather look the other away and keep their heads down. It was sad, but it told him everything he needed to know. You can't help those who won't help themselves.

15

Armando was setting up a couple of tables outside his taberna, wiping down surfaces with a wet cloth, when he spotted the Englishman at the end of the street. He was wearing the same grey linen trousers and cream shirt he'd been wearing the day before, but today his hair was more tousled and his expression stern; angry, even. As he got closer, he noticed Armando watching him and raised his head, offering him the sort of smile you might give to a grieving friend at their father's funeral.

"I see you didn't take my advice," Armando remarked, straightening.

"About leaving town?" Mike replied. "I was actually in two minds, but now I'm starting to believe you were right. I'm on my way to the hotel to get my things." Up close, Armando realised it wasn't anger but disappointment that was twisting the Englishman's features.

"Something happened?" he asked.

Mike hunched his shoulders. "Not really. That's the problem."

Armando leaned back to better take him in. "Are you okay,

man? You look like you've got the weight of the world on your shoulders."

"I think that's just my default look."

Armando chuckled. Mike didn't. A silence fell between them, but as the Englishman glanced up the road, Armando was compelled to keep him talking. Lina's words echoed in his head as he moved around the table to face him.

"Listen, man. I'm sorry again about what happened. I know you were only trying to protect my customers and my bar."

"It's fine. I understand."

Armando rocked his weight from foot to foot. He felt as if he had a lot to say but was finding it difficult to form the right words.

He might be able to help us in some way…
God knows we need it, Armando…
We all need it…

He glanced down the street. Next door, Josefa was dragging a display rack of pottery trinkets onto the pavement. Their eyes met; Armando forced a smile – the same funeral-smile Mike had offered him a few minutes earlier – but Josefa looked away without acknowledging him. Once they'd been friends. Not close, but close enough that they'd chat for a while in the mornings, share a joke or two. But no more. Under Emilio Silva's menacing shadow, even simple interactions felt strained.

He looked back at Michael Day, a man who could clearly handle himself in times of trouble and who seemed to genuinely want to help.

We all need it…

Even when Armando had explained to him about the family whose sights he'd put himself in the firing line of, he hadn't faltered. If anything, he'd only become more curious, more eager to know about the Silvas and why no one was standing up to them.

Armando felt a familiar pang of shame. He'd been a soldier. And a good one at that. In his military days he was considered heroic and respectable. But now he found himself paralysed like the rest of the town, unable to resist the oppressive weight of the Silva reign.

He regarded the Englishman. Could he ask him to stay? Should he?

He'd had conversations before with people he trusted, men who he felt might be willing and able to rise up against the insidious cancer spreading through the town. But nothing had ever come of it.

"I was thinking about what you said…" he blurted out, not knowing where it was going but needing to say something. "About the Silva family, I mean. It's just…" He trailed off, a flood of emotions competing for control in his system. Anger, compassion, a desire to protect his wife and business… that old friend, shame.

Mike lowered his chin, his intense blue eyes scanning Armando's face. "Don't worry," he said. "I understand. You've got a lot to lose."

"We have a lot to gain though too, right?"

"I'd say so. But you have a family. This is your home." Mike frowned and chewed on his lip as if thinking hard about something. "I just don't get why no one has stood up to them. Yes, they're powerful and have been strategic in the way they've tightened their grip on the town, ruling with fear and the threat of failure. But how many of them are working for Silva?"

"I don't know. Twenty. Maybe twenty-five. Most of them are ex-military. Tough guys. Men you don't want to cross paths with. That's how he keeps such a hold over people."

Mike swayed his head from side to side. "Well, if there was twenty-five of them, there are only nineteen now."

Armando's eyebrows shot up. "Are you serious? You took out six of their men?"

"Three on my first night here, one last night, two just now on the beach. At least three of them won't be walking for a while. The other three will be nursing bruised egos at the very least. And that's seven if you include Rodrigo." He smiled. "My point is it's possible. Yes, they rule with fear, and from what you say, they aren't afraid to kill those who oppose them. But with a strategic approach and a little courage, you could deal with this problem once and for all. Silva most likely has links to other organisations, bigger fish in the food chain, but once those organisations become aware that their minnows are encountering dissent, they'll drop them in a second. It's not worth their while, and it's not something for you to worry about. If anything, it will strengthen your hand."

Armando nodded. The Silvas being involved in bigger, more nefarious operations was something that had crossed his mind recently. Especially now people were going missing more and more. It was one reason why his heart told him he had to act now before things got worse.

"It's a lot to think about," he said, his voice low.

"Yes. I know it is."

Armando looked down at his hands. The cloth he'd been wiping the tables with was now coiled tight around his fingers. He sensed the dismay in Mike's voice, the irritation he felt towards Armando and the rest of the town for not even trying to help themselves. Yet, as he stared into the Englishman's searching eyes, he still couldn't bring himself to commit. He thought of Lina, of his bar; he thought of all he'd already lost and what he could stand to lose…

Patético covarde!

"I'd better be making a move," Mike said. "You take care of yourself, okay?"

Armando held his hand up to wave, feeling more pathetic and cowardly than ever. But then he remembered something.

"Hold on, Mike. I almost forgot. Come inside a second. I've got something for you."

"Oh?"

Armando headed into the cool interior of the taberna, glancing over his shoulder to make sure the Englishman was following him. The lights were off – anything to save money – but there was enough sunlight coming through the windows to cast the room in a dull glow. Armando walked around the back of the bar and retrieved the small brown envelope he'd propped up against a bottle of dark rum.

"Found it here this morning," he said, holding it up. "It had been slid under the door." He handed the envelope to Mike, the word *Ingles* scrawled in black pen on the front.

Mike studied the envelope. "From the Silvas?" he asked.

Armando shrugged. "I have no idea. I didn't see."

"Yeah. Maybe not." He turned the envelope over in his hands, a deep frown creasing his brow. "They don't strike me as the kind of people who send letters to those they're trying to intimidate. Well, best see what it's all about."

He tore the envelope open and pulled out the piece of folded paper inside, seemingly not the least bit troubled by this new development. Armando chewed on a gnarly bit of thumbnail as he watched him unfold the note. He very much envied the guy's unflappableness.

"Listen, Mike, I meant what I said before…" he started, his voice quiet. "I have been giving a lot of thought to what you said. About standing up for ourselves. And maybe… I don't know… if you were to stick around…" He trailed off as he realised Mike was too engrossed in the letter to be listening. Armando watched him as his eyes darted from left to right, mouthing the words to himself.

Now he looked a little less unflappable.

"What is it?" Armando asked.

Mike didn't look up. He frowned, shook his head and stuffed the letter in his shirt pocket.

"Is it bad?"

"I don't know…"

It was clear he didn't want to divulge the contents. But something was wrong. Armando's stomach turned over as he felt his last chance at redemption slipping away from him. "Listen, Mike, I can see you've got things on your mind right now, but I'd like to talk some more with you. Perhaps later?"

The Englishman looked up, a distracted expression tilting his eyebrows. "Sorry, Armando. I've got to go." He turned and headed out into the afternoon sun.

"Cool. No worries," Armando called after him. "You be careful now." He walked to the doorway and watched as the Englishman hurried down the street and disappeared around the corner. He hoped it wasn't the last he'd see of him.

He really hoped that.

16

Emilio Silva reclined on a sun lounger beside his large kidney-shaped pool, savouring a cocktail of his own creation, a concoction of exotic fruits and premium alcohol he'd christened *Rei Do Mundo*. King of the World. The sun, directly overhead, was like needles against the freshly plucked areas of bare scalp, yet it was a sensation he found oddly pleasing. Not in a kinky, masochistic way. But it made him feel alive, vital, real.

The surrounding ambience provided a cocoon of tranquillity. The gentle trickle of water cascading down the fibreglass waterfall on the far side of the pool, the chirruping of distant birds, the whisper from the palm fronds overhead as they rubbed together in the gentle breeze. It was the perfect setting for someone like Silva, a man readying himself for the next stage of his evolution. His mansion, his sanctuary, represented both affluence and power, a far cry from his chaotic beginnings.

Yet even in this relaxed state, Silva's mind was never idle. He was a predator, always watchful, his thoughts filled with new plots and strategies. The looming deal with Barbosa and the cartel kept him on edge, especially with the clock ticking ever closer to the deadline. He was still waiting on confirmation from Raul that the shipment was ready, but was confident they'd fulfil their part of the deal in time. They had to.

In exchange for the goods they'd be delivering, a cache of assault rifles and uncut, pharmaceutical-grade heroin would be theirs, tipping the power scales further in Emilio's favour. Now he could finally make a move on the Gadelha group up in Amadora, and the Velez family over in Cascais. Both organisations had grown flabby and complacent whilst he'd been sharpening his tools on the sidelines. These fools wouldn't know what had hit them. What Emilio had accomplished in São Lourenço would be nothing compared to what he could achieve once he had full control of the Lisbon District.

He took another sip of his drink, smiling to himself as the sweet nectar and sharp alcohol danced on his tongue. He relished the power he had over the townsfolk here; the fear he saw in their eyes was intoxicating. Their betrayal of the Englishman who dared harm his wayward son – eagerly directing his men to his whereabouts – only reinforced his control over them. Although, Rodrigo, the egotistical little prick that he was, had become more subdued and less annoying since it happened, so maybe he should be thanking the foreigner. Unfortunately, he was probably floating face down in the Atlantic Ocean by now.

Bastardo estúpido…

He was about to take another sip of his cocktail when a grunt of pain echoed through the courtyard. He looked up to see one of his men limping towards him, his vest stained with dirt and blood.

He sat up. It was Da Costa. One of the two he'd dispatched to deal with the Englishman. His broad shoulders were slumped and his face was bruised and bloody, the corners of his mouth twitching with pain as he walked. Silva set his glass down on the polished stone table next to him and got to his feet.

"What happened?" he barked. "Where's Mauricio?"

Da Costa hesitated, his eyes flickering between his boss and the ground. "He... the Englishman..." he began feebly, his voice raw. "I'm not sure what happened..."

"What the fuck?!" Silva walked over and grabbed Da Costa's head in both hands, examining the damage done. "He did this?"

Da Costa nodded. "He broke Mauricio's leg, shattered his knee joint. I just put him in a car and sent him to our guy up in Sintra."

Silva bared his teeth, resisting the urge to squeeze Da Costa's head and keep on squeezing. The man was twice his size, but he had four times the rage inside of him. That fucking Englishman. He'd already caused him enough trouble and now he'd disabled another of his men.

"Where is the foreign son of a whore now?" he asked, his patience dwindling with each passing second.

"I... I don't know."

A growl erupted from deep inside of Silva's soul. He let go of Da Costa's head and grabbed the lapels of his jacket, yanking him closer. "Find him," he hissed. "Take more men. Ask around, search everywhere. I want him disposed of today! Do I make myself clear?"

Da Costa nodded, fear evident in his eyes. "Yes, Boss."

"Good."

With a forceful shove, Silva sent Da Costa reeling backwards before closing his eyes and sucking in a deep breath. This was not what he needed right now. Not with Barbosa and the cartel breathing down his neck and the deal yet to go through. Who the hell did this damned foreigner think he was, some kind of fucking action hero? He'd been lucky up to now, but would not stand a chance against the entire might of the Silva organisation.

"Boss, do you want me to—?"

"What?" Silva's eyes snapped open. "Why are you still standing there, you fool? Get out of my sight and don't come back until you have the Englishman's head on a plate."

"Yes, Boss." Da Costa turned and limped away.

Silva watched him go, his hand reflexively rising to his hairline as a fresh rush of anger consumed him. He grabbed a large tuft from behind his right ear and pulled, the pain barely registering amidst the whirlwind of his emotions. The audacity of this Englishman was infuriating, but he would soon realise the cost of crossing Emilio Silva.

His gaze settled on the calm waters of his pool, the tranquil blue now in stark contrast to the storm raging in his belly. He was resolute. Anyone providing the foreigner with sanctuary would feel his wrath. This pathetic little town would witness violence and pain the likes of which it had never experienced before. He'd have his men turn the place upside down and burn it to the ground if they had to. But they would find the Englishman – and soon. They couldn't afford any more distractions, not now. There was too much at stake.

With a last glance at the retreating figure of his injured man, Silva turned on his heels and strode back into his mansion.

17

High up on the headland, overlooking the town, Beckett sat under the gnarled branches of a lone tree. Having wanted to escape the watchful eyes of the locals whilst he figured out his next move, he'd walked here from Armando's taberna and had been sitting for a few hours in quiet contemplation.

It was nice up here. Peaceful. The late afternoon sun bathed the town below in a warm, reddish glow, accentuating the weathered, pastel-coloured buildings spread out like rows of feeding cattle along the narrow streets. The coastal wind whispered through the leaves overhead, shimmering through the long grass and tousling his hair. He hadn't grown it this long since his university days and it was starting to annoy him. It was the hair of a traveller, not a soldier.

Another rush of breeze lifted the note from off his lap, but he grabbed it before it could fly away. He held it in front of him, reading the words once more despite already knowing them off by heart.

Michael Day.

I hope you get this message. We need to talk. I need your help.

But it is not safe in the town.

Please meet me on Thursday at 8 p.m. over the water in Almada, underneath the Cristo Rei statue.

Please come alone.

But please come!

Beckett crumpled the note and slipped it into his shirt pocket. He was well aware the meeting could be a trap laid by the Silvas, yet something gnawed at the edge of his intuition, suggesting otherwise. The handwritten note was shaky, with minimal pen lifts or flourishes. It told him that whoever wrote it was in a hurry. Desperate, even. This was personal for them.

But that didn't mean a Silva hadn't written the note.

Maria's face swam into his mind. Her dark eyes, full of spirit and determination. Could it be she who had written to him asking for his help? It was a possibility. But the last time they'd spoken, she'd told him in no uncertain terms that he should leave town.

Was it just that he wanted it to be from her?

No.

That was stupid.

Beckett shook the thought away, letting his attention drift once more over the rooftops of São Lourenço as he pondered what to do. Namely, should he meet with whoever sent the note?

He'd already run through all the possible outcomes, all the ways it could go down. It was a gamble going to Almada alone, not knowing for certain who or what was waiting for him there – but he'd been in similar situations over the years and walked away unscathed.

We need to talk. I need your help.

His instincts still told him it was on the level. He'd go and hear this person out, see who they were, but he doubted what they had to say would change anything. As far as Beckett saw it, the town was beyond help. If a once tough and noble man like Armando wasn't prepared to stand up to the family, what chance did any of them have? He empathised with the locals' plight, but it frustrated him a great deal that an idyllic town like São Lourenço had let this happen.

So he'd go to the meeting, satisfy his curiosity, and then leave. Get out of town like everyone kept telling him he should.

Thursday at 8 p.m.

He checked his watch. A little over three hours away. If he was going to meet this person, then he needed to leave now. He rose and headed down the hillside, walking east along the coastal road for an hour until he arrived at Cais do Sodré. He had almost a hundred euros in notes screwed up in his pocket, so was able to pay for the commuter ferry which transported him across the Tagus River to the southern margin on the opposite side. It was a brief, eight-minute crossing, but he relished every second, standing on deck and soaking up the briny air and the last throws of the day's sun. Across the water, Lisbon unfurled like a picture postcard. The evening light washed over the city, staining the buildings with shades of amber and gold.

Once at the other side, Beckett took a moment to find his bearings then set off, walking west. Most of the other ferry passengers were climbing onto a waiting bus that he assumed was going the same way, but he'd rather walk. It was a pleasant evening and he had over an hour before the meeting. Besides, he wanted to approach the rendezvous point from a different angle than was predictable and scope out the area first. He was almost certain it wasn't a trap, but until he was one hundred percent sure, he had to exercise caution. Besides, he never walked into a place without knowing how to get out of there if the shit hit the fan.

The evening air felt good on his skin as he trekked towards the huge statue of Christ where the meeting was to take place. Almada's streets were alive with excited chatter and the heavy pulse of music coming from the many tabernas lining the vibrant streets. This was the Portugal Beckett remembered, the one he'd been expecting to find in São Lourenço.

He stuck to the north of the sprawling municipality, keeping the sea in sight as much as possible. After another forty minutes of walking, he reached the outskirts of the city and saw the towering statue in front of him – *Cristo Rei*, Christ the King. Built after the Second World War, it had been a way of thanking God for sparing Lisbon from the bombings that had decimated other European capitals. Like Rio's Christ the Redeemer, which had inspired it, the gigantic monument had its arms spread wide as if embracing the capital city from across the water.

Beckett circled the site and entered the luscious greenery of the surrounding gardens from the south. He approached with caution, concealed behind a row of palm trees that bordered a narrow walkway leading to the base of the statue.

A few hundred feet away he stopped, claiming a vantage point behind a thick bark almost bouncy as he leaned against it. From here he had an uninhibited view of the rendezvous point. It being late in the day, the area was sparse with visitors, the tourist trade dwindling with the setting sun. Beckett counted twelve other people in total. Eight of them were in couples, whilst the remaining four appeared to be solo visitors. Almost all were in their fifties or sixties and none looked like the thugs he'd encountered in São Lourenço.

He realised if he didn't count Maria, he only knew what one of the Silvas looked like. Rodrigo, the youngest son. But if this was a trap, he doubted Emilio Silva would have sent someone recognisable. It was also unlikely he'd have travelled here in person to deal with him. So the elder son, Raul, perhaps? Yet from what Armando had said, there were only two years between each of the Silva siblings – Beckett was confident he'd pick up on the family resemblance.

And there was no one who fitted that description here, no one acting suspicious, no threatening presence. He remained in position, eyes fixed on the stone entrance at the south-facing side of the plinth; presumably the doors led to a visitor's centre but were locked for the night. Most of the stragglers were now wandering away and there was no one on this side of the gardens.

He glanced at his watch. It was almost 8 p.m. He pulled in a deep breath and held it in his lungs before releasing it carefully, slowing his heart rate in the process.

A minute went by. And another.

Then, as his watch ticked past the hour, he saw a lone figure approaching the statue over to the right. They had their back to him but he could see it was a man. A man he thought he recognised. Could it be?

Stepping out from his cover, he moved silently along the line of trees. As he got closer, the man turned in profile and Beckett stopped. His first impression was proved correct.

This was who had written the note?

He left the tree cover and walked along the paved causeway towards the base of the statue. As he neared he allowed his footsteps to grow heavier, and when he was twenty feet away the man turned around and saw him.

"Ah, you came," he said, with a relieved grin.

"Evening, Humberto," Beckett replied. "Fancy seeing you here."

18

Away from the gloom of Armando's bar, Humberto looked different, younger. The lines on his face were deep with age, but his eyes sparked with an intensity Beckett hadn't noticed previously. He was wearing pale blue trousers that appeared to be two sizes too big for him and a white short-sleeved shirt, unbuttoned to reveal a mass of white curls on a chest that was still broad and sturdy-looking. His thinning hair had been combed back with product, forming it into neat channels that showed off the tanned skin beneath. As he spoke, his gaze held Beckett's, steady and unwavering.

"Apologies for the mystery in getting you here," he began. "But I couldn't risk meeting in São Lourenço. People know me there. And now they know you, also. We would be seen. Silva would find out. It would be very bad."

Beckett frowned. He was starting to tire of hearing of this man and how scared everyone was of him. He regarded Humberto, noting the weariness in his posture, the tension around his eyes. "What is it you want?" he asked, keeping his tone and expression neutral. "Because I'm really not sure I can be of any help. I was planning on leaving town today and heading north; tomorrow at the latest."

Humberto sighed, a tired sound, full of resignation. "I was worried you might say that. But please, hear me out. I have a lot I need to say."

"I've already heard it all from Armando," Beckett told him. "And it sounds like there's nothing anyone can do to help."

"Maybe. But I'm done lying down in front of that family. I have to try. I have to do something."

Beckett folded his arms and glanced over Humberto's shoulder. There was no one in sight. He cast his attention around the area. They were alone.

"I suppose we're here now," he said, allowing his expression to soften. "Tell me what you have to say. You might start by telling me how you fit into all this."

Humberto sucked in a deep breath as if preparing himself for an important speech. "My name is Humberto Magro," he began. "I was born in São Lourenço and lived here until I was eighteen years old when I enrolled in the Portuguese army. My first deployment was a joint task force serving under NATO in the Middle East. I was a good soldier. I was brave… once." He held Beckett's gaze as he spoke, not blinking, not letting him look away. "Then in 1990 I was recruited to the Centro de Informações e Segurança Militares – the military intelligence service of Portugal – I served with them up until 2008."

"That's quite the service record," Beckett said, genuinely impressed. "But you'd only have been – what – forty then? Why did you leave?"

A sad smile twitched the sides of Humberto's mouth. "My wife died and I gave up work to raise our daughter. She was fourteen at the time. It was the biggest challenge I've ever faced."

"I'll bet." Beckett's thoughts drifted briefly to his niece, Amber, his only living relative, now safe in the bosom of the

Santos family over in Spain. "Bringing up a teenager single-handed has to be a tough job."

"It was. She was a good girl, but her mother's death hit us both hard. I was fifty-one when my wife died. I found it hard to relate to my daughter and her needs. I tried to protect her, to guide her in life, but as she got older and became a young woman we clashed often, finally with catastrophic results."

Beckett raised his head. "What do you mean?"

"The more we fought, the more I pushed her away. She was strong-willed like her mother, and also very beautiful. Boys began to notice her. Soon she became captivated by a young man who had just moved into the town. You might have heard of him. Raul Silva."

"Shit. So she's…?"

Humberto nodded. "They married seven years ago."

"I met her," Beckett said, an image of the woman from the mountainside flashing in his mind, Maria's friend. He thought of the timid way she'd reacted to his presence, the purple bruise visible behind her sunglasses. "She didn't look too good." He raised his hand to his eye, enough for Humberto to get the message.

"I hate that she's with him," he admitted, the anger and shame he was feeling unmistakable in his expression. "The last time I saw her was three months ago. She had a bandage on her arm, her lip was split and swollen. That bastard… But it was I who failed her. Antonia was broken-hearted after her mother died and I was unable to bridge the void that opened between us. I practically drove her into his arms."

"I'm not sure you should blame yourself," Beckett replied.

"Well, I do. The Silvas were not what they are now, but I already could tell the family was bad news. I warned her not to marry Raul but she wouldn't listen. She thought she loved him. With him whispering in her ear, she decided I was bitter and only wanted her to stay home so she could look after me. He convinced her I didn't want her to find happiness. I wasn't even invited to their wedding. Since then I have had to watch on, helpless, as Emilio Silva and his sons have grown more powerful and my beautiful Antonia has faded into the shadows."

Beckett unfolded his arms. "Why are you telling me all of this, Humberto?"

"Because I recognise something in you," Humberto replied, the fire in his eyes returning. "I saw how you dealt with Rodrigo and his accomplice in the bar. I know a man with Special Forces training when I see it."

Beckett's lips tightened. He didn't confirm Humberto's suspicions, but he didn't deny them either. "What do you want from me?" he asked.

"I want you to help me save my daughter! I want you to help me save my town!" His voice cracked slightly as he spoke. "I wake up every day fearful that today will be the day I get the news Raul has taken his beatings too far. That my beautiful Antonia is lying on a slab in a mortuary somewhere, beaten to a pulp or pushed down a flight of stairs. That family are growing more powerful all the time. They have to be stopped. If we don't act now it will be too late."

An icy anger had spread through Beckett's body as Humberto talked of his daughter's predicament. But he didn't let it show. "And you think I can stop them?"

Humberto nodded. "I can tell you are a man of means and ability. We need you. Antonia needs you."

A heavy silence fell between them as Beckett considered what was being asked of him. He gazed up at the statue of Christ, looming over them like a watchful protector, before returning his attention to Humberto. The older man's expression was one of desperation, but there was also something else in his eyes. Hope. A desire for redemption, for salvation. Beckett knew that feeling well.

"How do you see this going?" Beckett asked. "Do you have a plan?"

"I'm afraid I haven't thought that far. But after seeing you take down Rodrigo, I knew I had to speak with you. If we can garner support, if we can rally the people…"

"That's a hell of an ask, Humberto," Beckett cut in. "From what I see, the townsfolk are terrified of that family. What if no one else is willing to help?"

"We have to do something," Humberto insisted.

Beckett sighed. He'd planned on leaving São Lourenço that night, and he was a man who rarely deviated from his decisions once made. Yet here was a brave and desperate man asking him to stay, to fight.

"I need to think about it," he conceded.

"Time is not on our side," Humberto hit back. "The Silvas are growing bolder and more dangerous. And I fear recently there are greater forces at play."

Beckett lifted his head, his own theory confirmed. "You think someone else is pulling the strings?"

Humberto nodded. "I think Emilio Silva has big ideas and will not stop until he's taken over the country. I've seen too much, Michael. Too many 'accidents', too many silenced voices."

Beckett scratched his chin. He thought of Armando, of Maria, of the distress evident in Antonia up on the mountainside.

"Fine," he said. "I'm in."

Humberto exhaled and let out a breathy laugh. "Thank you, my friend…"

"Hey! Don't thank me just yet," Beckett told him. "But you should go now. We can't be seen returning together and I need some space to think this over."

Humberto gathered himself together. "Where can I find you?" he asked.

"I'll find you."

"Okay. But please don't wait too long. Like I said, every day counts."

"I understand."

Beckett waved Humberto off and then walked over to the railing that looked out across the river. In the distance the lights of São Lourenço twinkled in the twilight. Despite his intentions to move on, it seemed fate had anchored him here a while longer. There was a new battle to be fought, a darkness to be purged. But that was what he did.

It was who John Beckett was.

19

Humberto sensed the Englishman watching him as he ambled away, but he resisted the urge to look back. Partly because he didn't want to jinx the situation, have him change his mind at the last moment, and also because he wasn't ready to confront the pity he anticipated seeing in the younger man's eyes.

Yet he had agreed to help him.

That was all that mattered.

Humberto's soul was heavy with a mix of dread and newfound determination as he made his way across the open plaza. Like most tourist attractions, the Cristo Rei monument had ample parking provision, but he'd parked on a quiet avenue over to the south. He wasn't taking any chances. As he left the gardens he turned around. From this distance, all he could make out was the tall outline of the Englishman as he looked out over the river. In that proud, broad-shouldered silhouette, Humberto saw a shadow of his younger self. A man in his prime, wearing the distinguished uniform of the Centro de Informações e Segurança Militares.

Tempos diferentes...

He shook his head, brushing off the remnants of his past as he continued on his way. Those days were long gone and had been replaced by a much darker reality. His life as a soldier, however dangerous, had been a simple one. He was given orders and he followed them. That was it. He missed the clarity of that life. And the purpose it gave him.

Yet he was certain he'd done the right thing in approaching the enigmatic stranger. Regardless of Michael Day's reticence to own up about his past, it was clear to Humberto he was someone who could help. And hell, did he need it.

He reached his battered old Peugeot and climbed into the driver's seat. The worn-out leather groaned under his weight, the once vivid upholstery now faded and cracked from decades of relentless sun. Despite the wear and tear, the car had served him well over the years. He and Carla had travelled far and wide in this car. Antonia, too.

Tempos diferentes...

Different times. Happier times. The car had seen better days but it was reliable, just like him.

He turned the key in the ignition and the engine roared to life. As he drove away, he glanced in his rearview mirror at the grandeur of the Christ statue looking back at him and took it as a sign he was doing the right thing.

Navigating the road leading out of Almada, a rare feeling of optimism bubbled up inside him. Day's willingness to help had only strengthened his own desire to take a stand. As he drove across the Ponte 25 de Abril, his mind replayed the scenes in the taberna, the swift and clinical way the Englishman had taken out Rodrigo and his buddy. It felt like a wake-up call from the universe. A flash of defiance in a town that had forgotten what it meant to fight back. The raw courage and skill he'd witnessed had roused him from the fear and sorrow-induced coma he'd allowed himself to succumb to the last fifteen years. Seeing the Englishman in action,

Humberto was reminded of the fire he himself had once had. Day was a reflection of who he'd been – a fighter, a saviour.

He hadn't been boasting earlier, he'd been a good soldier. Hell, he'd been a great one. The challenges he had faced, the lives he had saved and taken, had all added to his experience. Age and grief might have weathered him, but in any way he could, it was time to be that man again.

His grip on the wheel tightened as he reached the outskirts of São Lourenço. His town, now in the clutches of that bastard brood. A fizzing rage blossomed in his chest as he slowed the car through the winding streets, each avenue and alleyway carrying reminders of what once was and what it had now become. As he parked the car outside his modest home, his thoughts drifted to Antonia. His sweet, beautiful daughter, caught in a life no one deserved. His heart ached for her, the guilt of his past cowardice eating away at him.

But things were about to change.

And with the Englishman as his ally, he might just stand a chance.

Climbing out of the car, he looked towards the ominous silhouette of The Kingdom, Silva's sprawling estate looming in the distance. The sight no longer filled him with dread, but determination. Emilio Silva might wield all the power, but Humberto had one thing he didn't have – he was ready to die for his cause. If it meant Antonia would be free from those bastards' clutches, he would do anything.

He slammed the car door shut and somewhere deep inside of him the old soldier opened his eyes. It was time to end the Silva reign. It was time to save his town. And it was time to save his daughter.

Even if it killed him.

20

In a backstreet taberna near São Lourenço harbour, Maria Silva was sitting alone, sipping on a glass of ice-cold vodka. She'd chosen a table in the corner of the small establishment, a vantage point that allowed her a view of the entrance, yet distanced her from the main bar. She was glad but not surprised to find that, except for a couple of weather-worn fishermen propping up the bar, she was the only person drinking there that evening.

The bar was as gnarly and tired as the old sea dogs. The yellowing paint on the walls had long since started to peel, revealing the raw stone underneath, and most of the chairs – including the one she was sitting on – had torn upholstery, the leather pulled back to reveal its aged foam. Yet, despite its appearance, the bar still had a certain charm.

She watched the owner, a man she knew as 'Sancho', as he wiped down the countertop. It didn't need cleaning. It was more a ritual than a necessity, something to occupy himself with as time ticked away. As she watched, he glanced up and their eyes met briefly before she looked away.

Poor Sancho.

He knew who she was, who her father and brothers were, yet he'd still greeted her with warmth and kindness this evening. He was a good man. He didn't deserve for his business to crumble away like it had done these past few years. No one did.

She turned her attention back to the door. Waiting. Mainly she'd chosen Sancho's place for strategic reasons – it was a far walk from the centre of town and even further from the Silva estate – but also nostalgic ones. Once, it had been a thriving venue frequented by locals and tourists alike. Maria had come here often when they first moved here. None of her family came this far out of town, so for her it was a refuge, a place to hide from the world outside and its burdens. Plus, Sancho was a good cook and his food was wonderful. There was live music some nights.

And she'd *danced*.

Oh, how she'd danced. Dancing to forget her problems. Dancing to forget her past, her present.

Dancing for her life…

But life's harsh realities could only be ignored for so long. And that wasn't just true for Maria but for the entire town. The old taberna, like many places in São Lourenço, was on its last legs and she expected it would close soon enough. Just like everywhere else.

Maria had arrived in São Lourenço at twenty-five hoping for a fresh start in a new town. But over the past decade, her father and brothers had done their best to destroy every single thing that was good about the place. They'd grown powerful whilst the people suffered. Grown rich whilst the town fell into decay. And from what Maria could tell – from what she'd picked up from snippets of whispered conversation – things were only going to get worse.

But she'd be okay, wouldn't she? She'd be fine. She was a Silva, after all. They looked after their own.

The bastards.

She sneered at the thought and drank more vodka. She always drank it neat. She liked to feel the burn in her nose as she brought the glass to her lips, feel it in her throat once she drank. This wasn't the good stuff, but it was cold and viscous and it would do the trick. Dutch courage. That was what she needed right now. That and a miracle.

She looked at her watch.

Where was she?

Had she had second thoughts, perhaps?

Maria wouldn't have been surprised. She sat back in her seat, her eyes falling on the old jukebox next to the bar. It had once been the centre of the action here but now sat quiet, its lights switched off, its chrome surround dulled and scratched. Most of its selections were outdated songs of long ago, and a tattered old handwritten sign taped over the money slot announced it was *'fora de serviço'* – out of order.

Maria checked her watch, about to finish her drink and leave, when the door creaked open and Antonia peered her head around it. Despite the darkness outside, she had on the same oversized sunglasses she'd worn the day before.

"Hey," Maria called softly, raising her hand. "Over here."

Antonia's head snapped left and right as she scoped the place. She saw Maria and hurried over.

"It's fine," she whispered, as Antonia pulled out a chair and sat. "None of these people know who we are."

Antonia nodded but didn't look convinced. She was wearing a thin yellow summer dress with a pattern of small red flowers, which hung on her slender frame. Whilst she had always been slim, over the last few months she'd lost more weight than was healthy. Maria hadn't said anything and she wouldn't, but the poor thing looked more fragile than ever.

"I didn't know whether to come," Antonia whispered. "If Raul knew I was out alone at this time, then…"

"He won't find out," Maria cut in. "And all we're doing is having a drink. Sisters-in-law having a catch-up. If he has a problem with that, you tell him to come see me."

Antonia forced a smile that seemed to take a lot of energy. "Thank you."

"Please, try and relax," Maria assured her, her own voice trembling slightly. She raised her hand to signal Sancho over. "We're safe here," she added; then to the barman, "Another vodka, please, and whatever my friend wants."

"Just a small wine," Antonia said, not meeting his eye.

Sancho nodded and sauntered off to prepare the drinks as a silent tension settled between the two women. It felt awkward. But the first few minutes of their meetings always did. Maria and Antonia wouldn't have been friends if they weren't related by marriage. As it was, however, Maria found she needed her sister-in-law more and more. And Antonia certainly needed her.

"Are you going to keep those on all night?" she asked, gesturing at the sunglasses.

Antonia sighed and removed them. The bruising around her eye was still purple but the swelling had gone down. A faint tinge of yellow spread down her cheek to just above her lips. She leaned closer to Maria, her voice urgent. "They'll know, Maria. They'll find out. I shouldn't have come."

"No one will know," Maria snapped. "Clearly Raul was not at home or you wouldn't be here. My father rarely leaves the estate unless he's visiting one of his hotels. I imagine Raul and Rodrigo are at the house with him like usual. You'll be home well before he returns."

They sat in silence for a moment, the only sounds the clinking of glasses and the low murmur of the other patrons. Sancho appeared and placed the fresh drinks down before retreating without saying a word.

Antonia stared at her drink, her hand trembling as she

picked up the glass. "I don't know how much longer I can live like this."

"I know." Maria looked away, blinking back tears. She was angry — not at her sister-in-law, but at the life they were forced to lead. A life that seemed to have no escape. She'd wanted to leave many times in the past, but each time her father had threatened to cut her off financially. She could live with that. She was bright, she could find a job, and she already hated herself for taking her father's blood money. But he'd threatened her in other ways, too. Not overtly, but he'd made it clear that if she left, if she embarrassed the family in any way, she'd regret it. She sucked in a deep breath as she turned back to Antonia. "We'll find a way out. We have to."

Antonia scoffed. "You really believe that?"

"I have to believe it."

A hush settled over them. Antonia sipped at her wine. Maria swished the vodka around in her glass, clunking the ice cubes together. She had a lot she wanted to say but suddenly felt strange saying it out loud.

Screw it.

She took a gulp of vodka and began. "I saw him again — the Englishman."

Antonia frowned. "The one who helped us with the car? Where was he?"

"At a café in the square. But that's not important. Did you know he fought with Rodrigo? He stood up to both him and his man Varella and walked away unscathed." She leaned in, not taking her eyes off her sister-in-law. "From what I hear, they couldn't say the same for Varella — or my brother."

"Did he know who they were?" Antonia asked, sitting forward also, her eyes widening.

"Yes. He did. And he doesn't seem to be scared of my family one bit."

"Then he's stupid."

"Maybe. But I don't think so. I think he could be helpful."

Antonia's eyes narrowed, a playful grin tugging at her lips. "Have you fallen for him or something?"

"No!" Maria snapped. "Of course not."

Yet he'd occupied her thoughts all day. There was something incredibly intriguing about Michael Day. He was self-confident in a way that wasn't about ego. It was like he knew he'd earned the right to be.

"I told him that he should leave town for his own safety but he didn't seem to care," she added. "And now I can't help but wonder if maybe he could help us... you know..."

Her sister-in-law's playful demeanour faded. Her eyes flicked to the door. "Stop it, Maria," she hissed. "Just stop!"

"Why? Don't you ever wonder... what if?"

Antonia shook her head. "What are you talking about?"

"The Englishman could help us."

"Help us?" Antonia's voice was high, panicked. "Maria, you have to stop talking like this. It will get us nowhere."

"Don't you hate Raul?" she asked.

"Hate? He's my husband, Maria. Your brother."

"That's not an answer," Maria snapped, and frustration creased Antonia's forehead.

"You don't understand. Your father doesn't make things easy for him. He struggles...

"And that's an excuse for him to take it out on you, is it? Jesus, Antonia, don't you want a better life for yourself?"

"Yes, of course, but..." She trailed off and looked away. "It's too hard."

Maria's gaze never wavered. "I hate them, Antonia. All of them. My father. My brothers. I hate them all. I can't live in their shadow any longer, knowing what they are doing to this town, to these people." She waved her hand around the room. "Look around you. It is not right what they have done. But the

Englishman – Michael – he could be the answer we've been waiting for."

"The answer to what?"

"To… everything." Maria's voice was firm. "To getting out from under the weight of this fucking family."

Antonia glanced at her watch. Her face was pale, her lips quivered. "I'm sorry, Maria. I can't do this." She reached for her glass and swallowed the wine in one gulp. Placing the empty glass down, she got to her feet. "I have to go. Please forget this. I mean it. It's too dangerous. People will get hurt." With that, she placed her sunglasses back on and hurried from the bar.

Maria watched her go, a sneer forming on her lips as she lifted her glass and pictured Michael, his confident stride, the way his piercing blue eyes had met hers. Stranger though he was, he was the first man to have stood up to her family and walked away. The sneer turned to a secret smile. He could help them. She was sure of it.

Antonia made a good point. It was dangerous. Very dangerous. And yet, the thought wouldn't leave her.

What if…?

What if…?

She downed the vodka and gestured to Sancho that she wanted another. And maybe she'd have another one after that. And another.

It was going to be one of those nights.

21

The air was cool against Beckett's skin as he climbed off the last train to São Lourenço and made his way back to his hotel. The day's events consumed his thoughts. The meeting with Humberto had made his decision to stay an easy one, but now there was plenty to consider. Two things stood out: he had to help the locals remove Silva from his self-appointed seat of power; and it wasn't going to be a walk in the park.

Still, as he walked he felt something awaken further inside him, a dormant aspect of his persona that had been quiet since he left England behind four months ago. Humberto's unwavering resolve reflected something within himself, and it was a familiarity that extended to Armando also. Because it was true what they said – kind recognised kind. Even if years of grief and stress had broken the ex-soldier's spirit, Beckett sensed Armando might still have some fire in his belly. He just needed a spark, and Beckett was happy to provide it. Hell, going up against a crime family whose operations were not yet fully understood – and who had possible links to larger organised crime syndicates – he would need all the help he could get.

His senses were as sharp as ever as he reached the centre of town, every shadow cast by the streetlights, every rustle of the wind logged and assessed. He was a man on high alert, prepared for anything in the moment even while his mind considered all the ways this conflict could play out.

Beckett had experienced the same manipulative strategies the Silvas were using six years earlier when he'd been sent to Sierra Leone to dethrone the violent warlord, Jean-Michael Jalloh. When he arrived, Jalloh had already taken over most of the eastern territories and his ambitions were set on the north of the country. Jalloh was a clever man with a greedy and brutal nature, but his control wasn't gained purely by force. Reminiscent of how the Silvas had operated in São Lourenço, Jalloh took control of the Kailahun and Kono regions by playing to their vulnerabilities, initially presenting himself as an antidote to corruption and instability. But where Jalloh exploited a political crisis in Sierra Leone, the Silvas exploited a financial one, lending money when the banks couldn't. By the time their snare tightened, it was too late; the townspeople, overwhelmed and oppressed, felt powerless against the family.

Stepping out from under this sort of control wasn't easy. Sometimes domestic and internal pressure helped, sometimes negotiations and non-violent resistance got the job done. Other times, like in Sierra Leone, you had to fight fire with fire. Show these people you weren't going to be pushed around any longer.

In Jalloh's case, it had taken the combined might of Sigma Unit, MI6, and a squad of US Navy Seals to take him out and remove his chokehold over the country. Beckett was currently a one-man army, with Humberto – perhaps – helping where he could. The odds weren't great.

But when were they ever?

Emilio Silva and his sons had strangled the life out of this once happy town, but they were just men. Men could be hurt.

Men could be killed.

Ever since Humberto left him at the foot of the Cristo Rei statue, Beckett had been piecing together an attack plan. Now his mind pulsed with ideas. He considered the family's behaviour, Rodrigo's actions, what he knew about Raul and Emilio – all of it pointed to a singular truth: the Silva's power came purely from the fear they'd sown in the town. If he could disrupt their operations before they had a chance to call in help from above, he suspected their house of cards would tumble and the town would be free.

Beckett was already sketching a rough outline of his strategy. All he needed was a little time and a lot of luck. But as he approached his hotel, an insidious prickle of danger halted him in his tracks. Something was off. Trusting his instincts, he veered down a side street and came at the building from a back alley opposite the main entrance.

And he'd been correct. Peering around the corner he identified four men standing in strategic positions around the hotel. They were acting nonchalant, just locals shooting the breeze, but Beckett could tell they were Silva's men. Two of them displayed the discreet bulge of a weapon under their thin shirts.

Beckett remained in position, watching, assessing. These men weren't amateurs, their stances were relaxed but vigilant, their predatory gazes fixed on the hotel entrance. One of them chewed lazily on a toothpick, a cruel smirk etched onto his face. Another, the largest of the group, stood with his arms crossed, his huge shoulders straining the fabric of his top. The third was a younger man with slicked-back hair, his eagerness for action visible in the way he bounced from foot to foot and kept reaching to his back pocket, perhaps grasping at the handle of a blade. The last one, an older man with a scar across his face, seemed the most dangerous. Sometimes it was just instinct that told you these things, but Beckett had learnt to trust his gut a long time ago. He could also see it in the man's eyes when he turned around. He had the cool, steady gaze of a seasoned killer.

Beckett withdrew further into the alley. Staying in the shadows, stalking them one by one, he could likely take them out, but it was still a risky play and if things went awry the subsequent conflict could tear the place apart in the process. Innocents would be caught in the crossfire and that was a cost he wasn't willing to pay. He turned and headed back the way he'd come.

But even as he retreated, a brief smile played across his lips. The fact that Silva had now sent four men to deal with him was telling. It meant he was wary of him. Threatened, even. And whilst today Beckett may have chosen to stand down rather than face these men, the wheels were already in motion.

The man in the big mansion was about to realise what happened when you messed with John Beckett.

22

Up in Porto, Salvador Barbosa was not a happy man. While he rarely allowed himself to indulge in feelings of joy or contentment – for him those were traits favoured by simpletons and fools – he usually exuded a kind of self-assured satisfaction.

But not this evening.

Tonight he roamed the corridors of his grand mansion with shoulders hunched and fists clenched, his face contorted by anger and unease. The ornate chandeliers rattled overhead as he made his way from room to room, slamming doors in his wake.

That fucking family.

His world, usually so orderly, was unravelling. Deadlines were looming with no hint of shipments being delivered on time, people who should have known better were not answering his calls, and to make matters worse he now had the cartel pressing him for answers he didn't possess.

This was not acceptable. Not by a long shot.

Were the Silvas messing him around on purpose? Or were

they – as Barbosa was beginning to speculate – nothing but a bunch of aspiring mobsters who'd got in over their heads?

Regardless, Barbosa found himself in a tight spot. He had vouched for the family, put his own reputation as well as his life on the line with Elvio Castellano, all based on the eldest son's eager reassurances. Raul Silva, with his suave words and big promises. He'd been very convincing, even impressive. Yet the current radio silence from both him and his father spoke volumes.

But low-level thugs or not, Barbosa wasn't about to relent. The Silva shipment had to be delivered on time. *Had to be!* If it wasn't, it meant he'd have to explain why to Elvio Castellano, and he wasn't prepared to do that. Those who crossed the Sangre de Dragón Cartel only did so once.

He reached his office and flung open the heavy double doors with a single push. Despite his diminutive size, Barbosa was deceptively strong, made stronger by the urgency coursing through his veins. Settling behind his large mahogany desk, he inhaled deeply, the familiar scent of his domain, of aged wood and leather, grounding him momentarily. Sitting here always made him feel powerful. The desk, purchased a few years earlier, was a statement of both status and beauty, displaying traditional craftmanship – and with legs shortened to accommodate Barbosa's frame and give the illusion he was taller than he was.

His fingers, freshly manicured and with perfectly arched cuticles, reached for the old-fashioned landline phone sitting top centre. The phone that connected him to employees all around the country and contacts all around the globe; strong men, dangerous men, men on his payroll who were ready to do his bidding in a flash, without discussion or demur. He lifted the receiver and dialled a number he knew by rote – the number he always dialled when he had an issue that needed prompt attention. The dial tone pierced the silence of the room before the call was answered after two rings.

"Mr Barbosa," Martim answered. "How are you this evening?"

"Not good. Not good at all," Barbosa replied. "I have a job for you."

Martim had been one of Barbosa's trusted allies since they were just street punks running scams in the heart of Porto. They had climbed the blood-soaked ladder out of the underworld together, their bond strengthening with each organisation they took down, with each rival crime lord they toppled. Martim: with his predator's eyes that spoke of the countless lives he had extinguished and his face a mask of bulbous scars, medals from battles fought in dark alleyways and behind closed doors. He was a man who had looked into the abyss of death so many times his own reflection stared back from it. But he was also a pillar of loyalty, and even after all these years still Barbosa's go-to man when he needed a problem solving.

"How big a job?" he asked.

Barbosa leaned back in his seat, the sense of panic that had gripped his stomach already easing. "The family down in São Lourenço, the ones I'm brokering the deal for with Castellano. They are... concerning me somewhat."

"I see."

Barbosa didn't need to explain the full situation; Martim would understand from the gravity of his tone. He'd seen more death than a cemetery caretaker and never faltered when Barbosa pointed a finger.

"You want me to put a permanent halt to their operations?"

Barbosa considered the question for a moment. "No. What I need is for them to grasp the magnitude of what they have agreed to. They've climbed into bed with powerful and dangerous people and now need to perform."

"Got it. I'll light a fire under them they can't ignore."

Barbosa smiled. He could hear the excitement in his friend's voice. "Good. But keep in mind, that this family could still prove worthy allies if they complete the deal on time. I want you to drive down there and find out what the hell is going on. Take Paulos with you and leave first thing in the morning. I'll email you all the information you need. If it's evident that Emilio Silva has just fallen a little behind but is still going to fulfil his part of the deal, then he might just need a little incentive to hurry things along but nothing more."

Martim cleared his throat. "And if he's fallen too far behind?"

"Then you take what exists of the shipment and you kill the entire family," Barbosa told him. "And anyone in their vicinity."

23

A thick plume of cigar smoke veiled the dimly lit study where Emilio Silva sat in silence. In front of him on the desk sat a small pile of black hair, freshly plucked from the area behind his left ear. His condition had been particularly prevalent this evening and the yanking and teasing more rigorous than usual. The raw skin on his scalp was stinging like hell, and when he reached up to tentatively touch the area, his fingertips came back dappled in fresh blood.

Plus, it had done little to ease the stress tightening his chest, sending his mind spiralling to the darkest corners of his psyche.

Footsteps in the corridor outside had him sit upright. He slicked his remaining hair with the flattened palm of his hand as whoever it was stopped outside the door. "Raul?" he barked. "Is that you?"

The door opened to reveal his eldest son standing in the doorway. He was wearing a black suit and tie, which presumably he thought gave him an air of authority. In reality, however, it made him look like he was on his way to a funeral. A bad omen, Silva thought. One more in a string of bad omens.

"You better have good news for me," he growled, as Raul closed the door and walked over to his desk, wafting the cigar smoke away like some pathetic girly boy. "Well?!"

Raul hesitated, not taking his eyes from his father's. He hadn't shaved for a few days, Silva noted; that was unlike him. "We still have twenty four hours before the deadline and—"

Silva smashed his hand down on the desk and Raul stopped; his eye twitched. "The shipment, Raul? Is it ready?"

Raul swallowed visibly, his voice a mere whisper as he answered. "Like I was just saying, we still have time. We will be ready."

"You guarantee this?"

"I've already told you I do!"

Fire erupted in Silva's chest, the heat spreading through his veins as he absorbed his son's insolence. His fingers toyed with the glass paperweight on the desk in front of him, the cold, hard glass such a contrast to the fury boiling beneath his skin. He grasped it tight in his fist, resisting the urge to smash it around the side of Raul's skull. Instead, he let the bitter taste of frustration simmer on his tongue as he rose from his chair and walked around the desk so he was standing less than a foot away from his eldest son.

"Raul, we both know this is the most important deal we have ever been involved with," he said, keeping his tone in check. "If we mess this up, it's not only our business that is in jeopardy. You assured me everything would go to plan, that you had it all under control."

"And I do! I just need a little more—"

His words were cut off by a sharp backhand from his father that whipped his head to one side. Raul took the hit silently, a red imprint blossoming on his cheek, as hatred burned in his eyes.

Good.

Silva relished that fiery glare. Hopefully, it would stoke the flames of ambition and drive in his son.

"The shipment will be ready on time," Raul said through gritted teeth. "I want to make sure we are supplying the Mexicans with the very best on offer. This way they will use us again in the future. Isn't that what you want?" He glared at his father, the space between them fizzing with heat energy.

The older man returned to his chair. Raul was damned lucky he'd put the paperweight down. "Nothing else can go wrong with this deal."

"It won't. But the more discerning we are, the more impressive we appear. We have to show these people we are a force to be reckoned with, Father. The real deal. Yes? Trust me. I have this under control."

"Do you?" Silva snarled. "Then returning to my question from a few minutes ago – do you have good news for me?"

Raul bowed his head. "I have news that everything is going to plan."

"What about the Englishman? Is he dead yet?"

The mention of the bothersome stranger in town appeared to suck all the air out of the room. Silva stared as Raul squirmed.

"Not yet," he replied. "But it's only a matter of time. I have four of our best men stationed outside his hotel. I'm confident as soon as he shows up they'll do what is necessary."

"How long has it been?" Silva enquired. "When did you give the orders?"

Raul shot a glance at the clock on the wall. It was ten minutes to ten. "Maybe three hours ago."

Silva slapped the desk once again as his temper flared. "Fucking hell! You idiot! He knows they're there. He saw them. That's why they've not seen anything of him. This damned nuisance, he's made fools of us again!" He waved a crooked finger at his son. "I want that man found and then gutted like a fucking fish. Do you hear me, Raul? We cannot have him slowing down our operations. On your mother's grave, I shall castrate every one of those men who failed to capture him tonight. Are you aware of what will happen if we fail to deliver for the Mexicans?"

"Yes, Father."

"Well, damn well act like it then! Find that man. Complete the shipment."

Raul scowled and opened his mouth, perhaps to protest, but the same finger stabbing through the air at him shut him up.

"I mean it. I want the whole town turned upside down. Do not rest. Do not sleep. Do not even take a shit until everything is in order. Understood?"

Raul nodded meekly, back to being a pathetic girly boy.

"Raul! Do you understand what I am saying to you?"

"Yes."

"Good. Get out of my sight and don't come back until you have good news. Now, go."

Raul muttered something under his breath and left, leaving Silva alone with his thoughts and the white-noise chirps from the cicadas outside his window. His hand went for his hair but he reached for the glass paperweight instead, gripping it until his fingers turned white. And then, with a roar of rage that did little to dispel the demons in his soul, he hurled it at the wall.

24

Along with his bag containing a few basic items of clothing – a toothbrush, his father's old watch and four hundred euros in used notes – Beckett's passport was also in his hotel room. It was still relatively early, but with Silva's thugs sniffing around the hotel, the wise option was to lie low for the night. He'd retrieve his belongings in the morning. He had another passport in a safe deposit box at Gago Coutinho Airport in Faro and six more in airports around the world. It was his father's watch that mattered the most.

He made his way north, heading for the rocky mountains where the wild, untamed space would provide perfect refuge. Night deepened as he reached the edge of town, the thin crescent moon painting the buildings in hues of silver and midnight blue. A warm, earthy scent filled the air. It was a pleasant night and he wouldn't mind sleeping rough at all. In fact, he was looking forward to settling down under the stars with the sea breeze on his face.

Beckett had slept in far harsher conditions. Compared to some of the hellholes he'd survived in, a grassy spot beneath a tree was luxury. Then tomorrow he'd reach out to Humberto, perhaps speak to Armando once more. Beckett understood why Armando was reluctant to face the Silvas, but he also believed with a little persuasion – and once he knew Beckett was sticking around and needed his help – the ex-soldier would come around.

However, as Beckett was making his way out of town, raised voices coming from a nearby street caught his attention. Two men and an older woman. They were too far away for him to hear what was being said, but he understood the tone and heard the fear in the woman's words.

Beckett stopped, his senses prickling as he placed the exact location of the voices. Retracing his steps, he slipped down a dim alleyway between two buildings that led through to the next street. He could hardly see where he was going but he moved slowly, guided by the sounds. As he neared the far corner he stopped, straining to hear the conversation.

Now up close, the aggression in the men's voices was unmistakeable. "If you are lying to us," one of them said, "we will hurt you. We will burn down your store and leave you with nothing. You will wish you were dead."

"Please..." the woman begged. "I do not know anything." Her voice was fragile, her vocal cords strained with age. Beckett's hand instinctively clenched into a fist as he peered around the side of the building.

The woman was older than he'd pictured, with leathery brown skin and a halo of snow-white hair. She was sitting in an old green plastic chair, illuminated by the interior lights from the small convenience store behind her. Presumably she was the store owner and had been sitting out front between customers, enjoying the evening air. That was, until the two goons standing over her had shown up.

Beckett instantly recognised them as two of the men from outside his hotel: the overly eager one with slicked-back hair and the one who'd been chewing on a toothpick. That same toothpick was now being brandished at the old woman, the idiot's overbearing demeanour making her recoil in fear. He also held up a grainy photocopied image, and even with its poor quality, Beckett recognised the face from his passport. That meant they had his belongings. They had everything.

"You must have seen him," Slick snarled. "You're always sat here and this is the main path to the mountains. That's where we think he's gone."

Tears welled up in the woman's eyes. "I have not seen this man," she cried. "Now leave me alone. I know nothing."

Beckett crouched low, sizing up the two men. They had athletic builds and were both about his height, and, except for their overzealous sense of status, appeared to be unarmed. He glanced at the moon, considering the way the shadows fell across the landscape. If he broke cover in silence, he could approach them on a wide arc without being detected. As he waited, the old woman tried to rise off her seat but Toothpick shoved her back, sending her stumbling to the ground with a cry.

"Pathetic bitch," he sneered, leaning down so he was mere inches from her face. "You know who you're dealing with, right?"

"Please, have mercy," the old woman wailed, the pain evident on her features. "I am old. I am sick."

At this the men both laughed and something inside Beckett snapped. There was no deliberation, no thought about the consequences. He couldn't stand by and watch this poor woman terrorised for a moment longer. Stepping out from the cover of the alley, he sidestepped around the back of the men without making a sound.

His jaw was clenched, his fists itching for action. The anger he'd been nursing was ready to boil over but he kept it in check, condensing it into a core of focused energy, ready to be unleashed.

"I'd say the real question here," he whispered, his voice steady, "is do you know who you're dealing with?"

Surprise tensed the thugs' shoulders for a second, but their smug expressions quickly returned as they shifted to face him.

"There you are," Toothpick sneered, his lips twisting into a feral snarl.

"Here I am. Now leave the woman alone."

Beckett's senses zoomed into hyper focus: acutely aware of the cool breeze against his skin, the distant crash of the ocean waves, the ripe scent of flowers drifting down from the hillside – that and the distinct whiff of fear coming off the two men in front of him. They were younger than he'd realised, but still tall and muscular. The one with the slicked-back hair carried an air of aggressive arrogance, the sort of attitude exhibited by those yet to lose a fight.

"You must be a real dumb son of a bitch," Slick said, his voice low and sinister. "A clever man would have left town by now. I mean… I'm glad you're still here. But it's going to go bad for you, old man."

He stepped forward and pulled a butterfly knife from his back pocket, opening it one-handed with a flick of his wrist. It looked impressive, but only because he'd most likely practiced the move daily in front of the mirror. Another hint for Beckett that these young punks were nothing but bluster and bravado. He leaned his weight onto his back foot, the veins in his forearms throbbing with anticipation. He was born for this.

Toothpick was first, swinging at Beckett without any preamble. He was the taller and broader of the two, but fast with it. Beckett ducked the punch and jabbed his open palm into the man's elbow, bending it inwards. The man howled as his arm buckled, his own momentum working against him. Capitalising on the shock and pain, Beckett drove his knee into the man's stomach, leaving him bent double on the ground.

One down…

Beckett shifted his attention to Slick, the younger man wielding the butterfly knife. He too was agile and full of energy. He lunged towards him, slashing the blade wildly, his movements emphasised with a heavy grunt. Beckett evaded the first attack, but a second swing found its mark, leaving a stinging gash across his forearm.

"Not so tough after all!" the man jeered, leaping back. "But don't you think about running away now. We'll find you."

"I don't run from people like you," Beckett replied. "Ever."

They circled each other, Slick jerking forward with the knife, trying to intimidate Beckett, goading him into making a wrong move. He remained alert, the muscles in his arms burning with tension as he judged his next manoeuvre – and that of his opponent. The younger man had grown cocky at the sight of blood.

But that was a good thing.

As Slick lunged again, Beckett sidestepped him, his hand darting out to catch the man's wrist. With a practiced twist he disarmed him, the knife clattering onto the cobblestones. Not letting go, Beckett twisted the man's arm up behind his back, applying an upward force. He heard a crunch and a crack followed by a scream; Slick's shoulder dislocated.

By now Toothpick was on his feet, raw fury evident in his eyes. He charged forward, intent on levelling the odds, yet it was clear he'd already given into desperation, and as far as Beckett was concerned, the fight was all but done. Maintaining his hold on the younger man he pivoted around, using Slick as a human shield. Toothpick's right hook, intended for Beckett, landed squarely on his buddy's jaw, knocking him to the ground, unconscious. Before the dumb bastard could right himself, Beckett lunged forward, slamming an elbow into the thug's temple with such force the impact was immediate. Toothpick's head snapped to one side and, as if a switch had been flipped, he was out cold. With no strength to hold himself up, he tumbled on top of his unconscious accomplice.

Outnumbered and unarmed, yet once again Beckett was the last man standing. But he'd known this would be the outcome before he'd entered the fight. With any other mindset he wouldn't have survived in this world as long as he had done. Still, the sight of the fallen thugs brought him little satisfaction. Their presence was just another sickening reminder of São Lourenço's descent into chaos.

Beckett kept his guard up, anticipating another wave of attacks as he stepped over to the old lady. She was still on the ground and had been watching the fight in silent awe. Beckett gave her a nod, his silent vow of protection, but as Toothpick and Slick regained consciousness they were on their feet and scrambling away, fear creasing their once bombastic expressions. As they hurried down the street, Toothpick glanced back at Beckett.

"You're a dead man," he yelled, his voice hoarse. "You hear me? Mr Silva will not let you live another day in this town. You are dead! DEAD!"

Unfazed, Beckett watched as Silva's goons disappeared into the shadows, their parting threats echoing through the dark streets. He rolled his shoulders back. Let Silva take his best shot. He'd learn soon enough what happened when people pushed John Beckett into a corner.

"You are hurt?" The old woman's voice pulled him back. He turned to see her nodding and pointing. "Your arm."

He glanced down at the wound, the sting intensifying beneath the fading rush of adrenaline. "I'll be fine."

"No. Please." She stepped closer, gently grasping his wrist and tilting his forearm to inspect the damage. "You need help. I have supplies."

Beckett hesitated, but the immediate threat had passed and he had no way of dressing his arm himself. He inspected the wound, feeling his pulse throbbing inside his flesh. It was deep. It needed attention.

"Okay," he told the woman, and smiled. "Thank you."

25

A tiny bell above the door tinkled as the old woman ushered Beckett into the shop. Once there, she shut the door behind them and locked it with a large brass key, dropping it back into the front pocket of her pale blue pinafore dress.

The pungent aroma of overripe fruit hung heavy in the air. On each wall, chiller cabinets teemed with drinks, vegetables and an array of different cheeses were all illuminated under harsh fluorescent lights. On the floor, the chequered linoleum was scuffed and faded from decades of foot traffic.

"This way," the woman told him, setting off down a narrow aisle.

Beckett followed, manoeuvring past shelves stacked with assorted goods: cleaning products, canned food, local wines, boxes of multipack crisps. The air became more humid as they ventured deeper into the store. The woman led Beckett through a beaded curtain hung across a doorframe in the far corner, and he found himself in a small backroom with no windows and a harsh naked bulb hanging from the ceiling. The room was cluttered but in an organised manner. Stacks of cardboard boxes teetered on the brink of collapse, while the lid of a chest freezer along the back wall doubled as a storage surface. In the middle of the room stood a plain wooden table and two green plastic chairs like the one the woman had been sitting on outside.

She gestured for Beckett to sit. "My name is Beatriz Rego," she told him. "This is my store. And those men will not intimidate me into leaving. No matter what they say or do."

"You know, Beatriz, I don't doubt it," he replied, noting the glimmer in her eyes as he sat. "And it's a pleasure to meet you. My name's… Michael. Michael Day. I'm afraid I've made a bit of a nuisance of myself in your town since I arrived."

Beatriz chuckled to herself. "Oh, I know who you are. I've heard all about the brave Englishman who humiliated Rodrigo Silva. Well… brave or stupid." She turned and met his eye, a knowing expression on her face. "But I think we both know which."

She rummaged around in one of the boxes and pulled out a metal tin with a white cross painted on top. Carrying it to the table, she opened it and lifted out a piece of gauze and a roll of bandage.

"That's going to need stitches," she told him, leaning over to inspect his wound again. "Give me a moment."

As she shuffled over to the far side of the room, Beckett held his arm to the light. The knife had cut him deep, but the incision was only about an inch long. As it usually did with deep wounds, the bleeding had ceased quickly and he could see where the blade had sliced through tissue and then muscle. Beatriz was right about it needing stitches.

"Thank you for this," he said. "And I'm sorry for what's happened to your town. I came here once when I was a lot younger. It was a lovely place then. Quiet, friendly, perfect."

Beatriz turned around, brandishing a darning needle and a bobbin of black cotton. "I'm afraid this is all I have," she said, returning to the table and sitting beside him. "Don't worry. I'll be careful."

"Oh, I've had worse done to me," he replied. "In fact, I've done worse to myself."

Sewing needles, superglue, electrical tape, rubbing alcohol – Beckett had used them all over the years to patch himself up in the field.

Whatever did the job, did the job.

The old woman picked a bottle of antiseptic lotion out of the metal box and sloshed some onto the wound. It stung like hell, but the heady stench of iodine revived Beckett's senses.

Next, she took a plastic cigarette lighter out of her dress pocket and ignited it under the needle, holding it there for a time and glancing up at him with a grin. "My mother was a nurse," she said, a soft smile playing on her lips, a touch of nostalgia in her eyes. "You're in good hands."

Beckett gripped the table with his other hand as she went to work with the needle, bracing himself through the worst of it.

"Has everyone in town heard about me?" he asked, as she threaded his flesh back together.

"It seems so," Beatriz replied. "We don't get many visitors anymore. The last of the tourist companies stopped sending people to São Lourenço last year. As if our ailing town needed any more problems." She stopped sewing and her expression dropped into a stern examination of Beckett's face. "Are you going to help us, Mr Day? *Can* you help us?"

Beckett inhaled deeply, considering his response as she finished the stitches. "Yes," he replied softly. "I am."

"And how will you do that?"

"That part I'm not entirely sure of yet. I have some ideas, but I need to know more about the family and their organisation – how they tick, what their operations involve."

Beatriz tied off the stitching and dressed the wound with a piece of gauze and the bandage. Once finished, Beckett flexed his newly sewn arm and nodded his approval.

But Beatriz's face only hardened some more. "Have you heard about the missing girls?" she asked.

"I've heard the Silva have killed those who stand up to them or get in their way. Men and women."

Beatriz shook her head morosely. "It's worse than that. You ask around. In the last few months, young women have vanished all over town. No one wants to speak about it too loudly for fear of what might happen to them. But behind closed doors we talk. People know." She glanced at the beaded curtain, and Beckett noticed the first hint of fear in her eyes. But there was something else there too. Sadness. She sighed. "My neighbour's daughter is called Telma. She was – *is* – a beautiful girl. Tall, slim, long black hair. Three weeks ago she disappeared and no one knows where she is. She is only twenty-two."

"What about the police?" Beckett asked. "I'm aware most of them are corrupt, but didn't they look into it?"

Beatriz sniffed derisively. "The police around here are useless. They're all cowards or they don't care. Plus, the closest police station is over in the next town. They stay away from São Lourenço if they can help it."

"That makes sense. I've not seen any patrols since I've been here."

"And you won't. My neighbour reported her daughter missing, of course, but the police dismissed her claims. Telma was a good girl, but she had gone off the rails lately and she and her mother had been arguing a lot. The police concluded she had simply run away from home. My neighbour begged the police to find her, but they said she was an adult and there was nothing they could do. But people had seen Telma hanging around with Rodrigo Silva shortly before she disappeared. He was buying her clothes, plying her with drinks in one of the hotel bars on the other side of town."

Beckett rubbed at the stubble on his chin. "You think Rodrigo killed her?"

"There has been no body found. But yes. I do. I think he's killed a lot of girls. I know of six, personally, that have gone missing in the last two months. The police are indifferent and most people here are scared to speak for fear of retribution. But some of us care, some of us still want to fight this virus that has infected our town. Rodrigo Silva is an evil and greedy man who only cares about himself, just like his father and brother. I think he takes what he wants from these poor young girls and disposes of them."

"Yeah," Beckett replied, a frown creasing his brow as he considered her words. "Maybe…" He trailed off as a sickening thought came to him. One that tightened his determination as much as it did the skin across his knuckles.

Beatriz held his gaze without blinking. "Don't underestimate that family, Mr Day. They are bad news. *Bestas malignas…*"

Beckett placed his hands on the table, the fresh stitches pulling slightly as he did. "I get it," he said. "I really do. But I've got to get going. Thank you again for stitching me up."

"I am happy to help," Beatriz replied. "As I hope you are, Michael Day. People tell me you are a brave man and strong too. We need people like you."

"I'll do what I can," he assured her, a renewed sense of purpose surging through his veins as he got to his feet. "You have my word."

As he stepped back into the dim light of the storefront, he spared one last glance at the old woman.

"Stay safe, Beatriz," he told her, before turning and heading out into the night.

But rather than head for the relative quiet and safety of the mountains, he retraced his steps towards the centre of town. Rest suddenly felt a long way off for John Beckett.

He had people he needed to speak to.

And he had plans to make.

26

Raul Silva could feel the tension clenching at his shoulder muscles as he strode across the gravel path separating his father's sprawling mansion from his own house at the bottom of the estate. He walked with care and precision, the crisp crunch of the rocks beneath his Italian leather shoes the only disruption to the heavy silence that hung in the air. Normally he liked being outside at this late hour, he liked the sense of serenity it brought with it, but tonight he was too angry to relax.

If his younger brother lived a life of chaos and bravado, Raul was all about control and structure. These were the cornerstones of his world and he hated feeling unsettled and at odds with himself.

As he got closer to the house he slowed his pace, sucking back deep, conscious breaths in an attempt to calm the indignant rage threatening to consume him. His cheek still smarted from where his father had slapped him, but it was the context in which it had been administered that hurt the most.

It was insulting. It was disrespectful.

And he didn't deserve it.

Raul hadn't been lying earlier when his father asked him about the shipment. He was one hundred percent confident they would be ready on time. The deal would go through. All would be well. The only reason the damned deal was happening in the first place was because of him. It was his ambition and tenacity that would propel the Silva organisation into the big time.

Why couldn't his father see that?

He moved off the path and entered his garden, the security lights flickering on as he approached, revealing the meticulously maintained lawns and flowerbeds. The firm grass beneath his feet was still damp from the sprinklers and as he got to his house he stamped his feet on the steps leading up to the porch, removing the excess moisture from his immaculate, polished shoes.

"Antonia?" he called out as he entered the house. "Are you home?"

There was no answer; the only sound he could hear was the soft hum of the central air conditioning. He slipped off his shoes and aligned them in their designated place inside the white lacquered unit on the wall – the symmetry of this action quelling the rage within, even if just for a moment. Raul's house was not the decadent and imposing fortress his father favoured, but a refined building of clean lines and modernist simplicity. Every surface was gleaming, free from the clutter of trinkets and personal effects. The furniture was expensive and carefully chosen, each piece different from the next but complementing the assembled whole. A home crafted to his exact specifications.

As he moved down the hallway he called out his wife's name once more, but received no answer.

Where the hell was she?

The kitchen light was on at the end of the corridor, but Raul moved into the lounge instead. Heading straight for his drinks cabinet, he selected a bottle of Cîroc vodka and poured himself a generous serving. He downed the drink in one go and slammed the glass down on the polished mahogany shelf like a pathetic college student doing shots. But screw it, he was feeling nihilistic this evening. He was tired of being the scapegoat, the punching bag for his father's insecurities. Being the middle sibling, he'd always been the quiet, unnoticed kid. Even as an adult and the rightful male heir to the Silva business, he still felt overlooked and denigrated most of the time.

He topped up his glass, filling it almost to the brim before taking a large gulp and savouring the lingering burn. He moved out of the lounge and down the corridor towards the kitchen, where he discovered Antonia standing by the sink looking out the window.

"You are home!" he sneered. "Did you not hear me calling you just now?"

"I was in the bedroom until a moment ago." She didn't turn around, just continued to stare out into the blackness of the night.

But she'd heard him. She had to have done. He took another sip of vodka. The bright kitchen lights accentuated his wife's silhouette, a fragile figure beneath her silk robe. Even to someone like Raul, who was not good with empathy or picking up on emotions, her body language told a story. She was closed off, cold, putting an icy barrier between them.

He walked over to her, holding the drink to his chest. "What the fuck is wrong with you?"

She glanced up at him. She wasn't wearing any make-up and the yellow bruising around her eye was still apparent. "Nothing is wrong," she said, looking away.

"You're not still angry about the other day. Come on, baby. I told you I was stressed. You shouldn't have pushed me. You know better than that."

Antonia sniffed and nodded at her reflection in the window. "Yes. I do know that, don't I?" Her voice was a hushed monotone.

"Antonia, sweetie, come on. Stop this. This isn't you. This isn't us."

He glared at the side of her face but she wouldn't look at him. Antonia was a good wife, Raul knew that. She put up with a lot. He looked her up and down, his gaze landing on her wrist at the point where the bone stuck out a little more than it used to after he broke it last year. He couldn't even remember now what they'd been fighting about, but he was certain she'd provoked him. She always did. They'd been married for almost a decade by this point, surely it wasn't too much to ask she try to understand him a little better. Raul was a passionate and sensitive soul. She should have given him more leeway, more support. She was his wife, after all. Was it not her job to care for him?

"Have you eaten?" he asked.

"I had some chicken and potatoes that were left over from yesterday," she replied. "I can make you a plate."

"I'll do it later. Come here, let me look at you."

He grabbed her shoulder and pulled her around so she was facing him. She was still a good-looking woman. Her nose had been a little wonky ever since she smashed it on the edge of the bathroom sink a few years ago, but if anything, it added to her beauty. He tilted his head to one side and smiled. She smiled back. It was almost convincing, except the loathing in her eyes, always there now, was hard to mask. They hadn't had sex together in a long time. Over a year.

"What do you want?" she asked.

"To look at my wife. There is no crime in that, is there?"

"I am tired, Raul. I don't need this right now."

He gritted his teeth. There she went again, dismissing his advances, making him feel like a damn fool.

They'd both wanted children. But after years of trying and failing, they'd given up; and after that, Raul had found it difficult to feel close to his wife. The constant sobbing and mournful looks didn't help. He found her moods both pathetic and insulting. It wasn't his fault she couldn't conceive.

But Raul enjoyed sex. He enjoyed the release it offered him. The girls he used these days, although pretty enough, were young and unresponsive. Maybe once the shipment was complete and the deal done, he would work on rekindling the fire in his marital bed. He would like that. So would she. He'd make sure of it.

Because despite the fear and disgust that now lingered between them, he needed his wife. He needed the semblance of normality she provided. The sense of order.

"Antonia, baby." His voice was soft, almost pleading. It made him feel ridiculous and angry with himself all at once but he pushed through it. His wife's silence hung in the air and she stiffened, her breath hitching slightly as he pulled her closer. "I'm sorry," he tried, the words like acid in his mouth.

"Let me go," she said, pushing him away. "I have things to do."

He held her out at arm's length, his fingers digging into the flesh of her upper arms. "Hey!" he hissed. "I'm under a lot of pressure at work, you know that. Everything I do is for you. For us."

He pulled her towards him once more. This time her body fell against his in defeated acceptance. He sensed she was sobbing, her back quivering as the silent tears fell.

"I know, Raul," she whispered. "But... I am not happy—"

"You're being unfair," he cut her off. "You know I can't talk about the business, but believe me when I say things are being put in place that will prove *very* rewarding for us. Just you wait. More money. More security. I'll make you happier than you ever thought possible."

But his words fell on empty air as his wife disentangled herself from his grip and hurried out of the room. The unfinished conversation hung in the air like another slap in the face.

How dare she?

He was done with this, he really was. Down went the rest of the vodka, setting his throat on fire, fuelling the storm within him. He would not be disrespected again this evening. Not by anyone.

With a determined stride, he stalked down the hall to the front door, panic and anger swelling in his belly. He needed a release. Needed to regain control.

And he would do so.

One way or another.

27

Beckett strode through the streets of São Lourenço and crossed the town square. It was late, almost midnight, and he was no longer sticking to the backstreets or alleyways. With Beatriz's story fresh in his mind, he didn't care if he encountered any of the Silva family or their men. Let them come. He'd put every one of them in the ground.

But none came, and as he neared Armando's bar the seasoned operative within him reasserted itself. It was reckless bordering on stupid to broadcast his movements to the enemy, especially now the stakes were getting higher. Two blocks from the taberna, he slipped into the shadows and approached the building from the rear, stopping in the passageway opposite to observe the surroundings and ensure there were no looming dangers.

Once satisfied, he made his way across the street and pushed open the heavy wooden door of the taberna, glancing over each shoulder as he entered. An airless heat hit him in the face, the low-lit room thick with the stench of stale beer and hint of body odour. A couple of stragglers, their eyelids heavy and their shoulders hunched, sat together at a small table at the back of the room. They barely looked up from their glasses as Beckett entered, and didn't acknowledge him as he let the door swing shut behind him.

Armando, standing in place behind the bar, had seen him, however. As had Humberto, who was sitting at the counter nursing the last few centimetres of a glass of beer. Whatever they'd been talking about was reduced to an abrupt silence as Beckett approached.

"Humberto. Armando." His tone held no room for levity as he gestured for them to follow him over to the corner, away from the remaining customers. "We need to talk."

"I was wondering when you'd show up," Humberto said, pushing off the bar and getting to his feet. "I'm glad you didn't wait too long."

They gathered around a small round table near the door to the kitchen.

"Have you told Armando what we discussed?" Beckett asked Humberto.

The older man winced. "No. I felt it would be better coming from you. Our new saviour."

Beckett held his gaze for a moment. He wasn't sure he liked that terminology. He was no saviour. Far from it.

Over the next few minutes, he updated Armando on recent events and the information he'd gathered since his arrival in town. As he described meeting Maria and Antonia, he glanced at Humberto, noticing the skin tightening around his mouth. He relayed what Beatriz had told him about the missing girls and concluded by looking both men in the eyes and stating, in no uncertain terms, that life for the people of São Lourenço was only going to get worse unless something was done to stop the Silva regime. And soon.

When he was done he sat back, allowing his words to sink in, giving the men space to reply.

Armando was first. He cleared his throat. He made a low

growling noise. He shook his head. He sighed. Finally, he said, "Listen, Mike, I told you already. No one wants to get rid of those evil bastards more than me. But this is crazy. They're powerful, connected, they have guns and men and are ready to kill anyone who tries to stop them."

"I know," Beckett said. "But people are dying. Girls are going missing. My father was a soldier too, like you. A good man. A brave man. One of his mantras, one of the things he drummed into me from an early age, was the importance of fighting injustice wherever one sees it. And another saying he liked: the only thing necessary for the triumph of evil is for good men to do nothing." He held Armando's anxious gaze. "The time of doing nothing has to stop. Today."

Armando held Beckett's gaze right back. "I know. I get it. But… I have responsibilities. This is dangerous talk."

"If Mike's staying around, we have to help him," Humberto chimed in. "You are staying, right?"

"For now," Beckett replied. "But not at the hotel. It's been compromised. Silva's men were waiting for me. They have my bag, my passport."

"That's why you want to hit these guys?" Armando muttered.

Beckett's face remained neutral. "It's very low down on my list of reasons, I assure you."

Armando nodded. "Where will you stay while you're in town?"

"Up in the mountains. I can stay out of sight better." Beckett's tone was dismissive, his mind focusing on bigger problems. "I probably won't be getting much rest for the next twenty-four hours anyway. In fact, Armando, I don't suppose your coffee machine is working, is it?"

He grinned. "Funnily enough… I managed to get it going again this afternoon."

"That's the best news I've heard all day. Strong and black if you've got it."

"No problem. There's already a jug on. Give me a second." He rose and wandered over to the bar, grabbing the half-full jug of coffee from under the machine and a large mug. As he poured and returned to the table with it, Humberto leaned over to Beckett.

"Thank you, Michael. I knew you'd do the right thing."

"I told you before, don't thank me yet," he replied, sitting back and accepting the coffee mug from Armando. "We've still got a lot to do. This isn't going to be easy."

"I was just thinking," Armando said, taking his seat. "I have a room upstairs here. It's full of boxes, but it has a cot bed along one wall. Why don't you stay there while you're in town? If you're careful, that is; I don't want the Silvas knowing you're here. But I guess it's the least I can do."

Beckett thanked him with a nod as he sipped the coffee. It was lukewarm but strong as hell and tasted good. "I'm afraid I need more than a room from you, Armando," he said, looking the bartender straight in the eyes. "An ex-soldier like yourself, still fit and able – I need your help."

Armando seemed to shrink into himself, his gaze falling to the wooden floor. "Man… I said it already. I can't help you."

Before Beckett could respond, Humberto slammed his fist down on the table. "For Christ's sake, don't be such a damned coward, Armando!" His face twisted into a scowl. "Think of everything we have already lost. The people, the trade – our self-respect! If we don't fight, what will happen to us? You heard what Mike said, those bastards are only going to grow more powerful and more dangerous. What, you want to wait around for the police chief to grow a conscience and do something about it? We both know that's never going to happen."

A tense silence fell over the table as Beckett regarded the

two men. He was a good judge of character, but at this moment he had no idea which way Armando would go. The man's eyes were filled with grim desperation, his mouth wilted in shame. He was torn. A man on the edge. Beckett knew what that felt like.

"We need to do this, Armando," he said. "And we need to do it soon."

Across the room, the two remaining customers scraped their chairs back and shuffled for the door, one of them calling out something in garbled Portuguese that Beckett didn't catch. Now it was just the three of them in the corner – the room and the night and the town's future stretching out in front of them.

"Fine," Armando whispered after what seemed like forever. "I'm in. What do you need from me?"

Beckett gave him a reassuring nod and leaned forward, resting his elbows on the table. "Firstly, how many men do the Silvas have? I've already met nine and I'd wager at least five of them are incapacitated for the time being. Going off that estimate, how many do we think are left?"

Humberto sucked in a breath and released it slowly, narrowing his eyes as if counting in his head. "I'd say they have a core army of around fifteen. If you've taken out five, that leaves ten men."

"Good. That's what I was expecting," Beckett replied. "Now, properties. There's the mansion and the estate over to the west. Any others you know about?"

"Emilio owns a couple of hotels up north, on the edge of town," Humberto replied. "He uses them as stash houses from what I hear – guns, drugs, anything illegal you can think of. Each building stands alone and is very well guarded."

"Very well guarded we can deal with," Beckett replied, turning to Armando. "Do you have a map of the area? And a pen?"

Armando rose without a word and walked over to the bar,

returning a few seconds later with an old bi-fold tourist map and a well-chewed ballpoint. "The map's not too detailed but it'll give you an idea," he said, handing it over.

Beckett opened it up and slid it in front of Humberto. "Mark all the locations for me."

"What are you thinking?" Armando asked.

"I need to get eyes on each of these properties to understand what we're dealing with and gather more intel. If we can hit them where it hurts – their resources, their pockets, their reputation – we'll stand a better chance of taking them down."

Armando scoffed. "You think we'd be that lucky?"

"I don't believe in luck," Beckett told him. He took another gulp of coffee and examined the map, noting the advent of the scrawled crosses courtesy of Humberto and already forming a strategic outline. "And what about the Silva estate?"

Humberto leaned in with the pen once more. "Here. That's Emilio's place, what people call The Kingdom. Rodrigo lives there too. And this"—pressing harder, the pen nib nearly puncturing the paper—"is Raul's place."

"Okay. Got it," Beckett said, eyes still on the map. "And what about the sister, Maria, where does she live?"

"In a big old villa over on the east side of town." Armando waved his hand at a vague location on the map. "She acts like she's better than everyone else, but she isn't involved in the family business. She's not so bad."

Beckett nodded but didn't look up. "Okay. Now if, as we suspect, the family are a smaller link in a much bigger chain, then I foresee those above them – the bigger fish – will likely cut all ties if they see how weak their authority is within their own town. Hell, if we can interfere with Silva's operations enough and disrupt whatever supply chain exists, the bigger fish might even take care of them for us."

"It makes sense," Humberto said.

"But we have to hit them hard," Beckett continued, "and soon. Before they have any inkling we're organising resistance."

Humberto nodded. "How soon is 'soon'?"

"Tomorrow. The day after at the latest. It doesn't give us much time."

"Shit! Tomorrow!" Armando blurted out, looking away and rubbing at his chin. "Are you serious?"

"It has to be fast and unexpected," Beckett confirmed, folding the marked map and tucking it into his pocket. He stared Armando out, hoping the urgency in his eyes was clear. There was no time for hesitation. "I'm going to head over to the hotel now. See what I can find out. It's almost midnight. Let's meet back here in a few hours. Just before dawn. Is that okay with you?"

The two men nodded sagely as Beckett glanced between them. Humberto cleared his throat. "It's all moving so quickly," he said, his gaze drifting to the door, "and that's what we need. But now the ball is rolling, there's something I have to do."

"Oh?" Beckett watched as the older man got to his feet. "What's that?"

"Something I should have done a long time ago," Humberto replied. "I'll see you later. Be careful."

With that, he walked to the door and exited without looking back. Beckett stared after him for a moment then got to his feet. The gears were in motion. He had work to do.

28

A thin new moon cast the sleeping town in an almost ethereal glow as Humberto prowled through the empty streets. The air was still, with the merest scent of salt coming in off the ocean, and the only sounds were his footsteps and the occasional scratch of a scurrying rodent. Humberto pushed his chest out as he walked, ignoring the darting shadows that would have once had him hurrying away to the safety of his home. Not tonight. São Lourenço was a place that had seen its fair share of darkness. But no more.

That was the hope, at least.

But he almost didn't dare consider it.

Memories of his military days had been haunting him all evening. Back then, he'd been a different man in a different world. Now a specific memory came to him, a mission that had taken him and his unit deep into the heart of Angola. Their task had been to infiltrate a well-guarded rebel stronghold and rescue a captured Portuguese diplomat before valuable information could be tortured out of him.

Humberto remembered the stifling heat and the relentless buzz of insects as if it were yesterday; the jungle, thick and disorienting and rife with hidden dangers. The rebels they'd been up against were experienced guerrillas, brutal and deadly, but Humberto had led his unit undeterred, his senses attuned to every rustle and hint of movement.

When they reached the rebel stronghold, it had been just him and one other soldier who had breached the perimeter, choosing stealth rather than force to get the job done. It had paid off, too. He remembered the heightened sensation, his pulse echoing in his ears as he silently took out rebel guards and located the diplomat.

Their exit had been less discreet. They were almost clear of the compound, but at the last moment a stray sentry spotted them and raised the alarm. In the ensuing firefight, Humberto had been a whirlwind of focused action. Some nights his dreams still echoed with the deafening roar of gunfire. Yet he had persevered, fought through the chaos, made sure his unit and the diplomat made it to the extraction point safely. His bravery that day had earned him commendations and a medal, but more importantly it had saved lives.

Back in the present, Humberto shook the memory away, bringing his focus back to the quiet street in front of him. Yet he held onto the feeling in his belly. A surge of extreme courage had driven him that day in the jungle, the same courage he called upon now.

Because fear was no longer an option.

"No more bowing down to those bastards," he muttered to the silent town, the sound of his voice ricocheting off the deserted buildings. "No more turning the other cheek."

Reaching his house, Humberto paused momentarily at the front door before continuing on his way. As he marched, his stride became more purposeful, his gaze unwavering. He could feel something changing inside of him, a shift in his mindset that was palpable. Like a soldier stepping into battle, preparing to face whatever came next.

As he ventured west, the ocean breeze bristled through the trees on either side. Humberto wasn't entirely sure what he was going to do when he reached his destination, but he pressed on regardless. When he got there, he would know. And now was the time for action, not cowardice.

A few minutes later he got to the house and slipped behind one of the large cypress trees that lined the bottom edge of the estate. Although not as big or as ostentatious as his father's mansion further up the hillside, Raul Silva's house was still grand and stood in stark contrast to the rest of the town. Humberto pulled in a deep breath. He'd stood in this same spot many times over the years – sometimes drunk and raging at his cowardly impotence, other times filled with sorrow and regret – but he'd never dared go any closer. He'd watched from a distance, a helpless father, as his only child, his daughter, became embroiled in the sinister world of the Silva family.

Tonight, however, Humberto felt the resurgence of a familiar bravery. The same courage and resolve he'd experienced on the way over here was still fire in his belly. He edged closer, sticking to the trees. The front of the house was dark, all the lights off except for a security lamp on the porch. But there were no guards in sight either. He circled around to the western side of the property, where a light from one of the rooms spread its orange glow over the lawn. Moving in a wide arc, he saw it was a bedroom, and as he watched on, a figure stepped into view, framed in the large picture window.

There she was.

His darling Antonia.

He gasped at the sight of her, and a sharp ache burnt through his chest like a bullet. Her beautiful face – so much like her mother's – was sullied by an ugly bruise that spread out beneath her left eye. He clenched his teeth, his blood seething with a new fervour. A father's rage.

Leaving his position, he stalked around the perimeter of

the property, moving faster than he had done in a long time. His jaw was rigid, his fists balled tight. But he saw no sign of Raul or anyone else.

Before he could talk himself out of it, he broke from his cover and headed towards the house. His throat was dry and his instincts screamed at him to retreat. But he pushed on, a father spurred on by love and duty. Though not just a father. Not any longer. The soldier in Humberto had awakened and he was ready for battle.

29

Emilio Silva steepled his fingers under his chin and spread his legs wide in his seat, drawing in deep mindful breaths.

Inhale... one... two... Exhale... one... two...

These were techniques supposed to make the user feel powerful and confident, but they weren't working.

Nothing was working.

His eyes burned with tiredness as he watched the antique clock hanging on the wall, the brass pendulum swinging like the sword of Damocles.

Tick-tock...

Tick-tock...

Each minute felt like a lifetime. It was now a few minutes past midnight. Friday. Leaving them just twenty-four hours to complete the shipment and honour their part of the deal.

He returned his attention to his phone lying on the desk in front of him. He'd been sitting here, shifting his focus from the phone to the clock and back again for what seemed like hours but was probably only thirty minutes. Time was a conundrum when it was working against you. Dread churned in his stomach. He stared at the phone screen, expecting it to light up any moment. The call he knew was coming.

Barbosa had called twice in the past twelve hours and Silva had swerved the calls each time, but it was fast getting to the point where he could no longer hide. Zero hour was approaching.

An unexpected knock on his door was a welcome distraction from his troubling thoughts. "Enter," he barked, his voice croaky.

He sat up, his relative interest in whoever this was turning immediately to anger as two dishevelled figures stumbled into his office. Cuba and Rego, two of the men that had been staking out the Englishman's hotel.

"What the fuck happened to you?" Silva growled, looking them up and down.

"We waited outside the hotel for the Englishman, like you told us," Cuba muttered. "But he never showed up. So after a couple of hours we got the call to return to Eagle."

Standing there all pathetic, he looked like a broken puppet, his bruised face battered by shame. Emilio rubbed his lips together, his nostrils flaring at the same time as he struggled to remain composed. He knew all this information already. What he wanted to know was why two of his – supposedly – toughest men looked like they'd been run over by a herd of stray goats.

"So why are you standing in my office?" Silva asked. "Can you no longer follow orders? You know Eagle in particular needs all hands on deck right now."

The stash houses of Eagle and Wolf, formerly hotels, were where the Silva organisation stored contraband and weapons – amongst other things. It was at Eagle where the Mexican's shipment was being stored until it was complete and transportation was secured.

"So?"

Cuba looked at Rego. Rego looked at his feet and

shrugged. He had a graze across his forehead and a nasty bruise on his cheek.

"We were on our way there," Cuba continued, "but we stopped off to get some food and decided to ask around, press the locals for any sight of the Englishman. We thought we were being diligent."

Silva's hand slid up the back of his neck, grabbing a tuft of hair from the base. "And…? Has anyone seen him?"

"Not exactly," Cuba responded. "This old bitch got mouthy with us and Rego got a little rough with her. The next thing we know he's standing behind us – the English prick. We gave a good fight, we really did. Rego slashed the prick's arm open with his blade but—"

"There were two of you!" Silva yelled, slapping the desk with his hand. "Two against one. You're supposed to be the best! And I take it from your wretched expressions and pitiable body language that he got the better of you."

The men looked at the floor and nodded. "He was like a whirlwind, Mr Silva," Rego mumbled. "You've not seen anything like it. We got away so we could report back… let you know he's still in town."

"I want him dead!" Silva snarled, yanking the hair from the back of his head and flinging it at his men. "If you couldn't finish the job, then you should be dead! Fucking idiots!"

He glared at them, wondering if he really should have them killed – held up as an example to the rest of his men that this sort of cowardly behaviour was not acceptable. But he dismissed the idea almost immediately. Despite the fact it would have appeased some of the rage bubbling inside him, his men were dropping like flies and he couldn't afford any more losses.

"We're sorry, Boss," Rego mumbled. "We'll do better next time. Just give us another—"

"Get out," he seethed, his voice a hoarse whisper. "Now. Before I cut your balls off myself."

The two men wasted no time in gathering themselves together and fleeing from his office. Watching their retreat, Silva felt a simmering rage that nearly consumed him. He needed to calm down. His blood pressure was already through the roof. Taking a deep breath, he buzzed the intercom on his desk. The deep voice of Delgado crackled over the speaker.

"Yes, Mr Silva?"

"Come meet me in my office. Now," he instructed. "Bring Gil and Lobo."

"Right away, sir."

Silva sat back in his chair. Moments later the three men entered the room. Their imposing statures and sharp eyes said they were ready for business, even at this late hour.

"Come, sit," he told them, gesturing at the chairs across his desk.

He watched them as they settled in. His inner circle. These three were the toughest and most experienced of his employees. Typically, he preferred to keep them close, safeguarding his home and himself. But at times like this, their skills were required elsewhere.

"Delgado, Gil, Lobo." He looked at each man in turn, his expression firm and eyes unblinking. "It appears the Englishman is still in town and still making us look like damn fools. We cannot have this go on a moment longer."

Delgado, a thick-set man with excessive body hair that gave him the appearance of a wild beast, nodded. "Do we know who this guy is yet?"

"No, we do not," Silva snarled. "But he's just one man. I was told I had the deadliest, most proficient security force money can buy. Are my men cowards or inept?"

Delgado didn't flinch. "We'll track him down, sir."

"That's right," Gil added, jutting his chin. "And then we dispose of him?"

"Oh yes, and in the most vicious and unpleasant way imaginable," Silva replied, his mind conjuring disgusting images of bloody retribution. "But at this present moment I'll settle on it being done as quickly and cleanly as possible. That man has gone from being more than just a thorn in my side. He's disrupting our operations, slowing us down at the worst possible time."

The three men exchanged glances and got to their feet. They understood the gravity of the situation.

"Our deal with the Mexicans is to take place in less than a day," he continued, as if they needed reminding. "If we can't assure delivery on time, we're as good as dead. At the very least we'll be cut off, a laughing stock, back to being petty crooks. Nobody here wants that. We've worked too hard, sacrificed too much." He glared at the men, letting his words sink in, noting the determination on each of their faces. He sat back and waved his hand. "Gil, Lobo – go now. Do what you're paid for."

The two men looked at Delgado and then left the room. Silva and his most trusted security detail sat in silence for a moment. Delgado shifted in his seat, the chair creaking beneath him while Silva tried in vain to gather his thoughts amidst the infernal ticking of the clock. It was no use. Standing, he ran a sweaty palm across his head, sleeking his hair back. The patches of bare scalp were getting larger, but his hair would grow back. It always did. And he had bigger issues to worry about than his appearance.

"I want you to drive me over to Eagle," he announced, glaring at Delgado with an intensity that froze any protests before they could be voiced. "I haven't been there in days and I want to check on operations."

It was going against his own rules, using his own supply, yet right now it might be the only way to calm his nerves and take his mind off Barbosa and the cartel. He needed a clear head. He needed to relax. He was reaching for his jacket when his phone rang, rattling against the table.

Silva froze, his heart pounding in his chest. Expecting it to be Barbosa again, he was momentarily relieved to see Rodrigo's name on the display.

But why was he calling at such an hour?

More upset? More problems?

"What is it?" he growled, answering the phone and pressing it to his ear.

Rodrigo's voice, garbled and bursting with excitement, filled his ears. "Father… I've done it… I've got it… The last one!"

Silva grimaced, struggling to process the cascade of words. "Slow down," he demanded. "I can't tell what you're damn well saying."

This was not doing anything for his blood pressure. After a few moments of gasping breaths, Rodrigo calmed down enough to properly relay his message.

"I've done it, Father," he said. "We have all twenty-five. I did it."

"Are you serious?" Silva asked. "The shipment is complete?"

"Yes. I'm here at Eagle now. All accounted for."

He glanced at Delgado, nodding excitedly. "Good boy," he told his son. "I'll be there in twenty minutes. Don't go anywhere." He ended the call. For the first time in a while, he felt something like relief, like achievement. They'd done it. He'd done it. The Silva organisation was going to be unstoppable.

He turned to Delgado who had remained seated throughout the exchange. "I've done it, my friend. I've fucking done it!"

"I knew you would," Delgado said, getting to his feet. "You're Emilio Silva, after all. So what now?"

Emilio clapped his hands, his giddiness a sharp contrast to the dark dread that had preceded it.

"Same as before," he said, putting on his jacket and grabbing his phone. "Take me over to Eagle. And fast. We've got a deal to prepare for."

30

Antonia's sobs filled the room – they felt as if they filled the entire world – as Humberto held her in his arms, her head pressed against his chest. His beautiful little girl. His daughter. A tear rolled down his leathery cheek. He didn't want to ever let her go.

Despite the intense feelings of joy he was now experiencing, he'd felt uneasy on his approach to the house. If Raul was home, it would have been like walking into the lion's den. Humberto had stood on the porch for what felt like forever, a pillar of silence in the darkness as he stared at the front door, willing Antonia to open it without him having to knock. When she didn't, he'd reached out, crooked fingers hovering over the brass knocker, gripping it as if clutching onto hope itself. Old instincts screamed at him to melt back into the shadows, to run. But he remained where he was. He had to do this. He was not here as a timid drunken loser, but as a father, and as a soldier with a mission to complete.

So he'd knocked and he'd waited.

It had felt like another lifetime before the door finally creaked open and Antonia was standing there in front of him.

She'd looked scared, then surprised, then she'd burst into tears, holding her arms out to him like when she was a little girl and had hurt herself.

And just like that, it was as if the past decade had never happened. Inside the house with the door closed they'd embraced more, a reunion that felt like a dream but was so much better than all the times Humberto had imagined it over the years. He hugged his daughter tight, breathing her in, the scent of her hair, her perfume. A heady mix of relief but also a painful reminder of what he'd lost.

"I'm sorry, Papa," she whispered into his chest. "I'm so very sorry."

"Oh my sweet girl, you have nothing to be sorry for." He stepped back, cradling her face in his rough hands. Her dark hair was cut short into a stylish bob, framing her delicate features, so like her mother's. But her large brown eyes were full of worry as she stared up at him, the skin around the right one yellow and bruised. He didn't need to ask how it had happened. He knew. The sight of it reignited the fire within him, reminding him of why he was here.

His eyes swept around the hallway. He took in the gleaming, white marble floor, the stark white walls undecorated except for a large modernist painting – a single, bold red stroke against a sea of monochrome. It looked expensive, aggressive, devoid of compassion. Much like the man who had hung it there. Through the open door to his left was the front room. Here, too, the décor was sparse and minimalist; the layout geometric rather than homely. Every piece of furniture, every fixture, looked to be meticulously placed. An oversized couch sat in the centre of the room, the black leather upholstery standing out against the white walls and cream carpet. The almost hospital-like ambience was barely softened by the low, ambient lighting that threw long, harsh shadows across the room. It was immaculate, but it was what the space lacked that hit Humberto the hardest. There was no feminine touch here, no children's toys, or even the lived-in mess that humanised a home. The house felt more like a museum. A cold, isolated place where his poor Antonia had lived for the past ten years.

He gazed back into his daughter's eyes. He could tell her for the rest of his life that he was sorry he'd failed her – and he hoped he'd get the chance – but right now action was needed.

"We need to talk," he told her.

She nodded. "Come into the kitchen." She led him down to the end of the corridor and through into a large open-plan space.

Glossy, steel-grey cabinets lined the walls, with a massive kitchen island topped with dark mottled granite sitting in the centre. Along the back wall, tri-fold patio doors looked out onto the rear of the estate. The spotless surfaces gleamed under the recessed lighting, but there were finally traces of domesticity here. To the right of the entrance, a coffee mug sat next to an open paperback book, its spine broken. Fresh fruit was neatly arranged in a glass bowl on the island, the vibrant colours breaking the monotone of the house. Humberto imagined this was where Antonia spent most of her time. That lazy bastard Raul probably never lifted a finger to help her.

"Do you want a drink?" she asked.

Humberto did. He certainly did. But he had to keep his head clear. And despite being up close with his baby girl after all these years, this was not the time for celebrations. "Just a water if you have it."

"Of course." He watched as she took two glasses from out of a cupboard and placed them on the island before going to the huge brushed-steel refrigerator that stood like a sentry at the side of the room. She opened it and took out a bottle of mineral water, filling up the glasses. Humberto noted how she moved with grace and composure and held her head up at all times, just like he'd shown her. It made his heart swell. She was still in there, his Antonia. This wicked family hadn't crushed her essence entirely.

She handed him one of the glasses and he thanked her, placing it down without taking a sip. "I'm sorry I let you down, my darling."

"No, Papa—" she started, but he held up his hand.

"Please. Let me say this." His voice was choked with regret. "Antonia, I should have done more. I know things were strained between us, but I was your father, I should have looked after you, guided you better. I was weak. Selfish. Still grieving for your mother. You should have been my only priority. I failed you…" He trailed off as his voice broke.

Antonia rushed to him. "I was young and hot-headed. Nothing you could have done would have changed things. It's me who's sorry." She placed her soft hand on his cheek, wiping away a solitary tear with the pad of her thumb. "And you're here now."

He raised his head. "Yes. And things are going to change," he told her. "I promise you."

She smiled at this, but it was the sort of resigned smile you might give to someone who was trying to win a game they'd already lost. "How, Papa? I don't know if that's possible…"

"Trust me," he said, finding his voice once more. "I have met people who can help us. Good people. Strong people. They want to remove this blight on our town as much as I do."

"But… Raul? Emilio? You know what they are like. No one can stand up to them. They will kill you." She stared into his eyes, hers now pleading. "Please do not do anything that will get you hurt."

"I have to," he said. "I've kept my head down for too long. We all have."

She stared at him for a few seconds longer but he didn't flinch, he didn't blink. Adrenaline, along with a decade of pain and regret, bubbled up in his system.

Antonia must have seen something in his stoic expression because at last she seemed to accept what he was saying. "How can I help?" she asked, pulling out two stools from under the kitchen island and sitting on one of them.

Humberto sat also. "The first thing you can do once I leave is to pack a bag. Can you do that without Raul finding out?"

"I think so. But what are you talking about? This is my home."

Humberto grabbed her hand. "Are you happy here, Antonia?"

Her eyes said no, but she hesitated several times before she spoke. "I hate who I've become. I hate the family, this whole business."

"And Raul?"

She dropped her gaze to where her fingers, trembling, gripped the glass between her hands, her knuckles white. That was all Humberto needed to know.

"Pack a bag, in secret. We're going to get our town back."

"But how?"

He paused. Currently he wasn't sure how to answer that question. But he had faith in Michael Day. Although cagey about his past, Humberto was almost certain his initial suspicions about the man were correct. Perhaps he'd retired and wanted to put his past behind him, perhaps he was on the run from someone and living under an assumed identity, but the man was a soldier through and through. Highly trained, strategic, tough as hell. He was Special Forces. Humberto would have bet his life on it.

"Can you provide any information at all on what Emilio and Raul are working on?" he asked Antonia.

"I don't think so," she said. "Raul is very secretive about the business. I know you tried to warn me a long time ago. But I know what he is now. What his father is. I try to stay away from that side of things."

She looked pained and Humberto felt a twinge of guilt as he pressed her further, but this was important.

"Anything you've heard or seen. No matter how small or insignificant. Any scrap of intel you have on their operations could prove invaluable."

Antonia's scowl deepened, her eyebrows meeting over her scrunched-up nose as she thought about it. In that moment, she looked so much like her mother it was almost unbearable. But then a flicker of remembrance sparked in her eyes.

"A few weeks ago. Emilio and Rodrigo both came to the house. They seemed excited, but nervous too. They went into the study and were in there for a while. I didn't listen, I didn't want to know what they were discussing, but as I passed by on the way to my bedroom I heard a name mentioned. Barbosa. They sounded fearful of this person; I remember because Emilio said something along the lines of them only having one chance at getting this right."

Humberto felt a chill run down his spine. Salvador Barbosa. It had to be. The head of the Barbosa Crime Syndicate up in Porto, rumoured to have links with the Sangre de Dragón Cartel in Mexico. The name was like a ghost from his past, resurrecting memories he'd rather forget. His mind reeled with the implications.

"That is useful," he told her, smiling. "Thank you. Now I must go. Pack your bags discreetly and wait for me to contact you. A storm is about to break over this town but you'll be safe. I'll make sure of that."

Antonia forced a smile as a silence fell between them. It was quickly broken by the faint growl of an approaching car. As it got closer Humberto slipped off the stool, his eyes meeting his daughter's in silent communication. Time was up.

Standing, he gave Antonia's shoulders a reassuring squeeze. "Stay safe, my sweet girl. I'll be back soon."

"Please be careful," she replied, but her eyes were now

wide with determination rather than trepidation. There was a fire there, a spirit he recognised – as resilient and fierce as his own.

Leaning down, he kissed her on the cheek before heading for the patio doors and slipping out into the back garden without another word.

His heart was pounding, but he had the ghost of a smile on his face as he hurried across the plush lawn and disappeared into the woodlands surrounding the estate. There'd been no hyperbole behind his words to Antonia just now. There really was a storm coming. A bloody war. But it was one he was more than ready for.

31

The conversation with Armando and Humberto was still swirling around in Beckett's mind as he wound his way through the sprawling undergrowth. He was up on the headland, moving west. Below him, the distant houses and cobbled streets of São Lourenço had given way to dirt roads and scrubland.

Although Armando had volunteered to join him on this initial recon mission, Beckett had opted to go alone. He trusted Armando and suspected he was more capable than he gave himself credit for, but given the unpredictability of the situation and the unknown challenges ahead, it was safer if he acted alone. This way he eliminated the need for communication and didn't have to concern himself with the wellbeing of his wingman.

His first stop had been Emilio Silva's mansion, a sprawling villa hemmed in by high walls, huge wrought iron gates and luscious ornamental gardens. Beckett had watched from the shadows, assessing entrances and exits, the areas that were most heavily patrolled, the weak spots. But after being there only a short while, the gates had swung open and a car had left the premises. It had driven close to his position, heading west. That was twenty minutes ago. After that he'd traversed the perimeter of the Silva estate in a wide arc and had spotted Humberto creeping around the second residence. His presence had initially been met with surprise and concern by Beckett. But on realising this was the home of Raul Silva, which he shared with Humberto's daughter, Beckett had kept his distance, trusting the older man's judgement and expertise.

Having observed no significant developments, Beckett had set his sights on the larger of the two stash houses, situated at the foot of the mountains on the west side of town. He moved with practised stealth, sticking to the cover of the trees and using the landscape and the darkness to his advantage. Even at this late hour the air was humid and the thin material of his shirt clung to his back. But he was more than prepared for what came next. In fact, he welcomed the familiar adrenaline rush that always accompanied these covert missions. With each step his senses sharpened. He felt alive, focused, ready.

This, despite Armando's warning to Beckett as he left the taberna. "From what I hear, those places are more than just warehouses," he'd told him, in hushed tones. "Yes, they keep weapons there, drugs, whatever other illegal shit those bastards are involved in. But they're heavily guarded and I've heard rumours it's where they take those who they want to get rid of. People go in. They don't come out."

"You think there's some kind of killing room inside?" Beckett had asked.

Armando had hesitated, then said, "Nothing's beyond those bastards. So be careful, Mike. I mean it. I know you can handle yourself, you've more than proved that. But everyone has limits."

Beckett had placed a hand on Armando's shoulder, reassuring him he'd be careful. And he'd meant it. He would be. And smart. He understood the dangers more than anyone.

Jumping in with both feet when you were unsure what you were dealing with was reckless. Suicidal.

Reaching the crest of the hill overlooking the stash house, Beckett positioned himself behind a jagged rock formation. It provided ample cover but with enough of a gap between the rocks to offer a clear view of the building below. The former hotel was a massive three-storey structure. It would once have been an impressive place to stay, but now showed its age. Constructed out of cream-coloured limestone, typical for the region, there were deep cracks in many of the walls and tiles missing off the roof. As Beckett took it in, he saw few ways of getting inside except for the obvious entrances. The windows were set in deep arches and the ones that weren't sealed shut were boarded up completely.

At the front of the building was an expansive courtyard lined with olive trees. Two cars – a black SUV and a pale blue Honda Civic – were parked alongside each other near the entrance. Further out, a high stone wall entwined with ivy surrounded the entire property, its top stones covered in thick shards of glass that glinted in the moonlight.

Beckett focused on the four guards patrolling the grounds, noting their synchronised movements and the AK-47s they carried. Each did a circuit of the building and stopped at a designated point for around a minute before retracing their steps. In addition to the patrol, there were two static guards in front of the main entrance and two stationed near the rear, all armed. Beckett also clocked movements behind the curtained windows, suggesting a deeper layer of security inside.

The place was more heavily guarded than he'd expected. That complicated matters somewhat; and it meant whatever was held inside was valuable.

As Beckett was assimilating this new information, a car pulled up to the property – the same one he'd seen leaving the Silva mansion earlier. He moved around the side of the rocks to get a better view as the driver got out. He was an imposing figure, both in stature and presence. Wearing dark trousers and a crisp navy shirt, he was dressed like a chauffeur, but his commanding presence and the way his piercing eyes scanned the environment suggested he wasn't just a driver. Despite being top-heavy, with broad shoulders and huge biceps visible through the taut material of his shirt, he was well-balanced and looked as if he knew his way around a punch. Beckett would have bet on him being ex-military. The clues were there in the way he carried himself, alert to danger, the way every movement was measured and precise as he stalked the length of the car.

The driver leaned down and opened the car's rear door allowing a second man to emerge. He was shorter than the driver but about the same width and exuded an undeniable air of authority. Whilst both men were undoubtedly powerful, there was a clear hierarchy at play. Beckett, ever the observant professional, knew better than to jump to conclusions. Yet part of his job was to anticipate and predict. If this was Emilio Silva, he looked nothing like the mental image he'd constructed of him.

He was too far away to properly make out, but his rotund belly and erratic movements screamed of ill health. He was wearing a jacket a size too large for him in the shoulders and two sizes too long in the arms.

As Beckett surveyed the scene, another man appeared from out of the building and strode towards the car. This one he recognised as Rodrigo Silva, the youngest son he'd encountered in Armando's taberna. He and the older man embraced, confirming his theory that he was indeed looking at Emilio Silva. The most feared man in São Lourenço.

The two men talked animatedly, Rodrigo gesticulating and slapping his father on the back before moving over to the driver and doing the same. They were all laughing at something. The mood felt celebratory. Then Rodrigo placed his arm around his father's shoulder and walked him over to the black SUV, grinning as he went. Beckett shifted his position as they approached the rear of the vehicle and Rodrigo popped the boot.

Damn it.

He couldn't get eyes on whatever was inside. Drugs? Money? Whatever it was, it had elicited excited claps from Emilio Silva as he peered into the boot. Beckett strained his neck, leaning as far around the side of the rocks as he could without giving himself away, but it was no use.

Rodrigo yelled something at the house, and a second later another man hurried out the front door and over to the car. He was big, but cumbersome, a low-level thug next to the barrel-chested driver flanking the elder Silva. He leaned down into the car boot and for a moment it was as if he was wrestling a wild animal, but finally he dragged the contents out onto the dusty courtyard. Illuminated by the interior lights of the SUV, Beckett could see it was a person. More specifically, a young woman.

The man lifted her to her feet and she stood on shaky legs, clearly disoriented. She looked from one man to the other. Her dark hair clung to her cheeks and forehead. Her summer dress was ripped and dirty. As realisation appeared to dawn on her, she jerked away in a feeble attempt to break free. But the thug had a tight grip on her upper arm and didn't expend any energy as he pulled her close and snarled in her ear.

Beckett held his ground, every muscle in his body throbbing with tension. He recognised the woman. It was the same one he'd defended from Silva's men on his first night in town. The bastards had got her.

Beckett watched on, helpless, as Silva approached the terrified woman, considering her like an object of value. The poor woman recoiled as he reached up and grabbed her face, moving it roughly from side to side, checking her profile, squeezing her cheeks together as if inspecting a pedigree racehorse. Satisfied after his scrutiny, he released her before speaking to his henchman, gesturing for him to take her into the property. As the thug dragged the shivering woman away, Silva couldn't resist one more degrading gesture. Leaning over he landed a crude slap on her upper thigh, sharing a leering grin with his associates as they revelled in the young woman's obvious distress. Then, still squirming and fighting against the big man's clutches, she was dragged away.

Beckett exhaled.

The night air suddenly felt a lot colder. He still had more intel to gather, but his instincts told him his suspicions were correct. The thing he hadn't wanted to be true. The town's young women weren't simply the victims of Rodrigo's violent temper. They were being systematically taken. The Silvas weren't killing these women. They were trafficking them.

32

Silva felt like a triumphant general surveying the spoils of war as he watched the last of the shipment being escorted up the steps into Eagle House. And what a prize piece of ass she was too.

A twinge of regret hit him as she was dragged, still struggling, through the main entrance and disappeared into the building. He liked them like that, still with a bit of fight left in them. There'd be no time now, though, to sample his wares. The deadline was fast approaching.

But they'd done it. *He'd* done it.

The shipment was complete.

A surge of triumph, bolstered by intense feelings of relief, swelled within him. Twenty-five girls, all under twenty-five. All fresh. All beautiful. That had been the Mexican's order. Not easy in a small town like São Lourenço, but he'd managed it and now the deal was sealed. He'd finally graduated to the big leagues, an associate of Salvador Barbosa, working alongside Elvio Castellano and the infamous Sangre de Dragón Cartel.

His lips curled into a satisfied grin as he turned to face his men. He felt invincible.

"You like this new one, huh?" Rodrigo asked, flicking up his eyebrows lustily. "She's a bit of a handful. But she'll learn. They always do."

Silva shrugged, ignoring his son's pointed comments. But he couldn't be too hard on the kid. He'd done well. Very well.

"And now we're all set," Rodrigo continued, changing tack, sounding professional for once. "That's all twenty-five and we're ready for the drop-off."

"I'm proud of you, Rodrigo," Silva told him, slapping him on the shoulder. It was as close as he ever got to affection with his sons. "Now, let us check on the shipment one last time and then I'll call Barbosa to confirm."

He gave Delgado a curt nod and headed towards the building. But he was still thinking about the new girl. Those legs, that ass, the timid way she'd eyed him through the strands of her hair. She had spirit, he could see that. Perhaps he should break her in after all? Because what was tonight if it wasn't a time for celebration?

One had to break the rules occasionally.

At the front door of Eagle he paused, nodding at the sentries on either side, waiting for one of the lantern-jawed thugs to open the door for him.

For Christ's sake.

Why was it so hard to find men with brains *and* brawn in this pathetic town? He made a mental note to speak with Raul and have him employ some higher calibre personnel, men more suited to his new status.

"Open the damned door," Rodrigo snarled at the guards, joining his father at the entrance. But before either could act, however, they were interrupted by the unmistakable sound of an approaching car.

Silva turned, shielding his eyes from the blinding glare of the headlights, both seemingly trained on him. He squared his shoulders, resisting the urge to find a tuft of hair, as an unwelcome prickle of anxiety spread across his chest and down his arms.

"Who is this?" he asked Rodrigo, but received only a shrug in response.

As the car pulled into the courtyard, he saw it was a Mercedes E-Class Saloon – the new model, in gunmetal grey. Once in sight of the building it slowed right down, crawling towards them like a panther stalking its prey, and came to a stop ten feet away. The windows were tinted black, so he couldn't see the driver or any of the passengers. The engine went silent and the lights died. But no one got out.

Silva glanced over at Delgado, whose eyes were also fixed on the car. His hand had moved discreetly inside his jacket, no doubt gripping the handle of the concealed firearm he always carried. Silva swallowed, directing his attention back to the car. The lights were still off and no one had emerged from inside. Beside him Rodrigo shifted nervously, blowing out each breath as if calming down after a heavy sprint. No one spoke. You could cut the tension in the air with a machete.

At last, the front doors of the Mercedes opened in unison. Then – slow, and calm, and more unhurried than anyone had any right to be in this situation – two men climbed out.

The driver, standing closest to Silva, was tall and wiry, with long angular limbs that seemed to have too many joints. His face was drawn, high cheekbones descending sharply to a chiselled chin. He was clean-shaven, wearing a tailored suit and round wire glasses, but despite his impeccable appearance, there was something decidedly unsettling about his gaze, something calculated and cold. He looked like a college professor, but one that conjured fear rather than imagination in his students. And whatever he taught, it would be intense and demanding. Certainly not humanities. He didn't look to have any.

In contrast, his partner had the appearance of a gnarly old

rockstar. He, too, was tall and he carried himself in that way people who didn't need to demonstrate power or aggression did. His mere presence did all that for him. He was wearing a sleeveless leather vest that showcased his muscular arms, covered in tattoos, and the tightest black jeans Silva had ever seen. His shaved head seemed remarkably large, and with his round cheeks he could have looked almost cherubic if it wasn't for the intricate facial ink that traced down from his left eye to his jaw – a pattern of thorns and vines that rippled as he raised his head. A smattering of facial piercings finished the look, rows of hoops in his ears, two in his nose and one on each eyebrow. The metal flashed in the moonlight as his eyes, hard and unyielding, took in the scene.

Silva cleared his throat, lowering his voice an octave. "Good evening. How can I help you, gentlemen?"

Neither man spoke. Together they walked around to the front of the car, moving in time with one another like it was some kind of dance.

Silva shot Delgado a look, glad to see his loyal enforcer's hand was still inside his jacket, poised for action. This gave Silva a sliver of reassurance. But the man with tattoos had seen it too and, with a jolt, he whipped a large handgun from out of the back of his jeans. At the same time, Delgado drew his piece, the tense atmosphere kicking up a couple of gears.

"Now, now," the man in the glasses said, unnerved and wagging a bony finger in the air. "We are all friends here, are we not? On the same side." He glanced at his partner who lowered his weapon. Then glanced at Delgado who wavered for a moment before doing the same. He chuckled, but there was no warmth in his laughter.

"I don't know you," Silva said. "Who are you?"

"My name is Martim," the man with glasses announced. "And this is my brother, Paulos."

"Brother?" Rodrigo gasped, incredulously.

"Well... half-brother," Martim said. "We have different mothers. But we look very alike, don't you think?"

Silva and Rodrigo nodded in unison, unsure if they were supposed to laugh or not. A bead of cold sweat trickled down Silva's back as he tugged at a piece of hair behind his ear. "I'm afraid I am still in the dark," he told the men. "What do you want?"

Martim grinned, displaying two rows of impeccable white teeth. "We are here as representatives of Salvador Barbosa. He is a little concerned at your lack of contact recently, and with the deadline imminent he worries you will not fulfil your part of the bargain. If this happened it would be bad. For... *everyone*. So he asked Paulos and me to come here and ensure everything was going according to plan."

"Everything is in place as agreed," Rodrigo snarled. "You have come here for no reason."

"Yet, here we are," Martim replied.

"Fine. Then step inside," Rodrigo said. "See for yourself."

"Please, Rodrigo, have some manners," Silva interjected, with a forced chuckle suppressing his annoyance at his son's brashness. "These men are only making sure everything is as it should be. Which it is. So, please, let me show you around. We have everything ready for you."

Gritting his teeth behind a big shit-eating grin, Silva led the men into the building, turning to gauge their reactions as they walked through the reception area of the former hotel. It was a spacious room, with a wide corridor opposite the entrance leading to the downstairs rooms and a broad staircase that spiralled up to the second floor. Silva quickly ushered the men past the boxes of counterfeit handbags, outdated electronics, and sweatshop clothing that were stacked against the wall – remnants of past business ventures that hadn't borne fruit.

"Through here, gentlemen," he said, beckoning them

towards the rooms. "I think you will be pleased at the quality of our... product."

The duo remained silent, their demeanour unreadable, as they followed him down the dim corridor lined with doors on either side. At each one he paused, pushing the door open with a flourish to reveal the young woman inside. Most of them were lying or sitting on the bed, their eyes vacant from drugs, their faces pale and drawn.

"As you can see, they are all young and very beautiful," he said, smiling and nodding in the hope Barbosa's men might reciprocate, or at least give him something to ease the tension gripping his chest. But their faces remained neutral. They looked at each girl as if viewing bundles of cocaine or numbers on a spreadsheet, their eyes searching and assessing without a hint of desire or lust.

Just as they reached the end of the corridor, the last door on the left swung open and Raul burst out through it. He saw the group and froze. "Oh—shit! You're here!" He slammed the door behind him and began stuffing the tails of his shirt into his trousers. "I was just... making sure that... all is well!"

"Thank you, Raul!" Silva stepped in front of him, clutching his hands together as he addressed Barbosa's men. "This is my eldest son. He is here checking everything is ready for Mr Castellano." He turned and glared at Raul, his dishevelled appearance leaving no doubt as to what he'd been doing in the room. "Meet Mr Martim and Mr Paulos, Raul, representatives of Mr Barbosa."

"Oh, I see," Raul said, wiping his hand on his trousers and holding it out. "Pleased to meet you, gentlemen. I had no idea you were coming."

The men remained stern-faced. Neither of them shook his hand. Martim turned his focus back to the elder Silva. "You have the same upstairs?" he asked.

"That is correct. Twenty-five girls in total. All ready for you. You can check them if you want."

Paulos, who hadn't said a word up to this point, stepped forward and mumbled something into Martim's ear. Silva watched their discreet exchange, trying desperately to keep his facade intact.

"Father?" Raul whispered. "I need to talk to you."

"Not now," he hissed back. "What the hell do you think you are playing at? Fucking idiot. You know the rules…"

"I'm sorry," Raul replied. "But I need to speak with you. It is—"

"I said not now!" Silva spat, raising his head and chuckling as Martim glanced over. "Is everything okay, my friends?"

Martim pushed his glasses up his slender nose. "Mr Barbosa was worried you were faltering, but I can see the shipment is good quality."

"Absolutely." He rubbed his hands together. "You can take them now if you want. They are ready."

Martim glanced at Paulos, who rolled his eyes. "We are not delivery drivers, Mr Silva. The deal was for you to deliver the shipment to Mr Barbosa's warehouse in Porto, where they will be placed in one of his shipping containers bound for Mexico."

"Yes. No problem. I apologise," Silva said. "I didn't mean to imply you should deliver them. Only that if you wanted to… you could." He shut up, his throat suddenly very dry. "We will deliver the shipment as arranged."

"Good. I shall let Mr Barbosa know. And you are on schedule?"

"When is Mr Barbosa expecting the shipment?" Raul asked.

Martim turned to look at him, as did Silva, curling his fingers into fists as he did. "Tomorrow," Martim said. "You know this."

"Yes of course." But Raul, not letting it go despite the

daggers Silva was sending his way, continued. "The only issue we may have is that we are waiting for our delivery vehicle to return from another job in Spain. It is due back tomorrow, but it could be late."

Silva's fists tightened, his fingernails digging into his fleshy palms. What the hell was Raul doing? It was true the damned truck wasn't yet in their possession and wasn't being delivered until late tomorrow afternoon, but Barbosa didn't need to know this. He clearly already doubted the Silva organisation's abilities. He didn't want him to think they were total amateurs. Yet he also didn't want him to know that until twenty minutes ago they were one light on the shipment and that half his men were in hospital because of that meddling Englishman. So maybe it was a good play by Raul, to buy themselves as much time as possible.

"Late tomorrow is fine," Martim said, picking a piece of lint from off the arm of his jacket. "We shall stay around to oversee things and inform Mr Barbosa once the shipment is on its way."

"No problem at all," Silva said.

"But any longer and you'll have to answer to both Mr Barbosa and Mr Castellano," Martim warned, regarding Silva over the top of his spectacles. "You do appreciate how much of a problem that would be for you?"

"It won't be a problem."

"Good," Martim said, rolling his head back. "We'll return tomorrow. Until then…" He turned and headed for the exit, Paulos following on behind him.

Silva held his breath until they'd left the building, then he let out a long sigh of relief.

Tomorrow.

It was going to go down to the wire but their reputations, and their necks, were safe.

"Father, I really need to—"

"*Shhht!*" Silva held his hand up to Raul. At least wait until they've left the premises. He gave it a moment then rounded on his son, baring his teeth.

"What the hell are you playing at?" he snapped. "You stupid fool, embarrassing me in front of those men. You shouldn't even be here…"

Rodrigo snickered but shut up quickly as Silva shot him a look. *Don't you start as well, boy.*

"I'm sorry, Father," Raul whimpered. "I've messed up… I didn't know what to do…"

"What the hell do you mean? What are you talking about?"

Raul's voice quivered. "It's what I was trying to tell you just now. We've got a problem. A really big fucking problem."

33

Raul steadied himself as his father and brother looked on, their eyes wide and expectant.

"Well? What is it?"

In the murky light of the old hotel, he was struck by his father's haunted appearance. The patchiness of his hairline, the glistening layer of sweat on his brow, plus his bloodshot eyes made him appear as if he had only hours to live.

But maybe he did.

That was the problem.

Raul swallowed the lump of apprehension stuck in his throat. It did no good. He scratched at the stubble on his neck as he attempted to put his thoughts into order, considering how best to say what needed to be said.

"Raul!" his father yelled. "Speak! What the fuck is going on? What is this problem?"

Maybe it was better to just show him. With a sigh, Raul stepped over to the door he'd exited through a few minutes earlier and eased it open.

"Here…" He stepped back, hanging his head as his father and brother moved closer so they could see into the room.

"No!" his father gasped. "No, Raul. You idiot. You stupid fucking idiot!"

Rodrigo simply made a whistling sound, which made Raul want to grab him by the back of the head and smash his face into the wall. The stupid bastard was wearing make-up to conceal the bruises the Englishman had given him, but he'd happily make some more.

Raul followed his father into the cramped room, a six-by-six-foot box with a boarded-up window facing the door. The only light came from an old lamp with a red velvet shade on the bedside table. It cast deep shadows into the room and across the body of the girl lying naked on the bed. She was a pretty young thing, with shoulder-length red-brown hair and big expressive eyes. Or, at least, they had been expressive until ten minutes earlier when things had gone too far and Raul had banished the life from them.

"I... I don't know what happened," he muttered.

His father spun around, his face red with rage. He leapt at Raul, grabbing him around the throat and pushing him back against the wall. "You don't know what happened? You killed her, you stupid bastard. That's what happened."

"I was just... I thought..."

"You thought what?" Silva yelled, slapping Raul around the head, emphasising each word. "What did you think, Raul? That you'd screw us all? Fuck up the deal? Get us all killed?"

"No!" he cried out, covering his face as he sidestepped away from more slaps. "It was an accident."

"Oh, it was an accident?" his father mocked, stepping back and grabbing Rodrigo by the shoulder. "You hear that, boy? It was an accident. Okay. No problem. We'll tell Barbosa and Castellano that's why the shipment is one girl down. I'm sure they'll understand."

"What was it, brother?" Rodrigo asked, not even trying to

hide the sly grin playing across his face. "Not getting enough at home?"

Raul shook his head and sighed. He had no fight left in him. "I was stressed. Angry. I just wanted to have a bit of fun. I thought it would ease my problems for one evening."

"Oh, I see," Rodrigo continued. "And how's that working out for you?"

"Go to hell."

But Rodrigo's smirk only widened, revelling in his older brother's mistake. Raul looked away, breathing heavily through his nose. He needed to keep his cool.

"What happened, Raul?" his father asked again, his voice now worryingly low and calm. "Tell me exactly."

Raul looked up, hesitated, then began. "Antonia and I had a fight. It left me on edge. I drove aimlessly, not really having a destination in mind, but ended up here. I decided to check on the place, make sure everything was in order. I thought work would be a good distraction. But when I got to this room – to her room – I don't know, there was something about the way she looked at me. She was sedated, but I gave her some ecstasy and put some music on my phone and she seemed to get into it. She didn't say much but she was… pliable.

"We started having sex and it was good. It felt like all my troubles were falling away. But then… I got a little rough. Too rough. I get like that sometimes when I'm really into it, you know? It's good. Girls like it. It helps me work out a few stresses too, it's a release." He glanced from his father to his brother and back again, hoping to catch a glimmer of recognition; empathy, even. But he received nothing but dark looks, plus another sly grin and a shake of the head from his younger brother.

He went on, staring at the floor as he spoke. "I put my hands around her throat, choking her. I thought she was enjoying it. I know I was. I know it's kind of kinky but I've done it before and it was fine. But I was so worked up, I guess. And the light in here isn't great so I couldn't tell she was going blue in the face. She was struggling. But that's usually part of it. Then all of a sudden she stopped struggling, and just went limp."

The room fell silent. Raul didn't look up.

"You pathetic, miserable wretch!"

A hard slap knocked Raul to one side, but this time he didn't even try to block it.

"You're an imbecile! A traitor! A fucking blight!"

Raul's senses dulled as his father cursed and spat in his face, calling him every slur under the sun. But he deserved this. It was all his fault. They had been so close to achieving their goal, and with this one selfish act he'd ruined everything. It had taken them weeks to gather a full shipment of women and now it was too late. He'd screwed them all. Himself. His father. His brother. Probably his wife, too, and all those who worked for them. Elvio Castellano wasn't going to accept anything less than what had been agreed. Which meant they were dead.

They were all dead.

34

Martim closed the door of the Mercedes and settled into the driver's seat beside his brother. The two of them sat in silence, their gazes fixed on the old hotel as the interior light faded to black.

"What are you thinking?" Martim asked.

Paulos didn't look away but emitted a low growl from deep in his throat, the sound he always made while in deep contemplation. Being the muscles of the operation, he usually left the thinking to Martim. But when he did engage his brain it wasn't an accident. It meant consideration was needed.

The brothers' shared history was as tangled as their family tree. There wasn't even a year between them and neither of their mothers had been married to the man who had spawned them – a cruel and vicious gangster with a roving eye, called Lucio Marcelo, a significant figure in the Faro underground. The two brothers had first met when they were in their teens, at their father's funeral, and had discovered that whilst each of them had been given their mother's maiden names, they both shared their father's Christian name of Lucio. Which was why everyone called them Paulos and Martim. Some of their early associates had jokingly referred to them as 'The Two Lucios' or 'The Lucio Twins', but none of those men were alive today.

"I think that family are full of shit," Paulos muttered, finally. "It's like what my mother always used to say – each monkey on its own branch."

"Indeed."

Despite Paulos being the quieter of the two brothers, when he spoke he was usually on point. Emilio Silva and his sons were so out of their depth they were already taking their last breaths. But maybe that was a good thing, Martim now wondered. Maybe they could capitalise on the situation. He started the engine and revved it a few times, gripping the leather-backed steering wheel.

"Come," he said, shifting the stick into reverse. "Let's get out of here."

He pulled the car around and drove away, Silva's crumbling stash house receding in the rearview mirror. These people must have seriously charmed and lied to Barbosa to have him broker the deal with Castellano. It was an oversight on the boss's part, but he and Paulos were here now. They'd make sure no one was embarrassed by this deal.

Heading into São Lourenço, they were met by a sad collection of run-down properties and dim streetlights. Martim's grip on the steering wheel tightened, his glasses reflecting the occasional neon sign from a dilapidated hotel or taberna, businesses still desperately trying to hang on in this dying town.

"What a dump." He peered out of the window, his eyes cold and unfeeling as they passed more downtrodden buildings.

Beside him Paulos grunted his agreement. "We'd be doing these people a favour," he said, echoing what Martim was already thinking.

He turned to look at Paulos. His face was covered in shadow, but every twenty yards the glow of a streetlight lit it up, highlighting the crisscross of scars on both cheeks, hidden most of the time beneath his facial tattoos.

"They were shaking like leaves," Paulos added. "But Barbosa will have our heads too if they mess this up."

Martim's eyes narrowed. "We'll make sure it doesn't come to that."

The car rolled deeper into São Lourenço, the shabby buildings and cobbled streets leaving nothing but a fleeting impression of a town that was old and worn out.

"I thought we'd have to kill them tonight," Paulos admitted, a note of disappointment in his voice.

Martim chuckled. Barbosa had sent them here with one specific instruction: if they suspected anything was off, anything at all, they should execute the entire family and clean up the mess.

"There's still time, brother. And besides"—he leaned closer to Paulos, his voice dropping to a whisper—"now we know where they're keeping the shipment."

He took the next left, signposted as the town centre. The disdain he was already feeling towards this pathetic broken town grew stronger as the car bumped and grumbled over the uneven surfaces.

"Seen any hotels?" he asked.

"None that I'd want to stay in," Paulos replied. "But we might have to lower our expectations, brother. We need to rest."

Martim eased the Mercedes around the next corner and they found themselves in the town's main square. It was lined mainly with sad, tired cafés and tabernas, their windows dark and lifeless at this time of night. But across the other side, he spotted what they were looking for.

"There," he said, pointing at the building opposite and the sign, 'Hotel Sol de Verao'. He drove across the square and pulled down a side street.

"Are you suggesting what I think you are?" Paulos asked, as Martim switched off the engine. "We kill them regardless, take the shipment ourselves?"

"Do you think the boss would go for it?" Martim asked.

"I think it's all about selling to him correctly. But you're good at convincing people. You always were."

A smile twitched on Martim's lips, but it died there almost as quickly as it appeared. If they were doing this, it was no time for merriment. Not yet at least. "So we're on the same page?" he asked, staring ahead into the deserted alleyway.

"Always."

"When Silva's delivery truck arrives, we'll kill them and drive the shipment back to Barbosa ourselves," Martim muttered, speaking to himself as much as his brother, thinking out loud. "He'll still get the commission from Castellano, but can also keep the weapons and heroin meant for the Silvas. He'll be pleased at this. We'll get ourselves a nice bonus and kudos for safeguarding his reputation."

"Or…" Paulos added, sounding almost giddy. "We sell the girls directly to the Mexicans ourselves. Cut out both middlemen."

Martim laughed at this. Paulos, too. It was unthinkable to betray Salvador Barbosa. He would skin them alive if he found them.

But what if he didn't find them?

What if they got to him first?

Martim opened the car door and climbed out into the cool night air. "Come on, brother," he said. "Let's get a room. We've got some thinking to do."

35

Beckett awoke beneath the shelter of a leafy cork tree, his body stiff from the night spent on the uneven terrain. After witnessing the grim proceedings at the stash house, he'd made his way back up the hillside on the east side of town and made camp for the night. He'd expected to be able to sleep easily enough – he was exhausted – but his mind had been plagued with dark thoughts and he'd stayed up for a few hours more, looking out over the town. He must have fallen asleep around two, and his best guess put it at around six now. Four hours wasn't the optimum amount of sleep, but it was better than nothing.

He got to his feet and stretched his arms wide. The beauty of the dawn was almost deceptive, casting the town below in pastel shades of orange and crimson. It looked idyllic, the São Lourenço he remembered from his youth. A once glorious place, now tainted with fear, crime, and the suffering of innocent people.

He raised his arms over his head, his shoulder muscles protesting after a night on the hard ground. The first order of the day was to properly revive himself and remind his body what it could do. He grabbed the bottle of water he'd procured from a bust vending machine on his way through town and gulped it down. The water was warm and chalky but did the trick.

Energised and hydrated, he dropped down into a push-up position. The ground was uneven, scattered with pebbles and sharp rocks that dug into his palms as he worked his chest muscles, but the discomfort only strengthened his resolve. He did thirty push-ups then rested for thirty seconds, then another thirty push-ups. He did this six times before flipping onto his feet and going straight into a series of burpees, that cruel combination of a squat, a thrust, and a leap. His side burned with a stitch after the fourth set but he pressed on, relentless. Sweat soaked his already damp clothing, his muscles quivering with exertion.

Pull-ups followed, his biceps bulging with effort as he hoisted himself onto one of the cork tree's lower branches. The tendons in his forearms throbbed, and his back muscles popped and rippled with every rise, but it felt good. He felt alive. Last was the plank, a test of endurance as he lay prone, his body a rigid bridge supported only by his toes and forearms. His face hovered inches above the dusty ground. Sweat soaked his already damp clothing and his muscles quivered with exertion, but he remained in position, closing his eyes and emptying his mind of thought. He had a lot to consider today, just not yet. Right now it was all about control and composure. The calm before the storm.

He didn't know how long he'd held the pose for; it could have been five minutes, it could have been twenty-five. He lowered himself to the ground. His body was spent and trembling but also sharpened, focused. Getting to his feet he stretched some more, sucking in deep breaths of mountain air fortified with a salty hint from the sea. The workout had done wonders for his state of mind. Like the way in which Beckett did everything, it was not just a workout, it was a declaration of intent, preparation for what came next.

But he wasn't done yet.

Lacing up his boots, he set off at a steady pace up the side of the mountain. Now, as he ran, he allowed his thoughts to drift back to the previous night. The image of that terrified young woman – her dignity stripped away at the lecherous hands of Emilio Silva – gnawed at his soul. Silva's vile plan was now undeniable.

Beckett pressed on, channelling his anger into speed and effort as the road got rockier and the gradient steeper. Sweat dripped from his brow and his breath came in ragged gasps as he pushed his body to its limits. But like always, the pain was cathartic. It was his church.

He thought of what Beatriz had told him, about her neighbour's daughter going missing.

Three weeks ago she disappeared…
She is only twenty-two…
No one knows where she is…

But Beckett now had a very good idea where she was. He thought of all the other young women locked inside that house; taken from their homes and subjected to prolonged and unspeakable horrors. Last night Beckett would have happily stormed into the hotel and gutted every single man working there, but he probably wouldn't have walked out alive and that wouldn't have helped anyone in the long run.

And now there was a new situation to contend with.

He'd seen the second car arrive. The silver Mercedes. He'd seen the two men get out and the reaction on the faces of each of the Silva clan. It was clear they hadn't been expecting them and were uneasy in their presence. Beckett's assessment was the men in the Mercedes had been sent by someone higher up the food chain to check on the operation. It meant he needed to tread even more carefully from now on, but they had clearly unsettled the Silvas. That was a good thing.

It took him another twenty minutes to reach the summit, his legs burning and his lungs aching. Once there, he paused briefly to take in the vastness of the ocean, the early morning sun dancing and rippling off the surface. Then, turning on his heels, he raced back down the incline to the spot where he'd spent the night.

From there he walked the rest of the way down the mountain and headed for the beach. The sun, still low on the horizon, was yet to make its presence truly felt, but Beckett was dripping with sweat after his gruelling routine. A public shower stood at the edge of the beach. It was an ugly contraption, a square of concrete with a bent metal pole sticking up on one side and its once shiny components now covered in rust. He'd spotted it the day before but no one had been using it and he wondered now if it was still functional. He twisted the metal handle and a reluctant jet of water sputtered out. Result.

As the water gushed forth more readily, he stepped under the jets without bothering to undress. It was ice cold but that's what he'd been hoping for. He let the water run down his face, through his hair, saturating his clothes. It was a basic cleansing, but it washed away most of the sweat and the grime, and in the heat of the morning he'd dry soon enough.

Once done, he shook himself down and set off, circling the perimeter of the town, walking anticlockwise and sticking to the backstreets. His clothes clung to him, but were already drying as he slipped down an alley he knew would take him to the centre. He moved quickly and with purpose, alert to threats – those working for the Silvas, either on their payroll or out of fear.

His belly grumbled as he walked. He hadn't eaten since yesterday afternoon, but with his bag gone he had no money for food. Sticking to the side streets and alleyways, it took him twenty minutes to cover a five-minute journey, but he finally reached Armando's taberna. He headed down the side of the building. Finding the back door ajar, he slipped inside and found himself in a small kitchen with a preparation station, four greasy hotplates and the usual kitchen equipment – a toaster, a kettle, a blender that had seen better days – plus a large steel sink.

A lingering smell of freshly toasted bread set Beckett's mouth watering. He moved through into the main room, where he found Armando sweeping the floor with an old wooden broom, his face contorted in a deep frown.

Beckett stood in the open doorway until Armando noticed him. When he did, he didn't seem to be surprised. Or if he was, it didn't alter his world-weary expression.

"Good morning," Beckett said. "You're here early."

Armando straightened to his full height and, ever the soldier, held the broom as if it were a rifle and he was in parade rest position.

"I couldn't sleep," he replied. "I thought my restlessness would be better served here rather than disturb Lina. She needs her sleep right now."

"You're a good man," Beckett told him. "And a good husband."

"I don't know about that." Armando nodded towards him. "And what are you doing up so early?"

"We need to talk," he said, moving closer. "I have news."

Armando leaned the broom against the counter. "Okay. Is it bad?"

"Yes. It's bad," he said. "And I'll tell you everything. But first, is there any chance of some food? I've not eaten and I'm absolutely ravenous. I could eat a cat."

Armando grinned, the light in his eyes flashing momentarily. "Sure, man, it'd be my pleasure." He gestured at the nearest table. "You sit down. I'll go fix you something."

36

Beckett grinned and rubbed at his empty stomach as Armando placed a steaming plate of beans and cubed pork in front of him, along with two slices of toasted bread.

"*Feijão A Portuguesa*," Armando announced. "It's not a cat, I'm afraid. But it's the best I could do."

"It smells wonderful," Beckett told him, grabbing up the accompanying knife and fork. "Thank you, Armando."

He scooped up a forkful of beans and ate. The sauce was rich and had a slight hint of spice, the beans were big with the right amount of bite, and the pork was tender and salty. For such a humble meal, it tasted delicious. Beckett wolfed the whole lot down and used the last piece of toast to mop up the remaining sauce. When he was done, he sat back and pushed the plate away.

"You were hungry," Armando said, raising his eyebrows.

"It's good to be a little hungry," Beckett replied. "Keeps a man on his toes." He rolled his shoulders back. "Listen, I don't want to be cheeky, but I don't suppose there's any coffee, is there?"

"Shit, I'm sorry, man." Armando strode over to the bar where Beckett had already clocked the jug of fresh coffee sitting under the machine. "I don't know what's going on with me today. I've got my head stuck up my ass."

"A lot has happened recently," Beckett said, as Armando poured coffee into a mug and brought the steaming drink over to the table. "And I know I'm asking a lot of you, making a stand against the Silvas. It's understandable you're feeling apprehensive."

He sipped the coffee. It was strong and bitter, not as nice as the last one Armando had made him, but very much needed. As he drank he regarded his companion, who was now sitting adjacent to him at the table. His eyes had a faraway look in them, as if he was somewhere else entirely.

"Your wife is sick?" Beckett asked.

It was a bold question – bordering on rude – and in different circumstances Beckett would never have asked it. But he needed to know where Armando's head was at.

"She... has... not been herself lately," he replied, still gazing at something only he could see. "But Lina is a good woman. She is strong. I have told her about you... about everything. She wants me to help you. She wants *you* to help *us*."

His eyes met Beckett's finally and he smiled. Beckett smiled back. Hearing that was enough for him.

"She sounds like a good woman."

"Oh, she is. The best. I'd do anything for her, man. Anything." Armando looked wistful for a moment, then his expression dropped. "But there's still something I can't quite understand – why are *you* doing this? Why risk your life for a bunch of people you hardly know?"

Beckett's smile broadened. It was another bold question. But one he'd been expecting at some stage. He placed the coffee mug down and ran his fingers over his lips, composing himself. He was about to begin when there was a loud knock on the door of the taberna. Both men turned as it opened and Humberto poked his head around the side.

"I texted him while you were eating," Armando said, gesturing Humberto over. "I figured whatever it is you wanted to talk about, he should hear it too."

"Good thinking." Beckett nodded at the older man as he approached. "How are you today, Humberto?"

"I've been better. But I've been a lot worse," he said, sitting in the chair opposite and eying Beckett's mug.

"You want a drink?" Armando asked him.

"Please. Coffee is good."

As Armando went to get it, Beckett studied Humberto. Despite his withering demeanour, he looked younger today than the last time they'd met. His posture was straighter, his shoulders pinned further back. He was also wearing a short-sleeved shirt that showed off his sinewy arms, tanned and leathery. They were the arms of a man used to hard work and toil. The arms of a fighter.

"I was just asking our new friend here why he was ready to jump into the lion's den for us," Armando said, returning with the coffee. "When he could easily have walked away."

Humberto looked at Beckett and stuck out his bottom lip. "It's a fair question."

"It is," Beckett replied. "And I suppose the easiest answer is what I already told you – that my father drummed into me the importance of fighting injustice wherever one sees it. But it's more than that." He smiled to himself. If this pair were sticking their necks on the line, then they deserved something more than that from him. "In truth, I suppose I came to São Lourenço seeking a past that's already gone. We had a wonderful time here, my father and I. I think a part of me hoped that if I came back I'd feel close to him again, maybe even find some answers I was looking for in myself. But all I've found is pain and torment, caused by that family. I can't sit back and allow them to destroy what was once such a vibrant and happy place in my memory." He looked up at Armando and Humberto in turn. "So, in some ways, this is personal for me too."

Both men met his gaze with warm, twinkling eyes, but it was Armando who spoke. "Sounds like your father had a real impact on you. He was a good man."

"He was the best. He was strict and tough, but always stood up for people less fortunate than him, when he could easily have walked away."

Armando glanced at the crucifix hanging over the bar. "My father was a good man too. Honourable. Brave. I guess that's another thing we have in common, Mike."

Beckett didn't miss a beat, picking up where Armando was going with that comment. "What else do we have in common?"

Armando glanced at Humberto. "Come on, man. You still want to be secretive, fine, but you can trust us. You're ex-military, right?"

"Perhaps."

"Perhaps?" Humberto said, his voice gruff. "I'd say some kind of Special Forces. Intelligence, even."

Beckett sipped his coffee. "You're getting warmer. But that's as far as I'm willing to go, gents. I hope you understand. I'm just Michael Day the traveller now. That's the way I want it to stay."

Thoughts of his past life flooded into his mind. His old handler and friend, Jacob Beaumont. His time at Sigma Unit. His niece, Amber.

He brushed them all away.

Not the time.

"Do you have family?" Armando asked as if reading his thoughts.

"No. Sort of," Beckett contradicted. He'd opened a can of

worms with this conversation but he owed the two men at least some explanation. They needed to trust him implicitly for what was about to happen. He just had to be careful how far he went.

"I have a niece. She got caught up in a lot of bad things because of me. Some people who wanted me silenced were trying to use her as leverage. But she's safe now. I've made sure of that." He gulped back the last of the coffee and placed the mug down.

Humberto asked, "Who wants you silenced?"

"Who doesn't? These days it's best I assume everyone is the enemy and live accordingly."

"That's no kind of life, man," Armando added.

Beckett shot him a half-smile. "We'll see, I suppose. I'm still finding my feet with it all." He sniffed and looked away, hoping that would be the end of it. He gave it a few seconds, and when no more questions arrived he drew in a deep breath and pressed on. "Anyway, gentlemen, back to business. I visited the largest of the Silva stash houses last night."

"Oh…?" Armando said. "They didn't see you?"

"No. But I saw plenty. Things I was expecting to see, and things I wasn't." He frowned. "From what I can piece together, the family are indeed involved with a more influential organisation, someone higher up the food chain. My guess is this person has agreed to supply the family with weapons, maybe manpower too, I don't know – but with the goal of spreading their control over more of the region. However… it's what the Silvas are providing in exchange that means we have to act fast."

Beckett scratched at his chin, giving his new allies a chance to respond. Neither did.

"Local women," he continued, a hint of anger piercing his usual calm demeanour. "Those that have vanished and are believed to be dead. I didn't get eyes on all of them, but my guess is they're still alive, held captive inside the main stash house. The young women are the leverage point with the bigger fish. Silva is likely going to trade them for something that will further his business. Weapons, drugs, power, who knows?"

He looked up to see Humberto's lined face tighten with rage. Disgusted, yes; but not surprised. "Salvador Barbosa," the older man hissed.

Armando coughed. "No. You think?"

"I saw my Antonia last night," Humberto said. "She told me she'd heard Raul and his father discussing business and Barbosa's name came up. He's the big fish."

Beckett leaned back. He wasn't going to mention seeing Humberto the previous evening, but it sounded as if the old soldier had done some recon of his own. Beckett knew of Salvador Barbosa from his time in Sigma Unit; and given the look on Armando's face, he could assume no further explanation was required there either. Barbosa was a vicious gangster who controlled most of the organised crime in the north of Portugal and had links to the Mexican Sangre de Dragón Cartel. None of which boded well for their current situation.

"I've heard of Barbosa," Beckett told them. "And if he is the bigger fish, that explains a lot. From the looks of it, he's sent his men to São Lourenço to oversee the deal. They arrived as I was scoping the place out. Just two of them, typical cartel heavies, but sophisticated. It was clear the Silvas weren't expecting them, but that tells me they're getting close to a deadline. The exchange is going to take place in the next twenty-four hours, maybe less."

"Meaning?" Armando said.

"Meaning we need to get those girls out of there," Beckett replied. "And we don't have much time."

37

São Lourenço was a dead town. A relic of a place. Dusty and broken and good for nothing. Everywhere Martim looked he saw degradation and decay. It left a sneer on his face and a bad taste in his mouth.

What was Silva's long game here?

Did he even have one?

Probably not. And that told him all he needed to know about these amateurs. They had raped the town of everything it had once been good for – trade, tourism, entertainment – leaving nothing but bones for the vermin to pick at. Clearly the family needed this deal to go down. They needed the guns and heroin Castellano was supplying them with in order to branch out and move into bigger towns and cities. Yet, why hang around so long in a place you've already decimated? Why live here? If it had been him, he'd have moved on years ago; left this dried-up husk of a community to salvage what they could from the ruins.

The Silva family had no clue what they were doing.

But that was good news for him and his brother.

He stopped in front of an old church in one of the main streets leading off from the town square. Case in point. Once, this place of worship would have been a central hub for the bustling town, but this morning it was empty, closed.

It was the same everywhere he looked. The stores and tabernas, worn down by time and disrepair, the paint on the windows and doors faded and peeling. It was a filthy, horrid little town, and only reinforced his contempt for those who continued to live here. The locals and the Silva family.

Martim considered himself a man of taste, accustomed to the lavish lifestyle that came with being one of Salvador Barbosa's top enforcers. He was used to the opulence of Porto's underground world, where money flowed like water, and power was wielded by those who knew how to rule. This place, with its grimy alleys and lowly inhabitants, offended his sensibilities. The locals moved sluggishly, their faces dour and uninteresting. Lazy and fearful, that's what they were. Scared of their own shadows.

"Can you believe this place?" Martim said, sneering at a pile of stinking black refuse bags dumped on the side of the street. "It's like going back in time fifty years."

Paulos grunted his agreement. "Disgusting," he spat, eyeing a group of children kicking a misshapen football around in an adjacent street. "Makes me want to swat these little flies so I don't have to listen to their shrill voices a second longer."

Martim chuckled silently to himself, placing a hand on Paulos's shoulder. "Easy, brother. We aren't here to have fun. This is business."

Which was true. As much as he loathed the place, they had work to do. After sleeping on it, Martim had come to the conclusion that double-crossing Barbosa was a very bad idea indeed. Not only had the boss been good to him and his brother over the years, but he was a vindictive and dangerous man. If they went for him, they'd only have one shot at it. And with the amount of security he surrounded himself with, the odds were stacked against them.

But that didn't mean they had to stick to the original plan. Once the boss knew the sort of people he was dealing with, he'd no doubt arrive at the same conclusion – kill the family, take the women, collect the commission from Castellano for brokering the deal. It was risky, playing the cartel in this way, but Martim felt it was doubtful they'd ever find out, nor particularly care if the Silvas were never heard from again. From what he could make out, the hapless gangsters had already pillaged every young, moderately attractive girl from the town. Once this shipment left the dock, there'd be no more business to be done here.

But to get Barbosa truly onside, Martim needed solid proof that his hunch was correct – that the Silvas were just small-time thugs with nothing more to offer once their women were locked in a shipping container bound for Mexico. He'd already spoken to a few locals this morning, enquiring about Emilio Silva and his two sons. People didn't want to say too much, but those that did, painted a picture of a ruthless but self-serving family, power-hungry and at the mercy of their egos.

One man, an old fisherman they'd encountered at first light down at the harbour, had been more vocal. Martim had liked that one. Chewing on a battered old pipe, he'd not seemed the least bit intimidated as he and Paulos towered over him. His skin was dark and weather-beaten and his watery eyes hinted at a life of pain and hardship. He'd spoken of the Silvas as opportunists, an affluent but weak family who had bought themselves power by hiring muscle to strong-arm the once peaceful town. But they were just playing at being gangsters, the old man had said; the sons were full of bluster and ego and the father was nothing but a narcissistic oaf.

It was as Martim had suspected and he'd thanked the old fisherman for his candidness. But he needed more. Something concrete to present to Barbosa.

As he was considering his next move, an old woman appeared from around the side of the old church. She was white-haired and bent over, another pathetic relic of the past. Her bony hands trembled as she pushed a cart of wilting vegetables in front of her. The two men watched her in silence as she shuffled towards them.

"Wait!" Martim told her. "I want to talk to you."

The woman didn't look up. She kept on walking.

"Hey!" Paulos snarled, stepping in front of her. "Stop."

The woman stared up at them. Her voice quivered as she spoke. "What do you want?"

"We have some questions," Martim said. "About the Silva family. You know of them?"

The woman didn't blink as she looked from Martim to Paulos and back again. Possibly she was playing for time, working out who they were and what sort of repercussions her answer might bring.

"Listen," Martim said, softening his tone. "We aren't going to hurt you – are we, brother?"

Paulos grinned, exposing two rows of yellowing teeth and four silver canines. "Of course not. We're here to help the good people of São Lourenço."

The woman frowned. She didn't seem convinced.

"We know Emilio Silva and his family have destroyed this once great town," Martim continued, leaning down to face the woman. "We know they treat people badly and take what they want from them. It's not fair. We want to help you get rid of them. That's why we are speaking to people, to find out all we can about this terrible family."

The woman lowered her head. "You are working with the Englishman?"

Martim shot his brother a glance.

The Englishman?

He grinned at the woman, clasping his hands together in front of him. "That's right. You're very perceptive. We are working with the Englishman. He is our friend. Can you tell me what you know about him?"

"I have not seen him myself," the woman said, a glimmer of defiance shining in her eyes. "But I've heard about him. He has only been in town a few days but has already put five of Silva's men in the hospital. They say he's unbreakable."

Martim straightened. A complication, but also a confirmation. If the family couldn't deal with one man, one solitary nuisance, what sort of organisation were they?

"Do you know where this man is?" he asked. "We arranged to meet with him but have lost contact."

The woman shook her head. "As I said, I have not seen him. I did wonder if he was just a story someone made up, a way to make ourselves feel better. But I've seen the bruises on Rodrigo Silva's face with my own eyes."

"I see. Thank you. Now go," Martim told her with a wave of his hand. "You have been most enlightening."

The woman hurried away as fast as her weary body would allow. Watching her leave, a cruel sneer spread across Martim's face. This was it, the evidence he'd been looking for. Whoever this vigilante Englishman was, he'd be no match for him and his brother. But if the Silva family couldn't deal with this one individual, their whole credibility became questionable. Association with such unsophisticated clowns would reflect poorly on both Barbosa and the cartel. Unacceptable.

And that settled it. He had to call Barbosa.

They set off back to the hotel, Martim's thoughts racing and a plan taking shape. The time for observation and information gathering was over. The time for action had arrived.

This town, along with those pathetic pretenders, had no idea what was coming.

38

Beckett crouched behind a row of cedar trees, their branches providing perfect cover as he peered through the wrought iron perimeter fence at Maria Silva's villa, which all but glowed in the early morning light.

It was certainly grand. The exterior was a blend of modern design and classic elegance, dominated by large whitewashed walls and a terracotta roof. Intricately patterned tiles around the entrance added bursts of colour, whilst contemporary floor-to-ceiling windows offered glimpses of the lavish interior beyond. In front of the house, the garden was a work of art in itself. Palm trees swayed gently, casting long shadows over the white gravel pathways and flowerbeds filled with native plants, their vibrant colours in stark contrast to the neutral tones of the villa.

As Beckett's gaze swept the area, he noticed subtle hints of security. Cameras had been placed at strategic points under the eaves and both the villa and main gate were alarmed. But from what he could make out, there were no guards on the premises.

He remained hidden, watching, waiting. He had to play this just right. A mistake here wouldn't just jeopardise the mission but Maria's safety too. He didn't want that. He knew Armando had his reservations about the woman, but the last time they'd met, Beckett had sensed a caring heart behind Maria's cool, brittle facade. She could be a worthy ally if his instincts were correct.

Keeping his head down he moved around to the back of the property, where he came upon a large swimming pool, its surface calm and undisturbed, mirroring the cloudless blue sky above. Beside it, an outdoor lounge area was set out with expensive-looking furniture; the scene of many an extravagant party, no doubt.

But no guards. No security detail.

He traversed the entire grounds and returned to his first position behind the cedar trees. After waiting five minutes more, he was certain there was no patrol and was about to break cover when Maria's presence at one of the windows caught his attention. She was in the kitchen, standing in front of the sink and staring out at the garden. Her thick brown hair was tied back in a high ponytail and she was wearing less make-up than the previous times he'd seen her, but her natural beauty was still evident. He observed her for a few moments, then as she turned from the window and disappeared from view, he scaled the fence and hurried across the lawn. Having already worked out where the security cameras' blind spots lay, he was able to make his way to the front door undetected.

He rotated his head left and right, stretching his neck muscles and allowing his shoulders to relax. Then he knocked on the door.

Footsteps could be heard in the hallway immediately. Heels clicking against a hard floor like distant gunshots. They stopped as they got closer, and Beckett stepped back so she could view him through the peephole as he imagined her doing.

A second later the door swung open, revealing Maria's shocked expression.

"What the hell are you doing here?" she snapped, grabbing his arm. "Get inside, you madman." She pulled him into the hallway and locked the door behind him.

"I was just in the neighbourhood," he told her. "Thought I'd drop in and say hello."

Maria glared at him. She hadn't blinked since she'd opened the door. "You're risking both our necks coming here, do you know that?"

Beckett's jaw tightened, any further attempts at humour gone. "Your father would hurt you if he knew we were talking?"

She pinned her lips closed and narrowed her eyes in silent warning before turning away. "Actually, I'm glad you're here. I was going to try and track you down."

Beckett followed her down the wide hallway and into the kitchen. Gleaming marble countertops stretched along each wall, their surfaces polished to perfection. A large island dominated the centre of the room, and above it a hanging rack held an array of copper pots and pans, reflecting the warm ambient lighting. A white and terracotta tiled floor added a touch of old-world charm to an otherwise modern design. Yet for all its luxury, there was a lived-in quality to the space. Jars of spices lined the shelves, cookbooks were stacked haphazardly on one of the shelves, and a faint aroma of garlic and herbs lingered in the air.

Beckett stopped near the island as Maria continued over to the sink and peered out through the large picture window, most likely looking for anyone who might have followed him here. They hadn't. He'd made sure of that.

"Did you know?" he asked.

She turned, a scowl creasing her brow. "Know what?"

Beckett gnawed on the inside of his lip, sensing his nostrils flaring. But, like always, he held it together. "Did you know what they were doing?"

Maria still looked confused, so Beckett took a deep breath and told her, his voice only cracking slightly as he explained about her father's hotel now being used as a makeshift prison for missing local women. When he'd finished, Maria's face had paled and her eyes were glassy.

"You had no idea?" he asked.

"No. I swear to you." Her voice was barely above a whisper. "But I can't pretend to be completely shocked by the revelation. I wish I was. I wish what you said sounded unbelievable to my ears, but I know what my father is capable of, Michael. Believe me, I know."

She scratched at her neck and turned back to the window, busying herself by placing a couple of used glasses in the sink. Beckett watched her, saw her reach up and wipe at her cheek.

"You're speaking from experience," he said softly. It wasn't a question.

The muscles in Maria's shoulders tensed, but she didn't respond.

"I'm sorry," he added.

The silence lingered. Then, still gazing out the window, Maria spoke, her voice steady and monotonous as if it was all she could do to get the words out.

"My mother died when I was eleven," she said. "And before you say anything else, I've heard the rumours. I don't know whether my father had anything to do with her death; I don't want to know. But after she died he would come into my room when everyone else in the house was asleep. At first he made a game of it, called it our 'special sleepover'. I was lonely, scared, I liked his presence. But then it turned into something else. Something that wasn't a game at all."

She reached up and wiped at her face again, her other hand turning pink as she clutched the side of the sink. "I remember his heavy weight on top of me, him fumbling around in my pyjamas. Then... I blanked it out, most of the time. I was good at that. I tried to think of other things – go to my happy place – that sort of thing." She laughed and it sounded so desperate, so feeble, it was worse than if she'd cried. Beckett shifted but didn't respond. Not yet.

"He was always drunk," she continued. "I could smell it on his breath. Hot and rancid. And then the next day he would act like nothing had happened... I did too. I still act that way, I suppose. It was the only way I could get through it."

Beckett made sure she was finished, then took a breath before speaking. "Is it still going on?"

"No," she said quickly. "The last time I was sixteen. A lifetime ago. I think by then he knew I was very strong-willed – despite or maybe because of what he'd done to me – and that he wasn't going to get away with it any longer. It is what it is. I don't think about it."

"Why are you telling me this?"

"I want you to believe me when I say that I hate him. I hate all of them." She turned and fixed him with an intense stare. Her eyes were bloodshot but there was no sadness behind them, only disgust. "My brothers are only a few years younger than me. They knew what went on but did nothing. They were scared of him then, just as they are now. But I despise him, and them, and I want you to trust me, Michael. Because I want to be rid of this family. For good. And I think you can help me."

Beckett narrowed his eyes, his heart aching and his mind spinning. "What are you saying, Maria?"

"I'm saying I want them dead," she replied coldly. "All of them. And I want you to help me do it."

39

Beckett studied Maria, deciphering the layers of emotion now visible beneath her cool exterior. Her words were unexpected, but resonated with Beckett's current focus. It was one reason why he'd come here this morning. But not the only reason.

I want them dead…

And I want you to help me do it…

"Funny you should say that," he replied.

Maria opened her mouth and then shut it again. "You… You'll help me?"

"I will. But I need something from you first." He took a step forward, shaking off any compassion he'd been feeling and shifting into soldier mode – strategic, clinical, cold. "I need information. Anything relevant you've heard the last few weeks relating to your father's operations."

Maria puffed her cheeks out but stared blankly at him. "I meant what I said before, I don't concern myself with his business. I try not to be around any of them as much as possible."

"Please think. Anything that you can give me that might be helpful, no matter how small."

Maria frowned, thinking. Then her eyes flashed with realisation. "Wait a minute. There is something."

"Go on."

"As I told you, I don't visit the main house very often, but my father likes to have people around on the first Saturday of each month – his associates, extended family, even his security team. He thinks it makes him a good leader. He read it somewhere. There are drinks, canapés. It feels like a party, except no one ever looks to be having much fun. He insists I attend and I do, for Antonia's sake more than anything. So she's not the only woman there." She scoffed, but regained her composure as Beckett leaned in. "The last time I attended was a few weeks ago. I heard my father and brothers talking about a truck they were planning to purchase – an ex-military vehicle. My father said it had to be large enough to fit thirty people inside. I wondered at the time why he needed such a thing, but I just thought…"

Beckett nodded. "It must be what they're using to transport the women."

He stared down at the worktop, tracing his fingers over the cold surface as he considered this new information. If the Silvas were involved in delivering the women to their intended destination, it kept the family in play longer, which was a good thing. It also meant he'd be able to track the whereabouts of the vehicle more easily if required. One of Silva's henchmen would talk. He'd make sure of that.

"Do they already have the truck?" he asked.

"No, I don't think so." Maria pressed her fingers to her temples, eyes narrowing. "Wait, what day is it?"

"Friday. The twentieth."

"Friday the twentieth," she repeated. "Yes! My mother's birthday was the twentieth – of November, not July – but the date sticks out because of that. I heard Raul say the truck was due to be delivered today. They were worried as it was very close to when they needed it." She glanced up, her concentration breaking as she realised the implication of what she'd said. "Oh, *merda!*"

"I already knew we were cutting it fine," Beckett replied. "But thank you. That's helpful. Anything else? Have you heard the name Barbosa mentioned?"

"Yes. He's not a good person though."

"Oh, I know that. In fact, he's downright dangerous."

Maria looked him up and down. "Aren't you scared? I know you've already handled some of them, but this is different."

"Fear is an overuse of the imagination," he told her. "I try to simply focus on what's happening in front of me. And what I need to do next."

"Yes, I get that."

Something shifted in Maria's eyes. Her lips tightened, her body rigid. It wasn't overt, but Beckett sensed it — a determination, a readiness.

"I want to help you," she whispered. "With more than just information."

"No. It's too dangerous," Beckett hit back. "I know what you said, and I believe you, but you're a civilian and these people *are* your family…"

But Maria wasn't giving in. She straightened up to her full height, the iciness Beckett had experienced on the hillside returning. "I mean it, Michael," she said, stepping closer until they were only inches apart. "I want to help take those bastards down. All of them. Whatever it takes. Whatever the outcome."

"Maria…" Beckett raised his chin. "I don't want anyone else getting hurt."

"I won't get hurt. And I can help. I know I can."

"How?"

"I can get you guns," she said, low and resolute. "I know where my father keeps them. He has a large store and I imagine there are plenty left over since you took out half his workforce."

"You can do that?" he asked. "We'd only need a few handguns, maybe a couple of rifles too. Plenty of ammo. But you could do that safely?"

Maria scoffed. "I may not like my family or what they do, but I'm still a Silva. For my sins."

Beckett nodded. As the shape of a plan formed in his mind, he couldn't help but smile. What lay ahead was certainly dangerous, but it brought with it the promise of redemption, a chance to eradicate the evil that had loomed over São Lourenço for too long.

"Okay then," he said. "Thank you."

"No, Michael – thank you. I mean it."

"Well, let's not get too congratulatory just yet. There's still a lot to do."

"I know."

Within Maria's steadfast gaze, Beckett saw a reflection of his own resolve. It was a resolve forged in pain, in betrayal, in a thirst for justice. He thought of his father, and then of Humberto and the torment he'd seen in the old man's eyes when he'd relayed all he'd lost because of these people.

"Actually, there's something else I need you to do for me," Beckett added, returning Maria's gaze. "But I'm afraid it's a big ask…"

40

Emilio Silva paced the cold marble floor of his bedroom, his silk robe with gold lamé stitching flapping loosely over his black cotton pyjamas. The evening wear was a new purchase, and an extravagant one considering hardly anyone but he would ever see it, but it was also a signifier to himself that he was moving into the big time. Or, at least, he should have been.

If his wretched son hadn't fucked everything up.

Dread gnawed at his gut, refusing to be ignored as he moved around the master suite, searching for distractions and answers in equal measure. His face, pale and drawn after a restless night, reflected in the low-lit mirror above his dresser. It wasn't the face of a frightened man – although fear certainly gripped him – but the face of a man on the edge. A man wired on desperation.

The first light of the day's sun shone through the cracks in his thick black-out curtains, but he kept them drawn for now, preferring to stay in this dim half-light of morning a while longer. If it wasn't yet Friday, he didn't have to panic. If it wasn't yet Friday, he still had a chance.

But the antique clock on the wall told another story. It was just after 10 a.m. Too late to call it early. Friday had well and truly begun, and in a little over nine hours the military truck was being delivered but with no longer a full shipment of women to load onto it. He paraded the length of his room, considered opening the curtains and decided against it. He marched back into the depths of the room. The tick of the clock filled his senses. Time was running out.

Silva prided himself on being a tough and ruthless individual, but the arrival of Barbosa's men was enough to upset anyone's sensibilities. Their introductions had been cordial enough, informing him they were there to help facilitate the deal – an extra pair of hands, nothing more – but Silva knew the real reason. Barbosa had sent them because he'd been swerving his calls and the deadline was imminent. They were here to ensure he delivered on time. And to make him pay a dear price if he didn't.

But that wasn't going to happen.

He still had time.

He entered his walk-in wardrobe, the overzealous air conditioning sending goosebumps down his arms as he pulled open drawers, his trembling hands fumbling through the assortment of clothes. Having Barbosa's men in town only added to his unease, but it was Raul's idiocy that had truly sent his anxiety levels soaring.

That fucking idiot!

They'd been so close. On the verge of getting everything Silva had ever wanted. Power, status, wealth, enough resources to take over the entire region. He'd envisioned people whispering his name with the same fear they reserved for Salvador Barbosa. And now thanks to his son's impulsive behaviour, it was all in ruins.

Silva selected a white vest and a pair of white underpants from the top drawer, then a pair of black socks from the one beneath. Dressing, he forced himself to focus on the task at hand – on the feel of the material against his skin, the softness of the red silk shirt he'd selected and the starchiness of his dark olive chinos – anything but the mess he found himself in. The shirt stuck to his back as he buttoned it, his mind spinning.

Maybe he should run.

He could change his name. Start over somewhere Barbosa would never find him. He could even have plastic surgery. He knew a guy over in Evora who would do it for him. Change his face, maybe get liposuction; he could get a hair transplant too. The idea tempted him, a ready escape from the web he'd woven around himself. But it was a fool's fantasy. You couldn't run from these people. Barbosa was a powerful man, with contacts all over the country. Elvio Castellano was even more powerful. They would find him.

So another plan was needed.

He slipped on black brogues and left the sanctuary of his bedroom, his heels clicking sharply against the floor as he marched down the hallway.

He found Delgado in the kitchen, standing to attention in front of the kitchen island. Emilio looked him up and down. "Have you been here all morning?" he asked.

"Yes, Boss. I got here just after eight. Raul asked me to—"

"No! Don't you mention that cretin's name in front of me right now," he barked. "But I'm glad you're here. Follow me."

They headed for his office, situated at the end of the hallway.

"Where are Gil and Lobo?" Silva enquired, not turning around.

"I put Lobo over at Eagle," Delgado replied as they entered the room. "Gil is on security detail here, at the front door."

Emilio settled himself behind his desk, gesturing with a wave of his arm for his man to shut the door and then take a seat.

"You realise we are all fucked?" he hissed, once the big man was sitting opposite. "My son has signed all our death warrants – you, me, him, everyone – unless we can find another young woman before this evening."

Delgado crossed one leg over the other. He was attempting an air of calm, but didn't quite manage it. "The two men in the Mercedes?"

"They're here to make sure the deal goes through – and take relevant measures if it doesn't. I'm sure of it."

"But we have time?"

"We have less than nine hours. Which is why I need you to get out there and sort this problem for us."

"Yes, Mr Silva."

"We need a replacement," he continued, his voice trembling despite his best efforts to keep it steady. "And at this point, I don't give two shits who they are or where they come from. We've been clever up to now, hiding our tracks, making it look as if these girls have run away or gone missing due to their own errors. But we can no longer afford to operate with such care. Just get me another girl. Even if you have to drag her off the street in broad daylight. We'll deal with that problem later. Do you understand?"

He sat back, watching Delgado process his request, the weight of what was being asked of him apparent in his widened eyes and furrowed brow. But he had to get with the program and fast. The time for subtlety was gone. They were now in survival mode.

"Yes, Mr Silva," he said, finally. "I understand." But his eyes still betrayed a hint of doubt.

"We need that girl today," Emilio snapped. "Or we're all dead."

The room fell silent, the magnitude of the situation hanging heavy in the air. With a brush of his hand, Emilio dismissed Delgado, who hurried out of the room with a new determination in his step. As the door closed, Emilio got to his feet feeling more alone, more vulnerable, than he'd felt in decades.

He walked to the window and pulled back the curtains, allowing with great reluctance the new day's arrival. Instinctively he tugged at a tuft of hair above his right temple. It was a big piece and made his eyes water as he yanked it out. But he needed more. More pain, more distraction, more control. His left hand found a similar-sized tuft on the opposite side. He pulled and tugged, the terror and anxiety he'd been trying to suppress finally breaking through. His hands trembled, his breath came in ragged gasps. With a cry, he ripped the hair from his scalp and stared down at it, held like a bunch of spider's legs in his sweaty fist.

He was terrified. The next nine hours would seal his fate.

But there was no turning back now.

41

The events of the last year meant John Beckett could never go back to the life he'd once lived. Indeed, whilst people like shady CIA agent Xander Templeton and monopolising criminal organisations like The Consortium were still active, he could never go back to being John Beckett. Yet there were some things they couldn't take away from him. His position and rank might now be pointless, but the attributes they demanded still remained. He'd been one of the British Secret Service's top operatives and an elite Special Forces officer. Which meant he was a soldier through and through, and a damned good one. So he knew to stay out of sight, cautious of every shadow, as he left Maria Silva's villa.

Even so, after seeing proof of what the Silvas were up to, a part of him – the part he kept hidden and under control as much as possible – yearned for a confrontation. A couple of Silva's goons; or even better, one of the brothers. Better still, both of them. He'd kill them. He'd kill them all. Slit them open and watch as they bled out.

Discipline prevailed as he made his way across the town square, channelling his anger into focused determination. His mind shifted gears, evaluating options, calculating moves. If Maria was correct, then the military truck – the key to Silva's deal with Barbosa – was yet to arrive. That meant they currently had no way of transporting the kidnapped women and no means of completing the delivery. It provided a window of opportunity to get the women out of the house and to safety. But he was talking hours, not days.

Beckett's stride didn't falter, the streets of São Lourenço moving past him in a blurred canvas of colour and life. The arrival of the men in the Mercedes added another layer to the problem. He was now all but certain they'd been sent by Barbosa to lean on the family and remove them from the equation if things didn't go to plan. There was the option to let this play out and have them do the work for him, but it was risky. There was a danger some of the women would get hurt in the process, and he still had the problem of how to get them to safety. He'd rather deal with the Silvas and all their henchmen – now proven to be as amateurish as he'd expected – than two practised killers. But there was always the possibility he'd have to deal with all of the above.

The stakes escalating also threw up another issue. The Silvas were under extreme pressure, their time running out, their moves questioned. Whenever that was the case, those involved got antsy. They made mistakes. People got hurt.

Beckett stopped as he reached Armando's taberna. For the first time in a while he felt the heavy weight of a mission on his shoulders, and the burden of responsibility. But in his heart there was no fear, no doubt.

He pushed the door open to find Armando standing behind the counter where he'd left him a few hours earlier. He looked deep in thought, which seemed to be the man's default setting presently. Whether this was his natural disposition or a result of the recent upheavals, Beckett wasn't sure.

Armando looked up. "Hey, you're back," he said, shrugging off whatever was concerning him. "How did it go?"

"Better than expected."

"You going to tell me where it is you went?"

Beckett slid onto one of the stools in front of the bar and rested his arms on the counter. "I went to see Maria Silva," he said. "She's going to help us."

Armando stared at him, his expression hard. "You're serious?"

"We can trust her," Beckett told him. "She hates her family, hates what they're doing even more. She wants to help. She's already provided useful intel." He told Armando about the truck and how it was yet to be delivered. He told him how Maria was going to the smaller of the two stash houses in order to provide them with weapons – guns and ammo, maybe explosives if she could find any. Once finished, he shut up and allowed his new friend and ally to process the information. But from the look on Armando's face, he wasn't too impressed. Or any less worried.

"I know I'm asking a lot of you," Beckett added. "But we can't let those bastards get away with this. We have to stop them."

"I get it," Armando replied. "And I'll do whatever I can. But going up against Salvador Barbosa wasn't exactly top of my bucket list. Hell, Mike, that's not just playing with fire, it's dancing into a damned volcano."

"Then we make sure we don't get burnt."

Armando's shoulders were slumped. "It's a lot though, right? There's only two of us; three if Humberto helps. I know you've depleted Silva's numbers, but we're still up against a large crew."

"Yes but they're disorganised, and on the back foot with Barbosa's men in town. We can exploit that. I intend to. And if

Maria delivers on her promise of weapons, we might stand a chance. I've taken on bigger crews before."

Armando raised an eyebrow. "So you are the real deal?"

"Yes," Beckett replied. "I am."

Armando puffed out his chest and smiled. It was a resigned sort of smile. The smile of someone who knew he was being reckless but was jumping in with both feet regardless. Beckett smiled back. He needed Armando in this mindset if they were to succeed.

"Okay, Mike – or whatever your real name is – count me in." He glanced at the clock. "What now?"

"Right now? Nothing. It's still early. Maria is meeting us here this afternoon with the guns. If you can get Humberto here at 1 p.m., that would work. From there we can plan our attack. Ideally we'd wait until it was dark, but we can't rely on the delivery truck being delayed. I want to be in position around the stash house before it arrives. Maria is also providing us with burner phones and hands-free kits we can use to stay in communication with each other. Once we know how many people we're dealing with and where they're situated, we'll move in. A classic extraction operation."

"Fair enough."

Beckett clicked his teeth. "I know it's not much of a plan. But sometimes the best plans are the simplest. Hit them fast, hit them hard. If we can take out the entire security team at the house before the truck arrives, we can get the women to safety. Then we go to the Silva estate and deal with whoever we find there."

Armando folded his arms. "You sure this won't come back on us? On me? On my family?"

"I wish I could give you a cast-iron promise," Beckett told him. "But my theory is once the Silvas are out of the picture, Barbosa will distance himself from the situation. The family are small-time gangsters trying to make it into the big leagues.

If there are bigger fish above Barbosa, they won't be happy about their deal breaking down, but I don't see Barbosa, or them, seeking revenge. Barbosa will twist the narrative to make out it was the Silvas at fault rather than outside forces involved. That way he appears as the dominant figure in the story. I've seen it happen a few times. Men like Barbosa like to think they're trailblazers, but most people go into self-preservation mode when their backs are against the wall."

"You sound like you have it all figured out." Armando picked up a cloth. "You going to stay here until Maria arrives?"

"If that's okay. Don't worry, I'll stay out of sight."

"There's the room upstairs," Armando said. "You're welcome to get some rest if you need it."

Beckett leaned back. He was wired, but he also knew the next twenty-four hours were going to be hell. "Thank you," he said. "That would be helpful."

"No problem, man. I'm going to head home for a while, but I'll lock the place up so you won't be disturbed."

"Everything okay?"

"Yeah," Armando replied, but he looked away as he said it. "I want to speak with Lina, convince her to go to her sister's place in the next town for a few nights. I don't want to have to be thinking about how she is whilst… you know…"

Beckett nodded. He got it. He understood.

"Also, Mike," Armando said, "if this Barbosa guy is involved, we need to be super careful. I've heard the stories. People say he's like the devil. I heard about this farmer who was on Barbosa's payroll. They used his fields to grow cannabis, or maybe even heroin poppies, I'm not totally sure. So the guy wasn't totally on the level but still a decent enough guy. I never found out what happened exactly, but he pissed Barbosa off somehow."

Armando didn't blink, staring off into the distance as he repeated the tale. "Barbosa's men wiped out the guy's whole family and his entire farm. The workers, the animals too. They burned the whole place to the ground. But they didn't just kill them, they tortured them, raped them, flayed them alive. People said you could hear their screams from miles around. But Barbosa left the farmer alive. After being made to watch his wife and children brutally murdered and having his entire livelihood destroyed, he was left to deal with his transgressions, every day a living hell. I've heard he's still alive, his body mutilated, his mind broken and he now begs for change in the street. Poor bastard."

Beckett listened to the story without comment or reaction. When Armando had finished, he gave it a moment before he spoke. "We don't know if Barbosa will get involved," he said, sliding off the bar stool. "But if he does – he'll regret it."

"I wish I had your confidence, Mike. Because that story isn't an outlier or some urban myth put about to scare people. I've heard many more stories just like it. That's the sort of man we're up against. A cruel bastard with a sick sense of humour."

"I know," Beckett replied. "But he hasn't met me yet."

"No," Armando said, an exasperated smile spreading across his face despite the panic still present in his eyes. "Not yet."

42

Rodrigo Silva couldn't sit still. His heart was a drum, thumping a victory beat as he steered his bright yellow Audi through the streets of São Lourenço. Music blared from the speakers, some fast-paced electronic beat that matched his pulse, but Rodrigo hardly heard it. His mind was spinning with what he'd just seen and his eagerness to act on it.

Scenes of the night before were still fresh in his mind. The panic, the confusion, his father and brother at each other's throats, scrambling like rats from a sinking ship. But now all of that seemed trivial, a minor blip on their journey to the big time.

Because he'd sorted it.

Him. Rodrigo Silva. The problem child. To many, a playboy rather than a player, lacking the cunning of his brother or the ruthlessness of his father.

But that was all about to change.

He'd been on his way to his sister's house when he'd spotted the Englishman hurrying down a back alley on the edge of town. At first, he couldn't believe his luck. But he'd have recognised that son of a whore anywhere. And here he was, alone and vulnerable, unaware he was being watched.

Seizing the opportunity in front of him, Rodrigo had parked up on a side street and followed at a distance. He could still recall the thrill of the chase; the way the sweat had clung to his brow as he'd tailed the Englishman back to the taberna where they had previously fought.

Bastard foreigner.

He couldn't believe Lopes was still associating with the Englishman after everything that had happened. The notion incensed him, but he'd deal with that treacherous prick later. For now, it was all about the Englishman.

Finding a dark passageway on the opposite side of the street, Rodrigo positioned himself with a clear view of the taberna's entrance. As the minutes ticked by, he wondered how he might use this new information – the Englishman's whereabouts – to his advantage. He wanted the bastard dead and would have loved to have been the one to do it, but he was still smarting from his beating and didn't want to rush in without a plan. Or backup.

He'd been crouched in that narrow passageway for almost ten minutes when the taberna door opened and Lopes stepped out. He'd looked troubled, his body tense, his eyes alert as he glanced up and down the street before locking the door behind him and moving away.

One in…

One out…

From his vantage point, Rodrigo had seen the Englishman through a window in the upper room of the taberna. But in keeping with his sense of self-preservation, he'd decided to follow Lopes instead, trailing him to his run-down shack on the far side of town. Once there, he maintained a low profile, watching from behind a line of trees as Lopes entered his house.

And then it had hit him.

His mind whirred and then clicked, and a plan had formed. A brilliant, devilish plan. A plan he knew would make his father proud.

With renewed purpose, Rodrigo had run back to his car, and as he sped north towards the family estate, his excitement was almost unbearable. He'd be the hero for once. The golden child. It was his time.

The scenery flew past in a blur. The run-down buildings turning to sun-soaked fields as he left the town behind. He'd be at the house in ten minutes, but… screw it. He couldn't wait. With eager fingers, he fished his phone from the plastic holster attached to the dashboard and hit Connect on his father's personal line.

"Hey, it's me," he announced as the elder Silva picked up. Rodrigo put the phone on speaker and placed it back in its holster. "Are you at home?"

"Where else would I be?" came the brusque retort. His father sounded even gruffer than usual, his voice strained. "What do you want?"

"I've had an idea," Rodrigo told him, grin spreading.

"What sort of idea?"

The road widened as Rodrigo hit the highway, the Audi's powerful engine purring as he accelerated, the landscape changing, rolling hills giving way to open expanses of barren wilderness. But his mind was elsewhere, on the Englishman, on Lopes, on the glory that awaited him.

"I've found the Englishman," Rodrigo said. "He's hiding out above a taberna downtown. The same one where he jumped me. It belongs to a guy called Lopes. I know him."

The line went dead, and for a moment Rodrigo wondered if they'd been cut off, but then his father spoke. "Is he still there?"

"Yes. I saw him in the upstairs window before he closed the

curtains. He'd taken his shirt off, looked like he was sleeping there, catching an early siesta. But that's not all…"

He paused, his head swaying from side to side as he delighted in the moment, in having his father's undivided attention for once.

"Enough with the bullshit," Silva hissed, as if speaking through gritted teeth. "What the hell is going on, Rodrigo? Talk to me."

But Rodrigo wasn't giving it to him that easily. This was his moment. "I'm on my way to you," he replied. "I'll be there in ten minutes and I'll explain everything then. But, Father, I think I've solved all our problems. All of them!"

"What do you mean?"

Rodrigo's laughter was wild, almost manic. "I've got a way of keeping the cartel happy, getting Barbosa's men off our backs and ridding ourselves of the Englishman once and for all."

"Tell me!"

Rodrigo flashed a look at himself in the rearview mirror. The cover-up foundation, along with his new Dolce & Gabbana sunglasses, made him look like a movie star and he grinned at himself, exposing two rows of perfect white teeth.

The game was on.

Victory was within his grasp.

"Patience, Father," he replied, reaching for his phone, finger hovering over the End Call button. "I'll explain everything when I get there. Just be ready, Father. Because we've won. We've done it!"

43

The bed was so soft, so warm. Still on the cusp of sleep, Beckett rolled onto his side but didn't open his eyes. A part of him knew where he was but didn't want to acknowledge it just yet. He preferred it here, in this hazy state where he was awake yet still entwined in the dream world he'd been inhabiting.

He'd been back in São Lourenço as a boy, his father by his side. They'd been wading in the surf with their trousers rolled up and their shoes and socks off, talking. His father had been telling the young Beckett how proud he was of him, and that if anything ever happened, he wanted John to look after his mother and sister. In the dream he'd looked up at his father, but the sun was so bright it had obscured most of his face and features. He didn't remember what his father looked like. And he'd also let him down. He'd not been able to save his dear mother from the illness that ravaged her body and took her from them ten years ago. He'd not been able to save his sister from the car accident that killed her and her husband and left his last surviving relative, Amber, an orphan at fifteen.

As his consciousness grew, he wondered briefly if there was

any lesson to be learnt here. Was his need to save others an attempt to make up for those he hadn't been able to?

Possibly. But Beckett was no psychologist and he didn't go in for self-exploration if he could help it. He knew what was needed in the moment. He knew how to act, how to help people, how to take down those who needed taking down.

That was enough.

He rolled onto his back, waking slowly, comfortably cocooned in the first proper rest he'd had since arriving in town. He stretched, his limbs heavy. The thin mattress felt like a five-star hotel bed compared with the dusty earth up on the hillside. But he couldn't lounge here forever. Maria was due at 1 p.m. with the guns. It was time to—

Beckett sat upright as an acrid smell invaded his nostrils, his sleep-fogged thoughts sharpening in an instant.

Smoke. Fire.

He was on his feet in a heartbeat, bare-chested and barefoot. With adrenaline flooding his system he crossed the room in two strides and yanked open the curtains. The air outside was thick with clouds of smoke. His best guess was the fire had originated in the kitchen or the main room. He had to get out. Now.

The window he was looking out of was the only one in the room and its frame was painted shut. It was also small and barred, the panes of glass too tiny to even fit his leg through. With some effort, he could perhaps kick out the entire unit but it would take time. Time he didn't have.

Down on the street below a crowd had formed, their wide-eyed faces just visible through the swirling plumes and their cries punctuating the air. Amongst them, Beckett spotted three stooped figures moving away from the scene, their movements too purposeful, too deliberate. His mind raced. Arson. Sabotage. The Silva goons. Right now it didn't matter. Survival was his only priority.

He backed away from the window, assessing his options. He checked the door handle; it wasn't hot. He pressed his ear against it. No sound of crackling flames. But the smell of smoke was stronger here, undeniable.

He pulled on his boots and grabbed his shirt off the floor, dousing it with the glass of water he'd brought up with him. Once soaked, he wrapped it around his nose and mouth and eased open the door. A bloom of thick grey smoke filled the stairwell as he hurtled down to the ground floor, the shirt around his face offering meagre protection against the toxic fumes. Moving into the main room, he found himself in a perfect vision of hell. The flames, like hungry orange snakes, crawled up the liquor shelves behind the counter. The wooden bar counter, the tables and chairs, the curtains too, were all ablaze. Everything was ablaze. The sheer intensity of the scene momentarily paralysed him. But years of military discipline rallied his senses.

Get out. Get clear.
Focus on survival.

The front door was nearest. He made for it, weaving between burning tables, but as he grabbed the door handle it didn't budge. It was locked. He threw his shoulder against it. Solid; as if there was some kind of barricade on the other side. But the fumes were getting thicker, the room hotter. His breathing became difficult as the acrid smoke invaded his lungs. He pictured the two CO_2 tanks Armando kept under the counter for the draft beer system, like ticking time bombs, and estimated he had about a minute left before he passed out from smoke inhalation, maybe less before the tanks exploded.

Then it would all be over.

The back door was his only hope. He raced toward the rear of the bar, jumping over burning debris and dodging falling timber to get there. But here too the door refused to yield. Someone had wedged it shut from the outside.

Those bastards.

Desperation narrowed his focus. A large window over the sink looked out onto the alley beyond. Without hesitation, he snatched an old metal stool from the corner and threw it against the glass. It spiderwebbed, but held. Gritting his teeth against the smoke and heat, Beckett battered the window again and again until, finally, it shattered.

Using the stool legs, he cleared the jagged shards from the frame and was able to clamber up onto the ledge just as a heavy explosion rocked the building, the CO_2 tanks exploding in a huge fireball. The shockwave propelled him through the open window and the ground rushed up to meet him. Instinctively he twisted his body in mid-air, executing a tactical roll to distribute the brunt of the impact. A shooting pain burst through his torso, but he was so pumped up on adrenaline the hurt was distant, secondary. He scrambled to his feet and sprinted away, darting down the passageway that ran between the taberna and the pottery store next door.

In the street beyond, the scene was chaotic but Beckett spotted Armando immediately, wild-eyed and shouting, directing people away from the danger. His eyes were fixed on the upstairs room, dread evident in his stare.

"Armando!" Beckett shouted, weaving through the crowd, his voice raspy from the smoke.

Armando turned, relief and confusion battling in his eyes. "Mike! Thank God!"

"They knew I was here," Beckett gasped, grabbing Armando's arm, steering him away from the scene. "This was no accident."

"Silva."

"Has to be. How did you know what was going on?"

"I was at home with Lina. I got a call to say the bar was on fire and I raced over here. The fire brigade are on their way, but they're stationed over in the next town." He glanced back, shaking his head. "There'll be nothing left of the place once they arrive."

As if on cue, another explosion ripped through the taberna, the entire frontage blowing out onto the street in a roaring fireball. Debris rained down as they dived for cover behind an old pick-up truck.

In the distance sirens wailed, the emergency vehicles getting closer.

Beckett helped Armando to his feet and then stopped. "Wait," he said. "Who was it who called you?"

"She didn't say," Armando said, brushing himself down, eyes still on his bar. "It was a woman. She just said there was a fire and I needed to get back here."

Beckett was silent. A woman? Maria? Had she known what was going to happen? Was she warning them?

But as the thought formed, another swiftly replaced it.

No. Not Maria.

But… who?

Unease settled deep in his stomach, making him more nauseous than he already was.

"You had no idea who this person was?" he asked. "You didn't recognise their voice? They didn't give a name?"

"She said she lived nearby, that's all." He grimaced at Beckett and then back to the bar. "Shit. It took hold fast, man. Gone in five minutes. Lucky for you the gas tanks held out long enough so you could get out before they blew. Another thirty seconds you'd be toast. At least that's something."

Yes, Beckett thought, but a nagging thought in his mind wouldn't go away. It told him he might have been lucky this time – but now that the Silvas were playing dirty, how long would that luck last?

44

Armando surveyed the charred wreckage of his taberna, just a smouldering shell now. Smaller, scavenger flames licked the blackened walls as smoke spiralled up into the heavens, turning the clear blue sky a dirty grey. His attention drifted to the gathered townsfolk, their pained gazes, the whispers of commiseration as they tried to find the right words to say. But there were no right words. There was nothing to say.

He had insurance, he could start again, eventually. But that wasn't the point. The taberna wasn't just bricks and mortar. It had been a fresh start after leaving the army. A vehicle for him to re-establish himself as a civilian, somewhere he could become the man – the husband, the father – he'd wanted to be. The taberna was a humble establishment, with no lofty aspirations, but it was a place of laughter and good times for many and salvation for him. Then after Ricardo died it became his salvation in another way – a place to pour his energy into, a place where he could escape the crippling pain of loss. Behind that counter he was simply Armando the barman, not Armando the bereft father, or Armando the man who couldn't find the words to comfort his grieving wife.

He'd even dreamed of passing the business on to his son one day. Now that dream, like his boy, was dead.

Pulling in a heavy breath, he wept.

Mike gripped his shoulder. "I'm sorry," he whispered. "This is my fault."

Armando wiped his eyes, regaining some composure as he turned to look at the Englishman, whose face and hair were streaked with soot. "It's not your fault," he said. "They did this. Cowardly bastards."

He'd worked so damned hard for this place, years of blood, sweat and tears, and these vindictive pieces of shit had taken it from him in minutes.

"We have to stop them," he added. "For good."

Mike nodded, a determined glint in his eye. "I agree. But listen, Armando... I'm concerned that—"

"Friends! Are you alright?" Humberto hurried towards them, his face creased with anxiety.

"Depends how you look at it," Armando told him. He quickly filled the older man in on what had happened – the phone call, the fire, Mike's escape, that they believed it was the Silvas that started the fire. As he spoke, Humberto's eyes bore into his, filled with the same age-old pain that was tightening Armando's chest and stomach muscles.

"Follow me," Humberto said, already pushing through the now disbursing crowds. "We'll go to my place. You'll be safe there."

Safe?

Would anywhere be safe from that family's wrath?

Armando suppressed a shudder. A sneer too, but it had been his choice to help the Englishman. Even if the weight of that decision now pressed down on him, he had to take ownership of it. His father would hate to see him like this, cowering, looking for blame elsewhere. Armando glanced to the heavens and said a silent prayer, asking his father for help. For guidance.

As they strode through the streets towards Humberto's house, Armando studied the Englishman. For someone who appeared perennially unflappable, even in the face of death, there was now a haunted quality behind his eyes. His face was rigid with contemplation.

"Are you sure you're okay, man?" Armando asked. "I mean, I know you just escaped a burning building, but you don't seem yourself. Maybe we should get you to the hospital."

Mike didn't look at him but stopped and pursed his lips. "I was just wondering about something…trying to get it clear in my head before I said anything."

"What is it?" Humberto asked, stopping and turning to face him. Armando did the same.

"It doesn't make any sense," Mike continued. "What have they got to gain by burning down your bar other than sending a message?"

"You were inside," Armando said.

"Yes, I was, and they'd wedged the door shut, but the window was there, easy to break. It's a lot of effort just to screw up at the final hurdle. The Silvas have shown themselves to be rather careless in the way they conduct themselves, but… I don't know… something doesn't add up and I can't quite put my finger on what it is."

"You think there's more to it?" Humberto asked.

The Englishman's eyes narrowed. "Possibly, yes."

"And what does that mean?" Armando asked.

"I'm not sure," Mike replied. "The phone call bothers me. Did the person call you on your mobile or at home?"

Armando frowned. "The house phone."

"Right. So they knew where you were and how to contact you. But you were already back at the bar when I escaped, so they must have called you the second flames were visible, or…?" He shook his head. "If it was a neighbouring business owner, why not announce who it was? What was their reason? Were they trying to get both of us in the fire, or was it… something else?"

Humberto and Mike continued to query the events, but their voices faded into the background as Armando closed his eyes and tried to remember the details of the call. It had happened so fast that he'd not taken much notice of the voice. Did he recognise who it was? What had they said exactly?

As usual at times like this – stressful times, full of worry – his thoughts switched to his wife, to his dear Lina. She'd been so tired today, unusually so. But that was expected, given her condition.

That poor woman. So kind, so loving. She'd been through too much already. How the hell was he going to tell her that their livelihood was gone? Literally up in flames. He pictured her in bed, asleep as he'd left. Even in his panic he'd leant over and kissed her on the forehead. She'd mumbled something but hadn't woken. The call hadn't even disturbed her. The call from the mystery woman telling him his taberna was on fire.

But who was she?

The Englishman's questions brought up a swirl of troubling thoughts. If only he'd probed her for more details. But there'd been no time.

"Unless it was all a diversion," he heard Humberto say.

Armando opened his eyes, shot him a look.

"That's what I'm thinking," Mike said. "But a diversion from what?"

Armando considered the question. He was about to say the same thing – that he had no idea – when a chilling thought hit him square in the guts.

Merda!

He brought his hands to his mouth.

No.

It couldn't be.

He felt sick and dizzy as if the air was stifling him, stopping his ability to breathe properly. "No…" he muttered.

"What is it?" Humberto asked.

Armando glanced around, desperately searching for answers where there were none. He opened his mouth, tried to speak, but no words came. He glanced at Mike, at Humberto. Raw fear gripped him, cold and relentless.

"I've got to go," he spluttered out, pivoting on his heel.

Ignoring Mike and Humberto's calls for him to return, to explain himself, he set off, running faster than he'd run in a very long time.

He hoped he was mistaken.

He hoped this was just his anxious brain playing tricks on him.

But if not, he hoped he wasn't too late.

45

Armando's lungs burned as he sprinted through the dusty streets, the scorch of the afternoon sun hot on his back.

Please, God, let her be okay.

He skidded to a halt as his home came into view. The sight of his front door hanging open turned his blood to ice. He scanned the area, up the street and down to the olive grove at the back of the property. He saw nothing out of the ordinary. There was no one else in sight.

As he got up to the house, the dread that had been budding in his stomach now bloomed like a nuclear explosion. The blue pottery vase that usually sat on their porch had been knocked over, the broken shards littering the entrance. Through an open window, the soft, floral curtains that Lina loved so much fluttered ominously in the wind – like silent witnesses to a crime.

Lina. Oh, God. Lina.

With his heart lodged in his throat, Armando burst through the front door, calling out desperately, "Lina? Lina, where are you?"

No reply.

His heart pounded against his ribs as he moved from room to room, hoping against hope she'd be there, that she'd answer him, that this was just a bad dream. He took the stairs two at a time up to their bedroom, praying to God she was still asleep. "Lina, my love!"

Still no answer.

On reaching the bedroom he stumbled. A cry caught in his throat. The sheets were tangled and torn and a lamp lay smashed on the floor. He spun around, frantically searching the room, heart hammering. "Lina!"

But she was gone.

Panic crippling him, he flew back downstairs, taking them three at a time. Out in the backyard maybe? In the bathroom?

He searched every room, overturning furniture in desperation, shouting her name. He burst out through the back door to check the yard. But the property was empty, devoid of life.

Lina was not here.

Finally, back in the living room, he collapsed to his knees as sobs wracked his body. His beloved wife was gone, taken from their own home. And it was all his fault. His choices had put her in harm's way. He should have protected his wife, kept her safe. He never should have gotten involved with the Englishman's crusade.

Images flashed in his mind, awful images that made him want to throw up. If those bastards had hurt her… If they'd…

No!

He couldn't think that way.

It would paralyse him and he needed to keep it together. However dire the situation, giving in to despair wouldn't help her.

He hauled himself to his feet and left the house, wiping the tears from his face as he went. She had been taken forcefully against her will, that much was clear. Someone must have seen or heard something.

Outside, the midday sun cast long shadows, giving the narrow street an ominous feel. Most of the neighbouring houses had their shutters closed, the once close-knit community now shut off from one another, too scared to get involved.

Armando's frustration boiled over. These people were once their friends, their neighbours. Why was no one coming to help? Why was no one sharing his panic? He pounded on the nearest door, shouting, "Open up! Lina's missing!"

No response.

He went to the next. Same deal. And the next. Nothing. Again and again he knocked, screaming and pleading for someone to help him. But he was met only with silence.

His anguish twisted into anger.

They were all cowering inside, too frightened to answer, to bear witness, to get involved. The neighbourhood that once thrived on shared meals and laughter now hid behind locked doors and closed windows.

"Please! Help me!" Armando yelled. "My wife has been taken!"

But still no one appeared.

"Cowards! All of you!" he roared.

In desperation he walked down to the end of the street and to the home of Senhora Cardoso. The old lady had lost her husband years ago, her only son taken by brain cancer at just thirty-two. Lina often took her food and helped tend her garden. Surely if she'd seen something she would help.

He hurried up the wooden steps and banged the side of his fist against her front door. "Senhora Cardoso. It's Armando Lopes. Are you there?"

He waited. Nothing. He was about to bang again when he heard shuffling from inside. A moment later a key scraped in the lock and the door creaked open an inch. The old woman peered out. She looked frail, her eyes clouded with age and sorrow. Yet she was the only one brave enough to open her door.

Armando's voice broke, the weight of hope and desperation clear in his tone. "Senhora Cardoso, have you seen Lina? Do you know where she is?"

Her gaze was steady, yet filled with sympathy. She nodded slowly, a gesture as painful as a sharp knife sticking into Armando's gut. "They took her," she whispered. "I'm sorry. I have to go."

Armando's world crumbled to dust around him as she shut the door. His legs felt like they were about to give way. He hesitated, hand half-raised to knock again, but what was the point? She was scared and she'd done all she could

They.

They took her.

She didn't need to say the name. Armando knew exactly who she meant. And if *they* had hurt his wife, *they* were all going to pay. Every last one of them. He'd make sure of that. Or he'd die trying.

46

The clock struck three. The day was pressing on and there was still no sign of Armando. Beckett sat in Humberto's sparse kitchen, his mind racing with strategies, interlaced with dark thoughts he tried not to focus on. He suspected why Armando had sprinted home in such a panic, but didn't want to say anything just yet. He was a realist, with a soldier's heart and an intelligence operative's mind, but with situations this precarious he didn't like to tempt fate.

Humberto was sitting across from him, his expression one of worry but also of determination. Beckett could see it in the set of his jaw, the tension in his neck muscles. The man was ready.

"Are you sure she's on the level?" Humberto asked, referring to Maria, after Beckett had just called to let her know the change of location. "She's still a Silva."

Beckett lifted his head. "I vouch for her," he said. "She wants rid of her family as much as we do."

"Yes, but rid of… how? She knows what we're planning?"

"She's providing us with weapons. I'd say so."

The older man stuck out his bottom lip but said no more.

Beckett leaned back in his seat. Humberto's home was modest and well-kept. The kitchen exuded an air of rustic charm: blue and white tiles on the floor, copper pans hanging from hooks, a window that looked out onto a courtyard.

"You know, I saw you the other night," Beckett said, when the silence got too much. "You were visiting your daughter."

Humberto stared at him, perhaps waiting for him to say more. When he didn't, he answered. "I had to see her. I was scared I might leave it too late. If things go to hell tonight and—"

"Don't talk that way," Beckett cut in. "You're going to see your daughter again. We're doing this for her, too. Remember that."

"I will." He looked into his leathery palms and shook his head. "I tried to get her to leave there and then. But she wouldn't. She said it was too risky, that Raul would burn the town down looking for her. But what if things get messy and she's hurt, Mike? I couldn't live with myself if I knew I was partly to blame."

"She wants to get away from Raul? From the family?"

Humberto nodded. "Yes. That bastard has laid his hands on her too many times. I hinted we were planning something and that she should leave before the trouble starts."

Beckett leaned forward, "And will she?"

"I don't know. She says she hates his family, but Raul has real control over her. My darling girl. She's been broken by them. Lived under their rules for too long. But it's why I'm more determined than ever to stop those evil bastards and get her back."

Beckett had more he could say on the matter, but as he opened his mouth to respond the kitchen door banged open. Armando lurched in, eyes wild, shirt stained with sweat.

"They've taken Lina!" he gasped.

Beckett got to his feet, but wasn't surprised, not really. He'd had a gnawing feeling in the pit of his stomach. "When? Did you see them?" he asked.

Fast and without taking a breath, Armando described finding his home ransacked and his wife gone. He spoke of his neighbours' silence and the old woman at the end of the street who had more or less informed him it was the Silvas who had taken Lina. When he finished, he slumped into a chair.

"If they've hurt her," he spat. "I will gut every single one of them. I swear it."

Humberto got up and placed a hand on his friend's shoulder. "Keep it together, son. We'll get her back, but we need to be smart about it."

Armando shook his head violently. "You don't understand. Lina is pregnant!"

Stunned, Humberto shot Beckett a look, but Beckett had no words. He felt like he'd been sucker-punched. He took a moment, composed a response. But before he could speak, Armando continued.

"She's only fourteen weeks," he said. "After Ricardo, we didn't think it would happen again… We tried for years, and just when we had given up… a miracle. She fell pregnant." His eyes glistened. "That's why I've been so distant lately, so caught up. I was scared of getting involved, scared of risking our new chance at happiness. And now…" The sentence hung in the air, unfinished but understood.

Beckett sat, giving it a moment before speaking "We'll get Lina back," he said, his tone allowing no doubt. "And we'll make damn sure those bastards regret ever laying a hand on her in the first place."

Armando wiped his eyes, a spark of hope penetrating his pain. "She's really weak right now. She needs rest. And she's everything to me, Mike. I'll do whatever it takes."

"And we'll be with you every step," Humberto vowed. "Those demons will regret they ever did this."

Beckett watched his new allies, noting the resolve in their eyes, the tension in their muscles. Lina's kidnapping meant the gloves were well and truly off. There could be no more half-measures. He leaned over the table, his keen mind working overtime. With Lina's life now in the balance, it would be easy to let stealth and precision give way to brute force. But he knew from experience that was dangerous. Foolish, even. Yet a part of him yearned for a bloody showdown with these cretins. He would tear that stash house apart brick by brick to free the kidnapped women. After that he would turn his attention to the Silva family. Show them what happened to people like them when people like him got involved.

"We'll get her back," he said softly, almost to himself. "We'll get them all back. But it needs to be swift and methodical. The situation is volatile. We'll roll with whatever we come up against, but we need a basic idea of what's going to happen. Like my father used to say – fail to prepare, prepare to fail."

Armando managed a shaky smile. "I'm ready to do whatever is needed."

"Good man." Beckett gave him a curt nod. "Things could get very ugly very quickly tonight. Barbosa has sent his men already, and there could be more coming. The Silva organisation is on the brink, ready to tip over. But if we're clever we can exploit that."

"I hope it does get ugly," Armando hissed. "For those bastards."

Beckett studied the man closely. Beneath the anguish, rage simmered – dangerous yet useful if channelled correctly.

"I know you're dealing with a lot," he told him. "But I need you to keep a clear head. You know it yourself, in the field a lack of focus gets you killed almost as quickly as a lack of experience."

"I'm ready to destroy those motherfuckers!" Armando

shouted, slamming his fist on the table. "Don't you worry about me."

The room fell silent. Beckett straightened, meeting Humberto's eye as a pulse of understanding shot between them, their shared worries, the recklessness of a man with nothing to lose. Maybe Armando saw it too because he sat back and patted the air.

"I'm not going to do anything stupid," he said. "I have too much to lose. But Lina is my world. She is carrying my unborn child. I cannot fail her when she needs me most."

"You won't fail her," Beckett told him. "We won't fail her."

"You know, my father was a deeply religious man but he was also a fighter," Armando said. "It was never about turning the other cheek for him. And he had sayings, too. One of them comes to mind now. He used to say – when the kingdom comes, there's only one thing you can do."

Beckett tilted his head, eyes narrowing inquisitively. "What's that? Pray?"

"No, my friend," Armando replied, his expression hardening. "You run for your gun."

Beckett grinned. He liked that. Armando was all in.

Those bastards wouldn't know what hit them.

47

Emilio Silva paced impatiently in the foyer of Eagle House, stopping each time he passed the entrance to glance out through the open double doors at the space beyond.

Where the hell was he?

Behind him, Raul leaned back against the old reception desk and lit a cigarette. He was trying to act cool and in control, but the shaky hand as he took a drag of nicotine and lifted the cigarette from his mouth gave him away. He was as nervous as any of them. And with good reason.

He said he'd be here…

Silva walked up to the entrance, holding onto the edge of the doorframe as he peered out. It was almost 4 p.m. and the sun's glare hung low in the sky, staining everything with its stifling orange hue. Time was ticking away from him. With each passing minute, the shadows lengthened across the rugged terrain, but still no sign of his useless youngest son.

"What did he say exactly?" Raul asked.

"He said he had good news," Silva snapped. "He said he'd solved all our problems. But I don't see him anywhere."

He walked back inside and checked his watch. Again. The delivery truck was due within two hours, and with Barbosa's men watching their every move, they needed to be ready once it arrived. That meant a full complement of twenty-five women bound for Mexico and the Sangre de Dragón Cartel's human trafficking ring. Only, they didn't have twenty-five. His insatiable eldest son, lacking in self-control, had seen to that.

He was still furious at Raul for what he'd done, could barely look at him. Later – if they still had hands and heads – he'd punish him severely for his actions, make him wish he'd never stepped foot into Eagle House that night. But for now he needed him.

A screech of tires broke the silence. Silva's head shot up, looking expectantly at Raul who took a final drag from his cigarette and flicked it away as he pushed off from the counter. They stepped out onto the porch together as Rodrigo's bright yellow sports car pulled into view.

He beeped the horn when he saw them, his grinning face behind the tinted glass sporting mirrored aviator shades. Silva remained still; his muscles ached with the strain of all he was carrying.

"Fucking idiot," Raul muttered to himself.

Silva shot him a sideways glance. Who was he to talk? Rodrigo was indeed a pampered playboy living off the family name, but if he really had solved their problems, he was twice the man his elder brother professed to be.

As Rodrigo pulled up in front of the hotel, Silva stepped down onto the dusty forecourt to greet him.

"You took your damn time," he growled, as Rodrigo opened the car door and climbed out.

"Apologies, Father," he replied, still grinning like the cat who'd got the cream. "But there is no need to worry. Everything is taken care of. I have done it." He removed his glasses and flashed his eyebrows at his brother, the subtext clear. *Fuck you. This is my time.*

Rodrigo was wearing smart black trousers and a white shirt, unbuttoned halfway to reveal his toned chest. Hours spent in the gym when he should have been working. He closed the door and strutted around to the rear of the car, gesturing for his father and brother to follow him. The way he moved, slow and with purpose, it was like he owned the world and everyone in it.

Biting his tongue, Silva shuffled over to join him. Up close, he saw Rodrigo's cheek marred by a fresh scratch, raw and bloody against his olive skin. The sort of wound made by a sharp fingernail.

Raul must have seen it too. "Looks like someone got the better of you," he said, jabbing his finger at the wound.

"Get the hell off me!" Rodrigo snapped, yanking his head away. "It's a battle scar. Nothing else."

"Whatever. You're a joke."

The air was thick with anticipation. The two brothers glared at each other. Silva wondered briefly if he should let them go at each other, see which one had the real worth. But now wasn't the time.

"Enough, Rodrigo," he said. "What the hell is going on?"

"You'll see." He leaned down and flipped open the boot with a flourish. Inside, a young woman lay bound and gagged, a dirty rag tied around her mouth. Her flowery skirt was torn and bloody and her dark hair was matted with sweat and grime, but her eyes burned with a fury and fear that excited Silva.

"Who is she?"

"Lopes's wife, the guy who's been harbouring the Englishman. After setting fire to his bar I got one of the bitches in town to call him, get him out of the house so I could grab his wife. Like I said on the phone, this way we complete the shipment and send a clear message. Don't mess with us. His bar is now nothing but ash, burned down with the Englishman inside."

"He's dead?" Raul asked, his sibling rivalry dissipating as his voice rose in excitement. "For real?"

Rodrigo cleared his throat. "I'm waiting to hear confirmation. But the way my men told it, there was no way anyone could escape that fire. We're all good."

Silva slapped Rodrigo on the back, laughing in giddy relief. "My boy! What a world. You were right. You've done it. Well done!" He raised his head, gesturing at his men standing guard at the front of the house. "Get her out," he ordered as they approached.

Lopes's wife tried to scream as the men hauled her from the car, but through the gag it was muffled. She struggled as they got her to her feet, though his men kept a firm hold on her.

Nodding to himself, Silva inspected the woman, looking her up and down, moving around the back to inspect the rear as she continued to whimper. "She's a hot little number. Maybe a bit old for the Mexican's brief, but I think they'll let it slide when they see the ass on her." She let out a high-pitched wail, and he laughed and yanked the cloth from her mouth, revealing raw, chapped lips. "You have something to say, my dear?"

She sucked in a breath, her chest heaving. "Fuck you," she hissed. "My husband... he will—"

"He will do nothing!" Silva yelled, slapping her across the face with a vicious backhand that silenced her instantly. "He is nothing against me. You are nothing."

"Please..." she whined, tears running down her cheeks. "I am pregnant. I have a child..."

"Shhh now, no need to cry," Silva crooned, changing tack. He stroked her hair almost tenderly and replaced the gag over her mouth as she tried to speak. "We have medicine in the house. Things that will take care of your... condition, and also make this whole experience much easier for you. You'll know what's going on but you won't care about it as much. You won't care about anything. Makes it better for you. Makes you more pliable for us. All good."

With a nod of his head, his men dragged her into the house still kicking and screaming through her restraints. He watched her go, the late afternoon sun shining through the thin material of her dress giving him a great view of her body. It was a shame he wouldn't get a ride on this one, but no matter.

He turned back to his sons and clapped his hands. "Thank Christ!" he said, sharing a satisfied nod with Rodrigo. For once, the boy had done good. The truck would be delivered within a few hours and the deal could go ahead as planned. The cartel would get their shipment and Barbosa's men would have to leave without their pound of flesh, or whatever they were here for.

The moment was broken by a high-pitched beeping sound. Raul pulled his phone from his pocket and answered it. Silva watched him as he took the call, nodding and asking questions as he paced up and down. He looked troubled, but when he hung up he was grinning.

"What is it?"

"That was Valdez," Raul said, checking his watch. "He's in town and has just spotted the Englishman with my dear father-in-law. It looks like the old-timer is helping him. Stupid old bastard."

Silva glared at Rodrigo. So, the son of a bitch was still alive after all. "Can you handle this?" he asked Raul.

"Yes, Father."

"I want him dead. Both of them."

Raul bared his teeth with glee. He hadn't looked this giddy since he was a boy.

"Actually, change of plan," Silva said, feeling a little giddy himself now the panic of the last few days was receding. "Bring them to the house. It'll be a nice way to celebrate once the shipment is finalised.

His eldest son gave a curt nod. "My pleasure. I have men in the area. They won't get away this time."

"Good. Go now. Take Rodrigo's car. It's faster."

The younger son opened his mouth to protest, but a sharp look from his father shut it for him. He was egotistical and self-obsessed, but not a complete fool. As Raul sped away, a dark chuckle bubbled up from Silva's throat.

It had been close. Damn close. But he'd done it.

He was in the clear.

48

Salvador Barbosa stared silently out the window of his black SUV as it sped along the coastal highway. Outside, the sun hovered low over the ocean, casting a fiery glow across the water, but Barbosa took no pleasure in the view. He recalled his recent conversation with Martim, his mind churning with questions that demanded answers.

Why was the deal stalling? Who was this Englishman interfering with operations? And, most importantly, why had Silva failed to eliminate him?

Such slackness could not be tolerated. If the Silvas struggled to deal with one man, they held no value to him. Weakness and incompetence were cardinal sins in Barbosa's world. And they always carried a death sentence.

He glanced at his Rolex. Two hours until they reached the town.

Salvador Barbosa considered himself a generous and reasonable man when treated with the appropriate respect. But insult his integrity or power, and you invited violence to your door. He was already pondering his next creation, the next tableau for his Theatre of Cruelty. Given his penchant for tailored punishments, he thought about chastising the family's vanity by mutilating them, cutting out their tongues so their smooth talking and lies were silenced forever. He thought about branding the sons' faces so their handsome looks were ruined.

But none of it was enough.

For their avarice, he could starve them to death, denying them sustenance and comfort. For their false sense of power, he could strip away all their wealth and status, reducing them to penniless beggars in rags.

But still, none of it was enough.

He shook his head. The more he thought of Emilio Silva and his two sons, the more enraged he became. They were smug, entitled, weak. Small-time thugs playing to a captive audience of nobodies. They were not like him. They were not in the same class. And now they were living on borrowed time, their days of playing mob bosses in their backwater town over. Barbosa and his men did not play games.

Beside him, Miguel, a hulking figure with a scar splitting his right eyebrow, shifted uncomfortably. Up front, his other two trusted enforcers, Luis and Rafa, whispered to each other in hushed, urgent tones.

"Miguel, you spoke to Martim before I did," Barbosa muttered, not turning from the window. "Did he tell you anything about this Englishman? Who the hell is he?"

"He only knows what he has heard from the locals," Miguel replied. "That this man has humiliated the family on more than occasion. That he is a thorn in their side and is slowing down operations."

Barbosa's eyes narrowed, a shark sensing blood. "One man against their whole organisation. Shit. They're even more pathetic than I realised."

He growled to himself.

What sort of low-level amateurs had he got himself involved with?

Rafa turned around to address his boss, choosing his words carefully. "Sir, don't concern yourself with this man. Once we're in town, we'll find the shipment and silence the family for messing us around. One problem gone. Then we find the Englishman and put him down, too. Two problems gone. No more problems."

"It shouldn't have come to this," Barbosa grumbled. "We shouldn't have to be cleaning up their mess. The only reason I agreed to broker this deal in the first place was because the son, Raul, assured me there would be many more shipments like the first." But then a grim smile pulled at his lips. It was a long time since he'd had the opportunity to kill someone with his own hands. He'd missed it. He sat back and waved a finger in the air. "I suppose at least now we know the truth. If they can't handle an easy shipment like this one, then they're of no use to me at all. Leave Raul to me. I'll make sure he suffers the most."

He chuckled to himself. When they arrived in São Lourenço they would paint the town red with Silva blood and deliver the shipment to the cartel themselves, reaping the full benefits of the deal. Suddenly he was excited. Castellano might question the change of plan, but as long as he got his shipping container full of young women, he wouldn't care too much about the details. If anything, this was a better plan. It was certainly more fun.

Because what else was he going to do with his weekend? He'd always felt a little blood sport was good for the soul.

With a sigh he returned to the window, gazing out across the ocean. The Englishman, however, was still an unknown quantity. If he'd been delving into Silva's business, he could know about the deal, about his own involvement. That meant he wasn't only a pest, he was a potential threat.

Barbosa closed his eyes, picturing the mysterious

Englishman having his tongue sliced from his mouth, and his eyeballs gouged from their sockets.

Aquele filho da puta!

He imagined his men holding the meddling bastard down whilst Barbosa poured molten metal into his ears. 'See No Evil, Hear No Evil, Speak No Evil.' That's what he'd call it. A grim amalgamation of those ridiculous carved statues of the three monkeys that people with no taste sometimes owned. He would silence everyone who got in his way. The whole town if he had to. He would leave no ties to him or the cartel.

He was smiling to himself when his phone vibrated against his chest. He pulled it out from the inside pocket of his silk bomber jacket and saw Martim's name on the caller ID.

Excellent.

He'd been expecting the call. At least his own men were reliable.

"Are you in position?" he asked, on answering.

"Yes, Mr Barbosa. We have eyes on the house, but no sign of the transportation as yet."

"Hold your ground," he replied. "I'm on my way. Have you texted me the location?"

Miguel leaned forward, waving his phone. "I have it, sir."

"Good work," Barbosa told both men. "Martim, let me know if anything changes, but you know what to do. Wait until I give you the word, then move in as we discussed."

"Yes, sir."

Barbosa hung up. He checked his watch. Not long to go. By the time he left São Lourenço, the balance of power would be clear for all to see. Everyone existed to serve Salvador Barbosa's interests. And those who failed to understand that essential truth forfeited their right to exist at all.

49

A sharp knock at the front door echoed through Humberto's home, causing the men sitting around the kitchen table to bristle into alertness. The urgency of their conversation had made them jumpy, their senses sharpened.

"Who is it?" Armando hissed.

Beckett held up a hand. "Relax," he said. "I'll get it."

He left them in the kitchen and made his way down the hallway, the old wooden floorboards creaking beneath his feet. As he got up to the door there was another knock, more insistent this time. His gut told him it was her, but he approached with caution nonetheless, the soldier in him not letting his guard down for a moment. He stopped. Listened.

"Maria?"

"It's me. Let me in."

He unlocked the door and pulled her inside. The large holdall she carried clanged against the doorframe as she stepped into the hallway. Once inside, Beckett closed the door and locked it once more.

"All good?" he asked, looking her up and down. Dressed in

a pair of jeans and an old t-shirt with a simple leather bag slung over her shoulder, she looked far removed from the glamorous mafia princess he'd met on the hillside, but there was still a sultry aura about her. He suspected the designer sunglasses and big hair were, in some respects, a shield. A way to protect her true self from the world. Everyone did it in some way or another. Today her hair was pulled back into a simple ponytail, and she wore minimal make-up, yet her natural beauty shone through.

"Any trouble getting here?" he asked.

"No, all quiet," she replied, placing the holdall down, slightly out of breath. "Nobody followed me."

"And you got everything?" he asked, gesturing to the bag at her feet.

She nodded, a nervous energy coming off her. "Yes. It's all there."

Beckett picked up the bag. Its contents were reassuringly heavy. Perfect.

He ushered her down the hall to the kitchen where Humberto and Armando waited like coiled springs. The reception was frosty; their stares a mix of wariness and distrust towards Maria. Setting the bag on the table, Beckett caught each of their attention in turn and shot them a stern look.

No time for old grudges. Not now.

He unzipped the holdall, revealing a collection of weapons wrapped in cloth. Five pistols rested on top: two Glocks, two Berettas, and a snub-nosed revolver. Beckett lifted out one of the Glocks, examining its slide, weight and chamber. All good.

Maria interrupted his inspection, leaning into him as she spoke. "I found some grenades, too. And I brought plenty of ammo like you asked, plus extra magazines."

Beckett continued his inspection. Three AK-47s lay at the bottom of the bag. Picking one out, he held it up and clicked back the bolt, noticing Armando's expression. "They won't know what's hit them," he said, by way of reassurance.

"They sure won't," Humberto muttered appreciatively. "And these will do nicely."

"Thank you, Maria," Beckett said, raising an eyebrow at the others. "You've done well. You've risked a lot."

Armando shuffled his feet.

"Yes, we… appreciate your efforts," Humberto managed. "Thank you."

Armando mumbled his thanks, but it was unintelligible and said to the floor. Beckett let it go. Armando was on the edge and Maria represented those who had taken everything from him. All things considered, he was holding it together remarkably well. He was a good soldier. He needed to stay that way.

"I'm just doing what I can," Maria replied.

Beckett lowered his voice. "And the other thing I asked you to do?"

"All under control. I'm going to her place once I'm done here."

Humberto looked puzzled. Beckett explained. "I asked Maria to get Antonia somewhere safe, just until this blows over."

Humberto's eyes widened. "She refused to leave when I asked her." He turned to Maria. "You're certain you can convince her?"

"She'll put up a fight, but I can be very persuasive," Maria said, a glint in her eye. "We're close. Close enough. I'll make her see it's for the best."

Humberto grasped her hand. "Thank you. I'm in your debt."

"It's fine. I'm sorry it has come to this."

She glanced at Beckett, who clapped his hands together

decisively. "It looks like we're almost set," he said. "Maria, did you get the other items I asked for?"

She nodded, hastily unzipping her shoulder bag and pulling out four burner phones. "Here," she handed them over. "I did as you explained."

Beckett smiled at her in thanks. Each phone had a number on the back written in marker pen. One to four. He handed them out, noting the number on each as he did. "I'm one." He passed the next to Armando: "You're two." Humberto received the third: "Three for you." And the last one went to Maria. He opened his phone and scrolled through the menu, checking all was well. "They have prepaid credit and Maria has programmed each phone so it contains only the numbers of the other three. They're set to vibrate only. If we need to contact each other we can use them."

It was a low-tech compromise. Beckett would have preferred walkies or, even better, earpieces. But in the field you made do. You improvised.

He turned to Maria. "You should go now. I'll be in touch when this is finished. Not before."

Maria's face was a complex mix of emotions: fear, determination, and maybe a touch of sadness. "Good luck."

She turned to leave but Humberto got up from the table and grasped her hand a second time. "Thank you again, Maria," he said. "Please, get my Antonia to safety."

Maria held his gaze, her voice almost a whisper, "I will." Then she pulled in a sharp breath and pulled her hand away. "I should go."

Beckett followed her into the hallway. At the door she stopped and turned back. There was an awkward moment – the air tense and electric – where it seemed as though she wanted to say or do something more. But she hesitated.

"What will happen to my father and brothers?" she asked.

Beckett didn't flinch. "They'll get what they deserve," he replied. No point in sugar-coating it.

Maria considered this a moment, then gave a grim nod of acceptance. She understood.

"Be careful," Beckett said, reaching around the side of her to open the door. "I'll be in touch when I can."

With a final lingering look, Maria slipped outside into the early evening gloom. Beckett watched her cross the street and disappear from view. Then he closed the door and returned to the kitchen where Humberto and Armando were checking the weapons with calm focus.

Beckett stood in the doorway and watched them, his tactical mind now whirring with ideas, running scenarios. The stash house would be heavily guarded. Just three of them against Silva's thugs. The odds weren't great.

But when were they ever?

"We need to move," he said.

Armando and Humberto looked up expectantly.

"Now?" Armando repeated. "Shit... I... Okay..."

Beckett gave him a reassuring smile. "No time like the present, my friend. It'll take us half an hour to reach the stash house. By then it will be dark. We need to hit them before the transportation arrives – while they're still waiting, when they're complacent. We'll park up far enough away that they won't hear us, and cover the last hundred metres or so on foot."

He picked up one of the Berettas, checked the mechanism and then grabbed three magazines from the holdall. He pocketed two and held the third up to eye level, noting the glimmer of brass, the first of the bullets nestled tightly together inside. Yes, Maria had done well. He slotted the magazine into the grip of the Beretta, feeling the satisfying click as it locked into place. Then he pulled back the slide, chambering the first round, and slid the pistol down the back of his waistband. Ready.

Across the table, Humberto and Armando were also tooling up in tense silence. Beckett watched as they loaded guns and pocketed ammo. Their expressions were grim, lined with worry yet underpinned by a steely resolve. Each man knew what was at stake tonight. Failure was not an option.

Humberto selected both Glocks and Armando took the remaining Beretta and slung one of the AKs over his shoulder. Beckett grabbed one also, releasing the curved magazine and checking for a full complement of rounds. There were no spare mags for the rifles so they had to make every bullet count. Satisfied, he aligned the magazine's lip with the rifle's front trunnion and rocked it back until it latched in securely. Drawing the bolt carrier to the rear, he let it snap forward, chambering the first round. The cold, mechanical motion of the rifle felt smooth, even comforting, in its familiarity. It had been a while since he'd fired one of these, but it was like riding a bike. A very deadly and powerful bike.

He glanced at the others. At his extraction team. They were a ramshackle trio, but the intensity in their eyes was apparent.

Their time had come.

They could do this.

Tonight the Silva organisation would learn what happened when ordinary men were backed into a corner and forced to embrace their inner monsters.

In his mind Beckett visualised the target location – the old hotel, now Silva's stash house, a prison for the women held captive inside. He was counting on four armed guards minimum, at least two more inside. They'd have to neutralise the external threats rapidly and with stealth, to avoid alerting the whole building.

Once inside, they would locate the captives and eliminate any resistance. Their initial goal was freeing the women and driving them to safety using the Silva's transportation, nothing more. Revenge and justice would come later.

Beckett glanced at his watch. 7:30 p.m. On the other side of the kitchen window, the sun had sunk towards the horizon, the sky splashed with faint wisps of pink and orange amidst an inky blue. He felt a familiar shift, the dropping of a metaphorical visor as his soldier's instincts took over. A sense of calm descended, steadying his hammering heart. He rolled his neck and squared his shoulders. *No time like the present...* "Ready?"

Armando and Humberto exchanged a tense look, then nodded. They were as ready as they'd ever be.

Beckett led the way towards the rear of the house, weapons concealed beneath their jackets. Exiting through the rear door, they crossed the courtyard and slipped into the adjacent alleyway. Humberto's car was parked in a nearby lot, their transport to the stash house.

They moved swiftly down the alley and across a stretch of wasteland. The car was in sight, but halfway there a sudden burst of intense light illuminated the space. Blinded and disoriented, they halted in their tracks.

"Don't move!" a voice shouted as they were encircled by armed men.

Armando and Humberto raised their weapons, but with the light shining in their eyes and their opponents mere silhouettes, Beckett knew it was hopeless. He gripped the rifle slung over his shoulder, assessed his chances of walking away from this, and lowered it again.

"Stand down," he muttered, raising his hands. "Do it!"

Reluctantly Armando and Humberto lowered their weapons as cruel laughter echoed around the open space. Through the haze of the spotlights, a figure came into view. It was Beckett's first time meeting Raul Silva, but he clocked him immediately.

"Well, well, look what we have here," Raul sneered. "The three musketeers. The three amigos. All ready for action but nowhere to go. What a shame." His grin widening malevolently, he walked right up to Beckett, his lips almost brushing his ear as he spoke. "You've fucked up big time, English," he sneered, as his men forced Armando and Humberto to their knees. "It's over. You're mine."

50

With Raul Silva's mocking laughter filling his ears, Beckett allowed the armed men to push him to his knees. His mind raced, searching for a way out. But there were four of them including Raul, all armed and looking for any excuse to open fire.

"You really believed you could take on the might of the Silva organisation?" Raul asked, delight dancing in his eyes. "I mean, it's brave. It's also very stupid. *Sim? Bastardos estúpidos.*"

He laughed and looked at his men, permitting them – or maybe ordering them – to join in. They did as they were told, emitting a low humourless chuckle.

Beckett remained poised, still analysing his options. But they were hopelessly outgunned.

Suddenly Armando spoke up, his voice cracking with raw desperation. "Where is she, Raul? Where's my wife?"

At this, Raul focused in on him, the smug grin on his face widening. But before he could answer, Armando leapt to his feet and pulled a concealed pistol from his waistband, aiming it squarely at Raul's head. "Bastard. What have you done with her?"

Chaos erupted. Raul's men snapped up their weapons, shouting and gesturing wildly at Armando, their shouts merging into a cacophonous roar. Time slowed. Beckett's focus zoomed into macro. He saw the killing rage contorting Armando's face, his finger tightening on the trigger of his gun, and he saw the men ready to blow him away the second he pulled it...

"Armando, put it down." Beckett's voice was stern, unwavering.

Eternity ticked by. Then, slowly, Armando lowered his gun.

Raul's men swarmed him, wrenching away the weapon as Raul backhanded Armando viciously across the face. "Don't worry, Lopes, you'll die soon enough," he snarled. "Along with your pathetic friends. But not yet. Not until my father has seen you."

Armando said nothing; he just glared at Raul with pure hatred in his eyes. Beside him Humberto had the same expression. As Raul's men stripped them of their weapons, Beckett stayed compliant. The situation was dire, with no obvious way out presenting itself, but he had to hold his nerve. He glanced between Armando and Humberto, communicating to them with a firm nod to stay strong, to remain calm. Armando's twitching jaw and clenched fists suggested another imminent eruption, but Beckett locked eyes with him and subtly shook his head. Rage wouldn't save them. They had to be patient. Their moment would come.

It had to.

The stench of sweat and gun oil surrounded them as Raul's thugs hustled them to their feet and shoved them forward. They were marched to the end of the yard and around a corner where a large black van was waiting, its rear doors open.

"Inside," one of the men growled.

Beckett did as instructed, climbing all the way in and sitting on the cold floor with his back to the wall. He watched as Humberto and then Armando clambered into the van, followed by two of the gunmen. Outside he could hear the caw of seabirds and the distant sounds of traffic, but his thoughts were elsewhere.

How had Raul known where they were?

He closed his eyes, searching for an answer. Did they know of Humberto's meeting with Antonia and had been watching him? Maybe; but Beckett didn't think so. The older man was haunted by his past mistakes, but he was also an ex-intelligence operative and that sort of training never left you. He would have been careful.

So, what then?

It could have been anything – a neighbour under Silva's control, a scout who'd got lucky. Yet Beckett couldn't shake a nagging thought…

Maria.

Had she betrayed them?

If so, it was on him alone. Emotions had clouded his judgement. That wasn't like him. A bitter resentment gnawed at his nerves but he pushed it down. He couldn't deal with it now. Later.

The doors of the van slamming shut jolted him back to the moment. As he looked up, the two gunmen grinned, their assault rifles trained on him and Armando. The van rocked as Raul and the third gunman climbed into the cab and the engine roared to life. No one spoke as they set off. No one moved except to allow for the sway of the vehicle as it negotiated the cobbled streets.

Beckett lowered his head. Positioned where he was behind the driver's seat, he could pick out low murmurs coming through the wall of the cab. He closed his eyes, straining to hear. They were speaking hurriedly in Portuguese, but he could pick out the salient points of their conversation.

"Are we taking them to Eagle House?" he heard the driver ask.

A pause and then Raul: "Normally, yes. But with the deal going down tonight and Barbosa's monkeys still sniffing around, we'll do this at my father's house. It might involve a bit of a clean-up on your part later, but it will be a nice present for him. Killing these rats will be a fine way to celebrate the deal going through."

Beckett exhaled slowly. Right now he saw no clear way of turning the odds in their favour. They were captives, being delivered to their executioner as part of the evening's entertainment. He had never felt so powerless. So filled with impotent rage.

He watched the night shadows slide past the van's tiny windows. His entire life had prepared him for situations like this. He would stay watchful, ready. If any opportunity presented itself, he would grab it. But time was running out and every second that ticked by brought them closer to becoming trophies for Emilio Silva.

That couldn't happen.

He wouldn't let it.

51

Beckett had been following the van's journey in his head as they drove out of town and headed north. Fifteen minutes later the vehicle slowed and he heard the crunch of gravel, signalling they'd reached the gates of the Silva estate. Raul spoke into the intercom and, after a pause, they set off again, ascending the sloping driveway towards the main house.

It took them another ten seconds to reach the top of the drive, and once the van had stopped for a second time, the back doors were flung open.

"Out," a voice said. "Now."

One of the gunmen shuffled to the back of the van and shoved the three of them out into the night, where they were bustled into a line-up facing the main building.

Raul stepped up to them, chin raised, up on the balls of his feet, his eyes gleaming in amusement. "Look at the three of you. Not so tough now, huh?" He stepped back and spat on Beckett's boots. "Dumb English fuck!"

He was after a reaction, a physical response so his men could administer a retort by opening up his lip with the butt of a rifle. But Beckett did nothing. He said nothing. Instead he glanced around, moving only his eyes as he took in his surroundings. The main residence was all one level, angular and sprawling, with huge windows and a flat roof. The lights were on in most of the rooms and through the glass he counted two armed guards, plus one more on the front door, making six including the three standing over them. On his reconnaissance outing, he'd counted six men in position at the stash house also. That was a lot of manpower. A lot of firepower, too.

They were nudged forward, rifle barrels digging into their kidneys as Raul led them through the main entrance of the house and into a vast hallway. The interior of the house was as Beckett had anticipated – cold marble, dark mahogany, artworks that screamed more of price than value. But while the grandeur was meant to impress, Beckett's trained eyes were assessing every surface and corner, looking for something he could utilise as a weapon or distraction. They passed by a door that led through to a large lounge area and what looked to be a dining room, but the rifles pressed against their backs allowed no openings.

Raul directed them into a room at the rear of the property that boasted a well-equipped bar, pool table and gym equipment. Displayed on the back wall was a neon sign: '*Salão de Jogos*' – Games Room. Huge bi-fold doors spanned the entire adjacent wall and the one opposite, suggesting that, when open, the room could blend with the outdoor area. A patio spread across the rear of the house, centring around a large pool, its waters shimmering with tasteful underwater lighting. Beckett noted the mountains in the distance, the dirt track running down the far side of the property, the lush grove of cypress trees over to the west. He'd already concluded this side of the house would be the optimum point of attack and would have been his next call after rescuing the women from the stash house. But that opportunity was now long gone.

He thought of the captive women, and the minutes ticking by.

He thought of Maria.

A sharp look from Humberto caught his attention as the largest of Silva's men herded them, rifle jerking, into the centre of the room. The remaining two thugs, their rifles now slung over their shoulders, carried the confiscated weapons to the pool table where they dumped them on the green baize.

One armed and ready, two occupied…

Beckett gauged the distance to the pool table. If he broke away, it would take him two seconds to grab the nearest Glock, another half-second to shift around enough to take out the man holding the assault rifle. But by that time the man would have opened up his chest with said weapon. Not an option. He stared at the guns for a moment longer, their cold steel reflecting the room's stark lighting as if mocking him.

Raul, relishing every second of the show, sauntered over to the pool table to examine the stash. "Wait. Are these… ours?" he asked, frowning, doing the whole 'dumb cop' routine.

"Fuck you!" Humberto hissed under his breath.

Beckett shot him a sharp look.

Raul picked up one of the Glocks and aimed it at Armando's head. Closing one eye, he puffed out his cheeks. "Bang! You're dead."

Armando visibly tensed, but held his tongue. Suddenly the door to the room swung open and an older man in a dark suit entered the room. Emilio Silva.

Previously Beckett had only seen him from a distance. Up close he was a real sight, his appearance almost unsettling. His yellowing skin looked to be pulled too tight over his hefty frame and his hair – jet black, the way only a bottle could provide – was coming out in large clumps, patches of his scalp visible across his rotund cranium. At first, Beckett wondered if it was the result of chemotherapy or alopecia, but as Silva circled the three men and then approached the pool table, he noticed him yank a tuft of hair from the nape of his neck.

So an anxiety condition, perhaps. Beckett had read about it somewhere. If that was the case, he only hoped he could add to that anxiety over the next few minutes. Because that's all he had – minutes.

At the sight of the guns, Emilio clenched his meaty fists and his face turned a shade of purple. "My own guns!" he growled, his grotesque double chin quivering as he spoke. "You steal from me and plan on killing me with my own fucking guns. How dare you!"

Damn it.

Maria had been adamant no one saw her swiping the weapons from the second stash house. But they must have. She hadn't betrayed them. It was a tiny, pyrrhic victory, but Beckett felt relieved.

Emilio Silva's eyes locked on Beckett's, heavy with loathing. "My own daughter, swayed by a snake like you. Turned against her father. Her family." He waved a finger in the air. "But don't worry, she will learn what happens to traitors soon enough."

Beckett remained still, but fury boiled inside of him as he recalled Maria's words, her childhood abuse at the hands of this monster. It took all his self-control not to lunge for the evil bastard and grab him by the throat. He'd crush his windpipe and rip it clean out.

"I know all about you," he replied quietly. "You think you're some kind of criminal mastermind, but you're just a vicious lowlife. A thug. You destroy lives, steal innocent people from their homes to sell for… what? Profit? Guns? Power? You're a father: how could you? But then, I also know what kind of sick and twisted 'father' you are."

Silva marched up to him, his eyes all but bulging from his head as he addressed him. "You shut your mouth, English," he snarled, spearing a finger into Beckett's sternum. "I'll make you regret every word. You'll rue ever walking into my town, believe me."

Beckett didn't flinch. "If you plan on killing us, get on with it then."

From behind his father, Raul let out a chuckle. "Hold on. Let's not get ahead of ourselves," he said. "You clearly think you're a big deal, a threat. But to us you are mere pests, vermin that we need to deal with – *at some stage*. Tonight, however, we have a more pressing engagement." He walked up to Beckett, a supercilious smile plastered across his face. "But don't worry, English. It will happen soon. You will all die."

"Oh yes. I'm going to enjoy very much killing you," Emilio hissed, his face inches away. "My men will keep you here until tonight's business has concluded. That way we will have more time. We can ensure the process is very long and very painful. You'll suffer for hours, maybe even days." He turned to include Humberto and Armando in his glare. "All of you."

"What about Maria?" Beckett asked. "Where is she?"

Silva glanced at his son and Beckett caught doubt flashing across Raul's face. It was only fleeting, but he was trained to notice such things. They didn't know where she was. That was good.

"Don't worry, my friend," Silva sneered. "We will find her. There is nowhere in the country she can hide from us. That girl has betrayed me for the last time. It pains me, but she will pay for this." He moved over to stand in front of Humberto, squaring up to him. "Her and your pathetic daughter."

Humberto let out a roar, like the noise a caged animal might make. "You piece of shit. You son of a whore." He spat in Emilio's face, sending the smug bastard reeling.

Beckett saw the punch coming before it happened. Raul surged forward, smashing his fist into Humberto's stomach and bending him in two. As Humberto doubled over, gasping for breath, Raul stepped back, ready for another strike.

No.

Leaping instinctively to Humberto's defence, Beckett positioned himself between him and Raul.

"What the fuck do you think you're doing?" Raul cried. He swung his hand towards Beckett's face, but Beckett saw it coming and caught his wrist in a swift counter.

"Fuck you!" Raul hissed as Beckett, his jaw rigid, applied pressure to the joint even though he knew the advantage would be short-lived. A second later a rifle butt slammed into his solar plexus, knocking the air from his lungs and forcing him to his knees.

From somewhere in the room he heard Emilio's laughter. "So, this is the brave Englishman everyone was worried about?"

He heard Raul telling someone to "finish him".

Bracing himself, he awaited the inevitable blow. It came fast, crunching against the back of his head and mashing his senses. It felt as if his skull had splintered open. It felt as if he was going to die. But he only had a split second to process the intense agony, before his face met the floor and darkness consumed him.

52

Way across town, Martim was waiting in the shadows outside the dilapidated old hotel the Silvas called Eagle House. Beside him his brother Paulos shifted with pent-up energy, like a well-trained attack dog straining against its leash. He was excited.

They both were.

Above them the night sky was empty of stars, just an endless void of blackness. A heavy stillness hung in the air, as if the night itself was holding its breath. The occasional scuttling of a rat or the distant hoot of an owl did little to break the men's concentration, waiting like two deadly predators for their night's work to begin.

"This is bullshit. What's taking them so long?" Paulos growled, his fingers drumming against the grip of his gun beneath his jacket.

Martim placed a restraining hand upon his brother's arm. "Patience. Our time will come."

A few moments ago Miguel had texted him from Barbosa's car. They were close and the plan remained the same: wait for the truck to arrive, then move in.

With pleasure.

Martim kept his eyes on the stash house and the two armed guards on sentry duty out front. He sucked in a deep breath, his senses on high alert, attuned to the slightest sound or movement. He was trained for moments like this, his skills honed over decades spilling blood on command without mercy or hesitation. Now in his forties, he was a master of his vile craft – killing wasn't just a job for him, but an art form. He took pride in it, refining his techniques and staying abreast of advancements in technology. He had studied human anatomy so he could kill more efficiently, learned how to paralyse his targets so he could prolong their suffering. He still got a deep thrill from watching the light fade from his victim's eyes.

It was safe to say he got real satisfaction from his work.

The growl of an approaching engine interrupted his thoughts. An old military truck rumbled over the hillside, making its way towards them. Paulos let out an eager gasp as it came to a stop in front of the stash house.

"This is it."

Martim smoothly drew his pistol from its holster and began to attach a suppressor to the muzzle. Beside him Paulos did the same, their movements synchronised.

They watched as the truck driver climbed out of the cab, his silhouette highlighted by the string of lights that ran around the perimeter of the courtyard. Oblivious to the eyes trained on him, he stretched his back, glancing briefly at the twilight sky. The smile on his face hinted at a job well done, perhaps the thought of a cold beer waiting for him once he'd signed off the delivery.

He could be an innocent, he could be part of Silva's crew, Martim didn't know. And he didn't care.

Silently Martim got out of the car, raising his gun as he approached. The armed sentries had now left their post and were speaking to the driver. But not for long. Three coughs in rapid succession, three flawless headshots, and the driver and the two sentries were eliminated in less than a second.

Alerted by the noise of the falling bodies, two more guards came rushing out of the building, fumbling to raise their weapons. But their fate was already sealed. With two clean shots, Paulos dropped them both, knocked backwards as if struck by an unseen force. Five seconds. Five targets. All textbook kills. Neutralised with ruthless efficiency.

Paulos led the way up the steps and opened the door for Martim to slip through. He entered the stuffy confines of the old reception area, his aim sweeping left and right. But the place was empty, quiet.

Too quiet.

He could hear the static hum of a radio playing somewhere, but that was all. Sticking to the wall, he made his way towards an open doorway that was once presumably an office. He leaned around the doorframe. There was no one in sight, but his heightened senses detected muffled breathing. He narrowed his eyes, listening. Two of them, no doubt pressed against the wall adjacent to the door, ready to take him out the second he entered.

Glancing over his shoulder, he informed his brother with a swift wave of his hand what he'd discovered. Moving past the doorway he pictured the two men on the other side of the wall, the muzzle of his pistol swaying up and down until he was confident of their positions. He fired. Four shots. One to the head, one to the heart of each man. He heard a gurgle, a cry, and then the unmistakable sound of two bodies hitting the ground.

Giving his brother a sly grin, he poked his head around the door. Two dead guards, just as he'd thought. He'd got one of them in the temple and the heart as planned, the other had been crouching lower than he'd imagined and had died from a single headshot above the ear. A good result regardless.

He beckoned his brother over. Six guards, dead. That was all of them as far as he was aware, but there was no room for complacency in these situations. Together they moved over to the entrance to the main corridor, guns drawn, eyes and ears alert for danger. The only light came from a stark blue strip light hanging precariously from the ceiling. Moving along the corridor they could hear muffled wails from behind the doors, still numbered from when the place was a hotel. Martim opened door number one, the young woman on the bed cowering under the covers as the light speared across the room.

Paulos opened the next door along and whistled. "Very nice," he said, chuckling to himself. "Hey, do you think we've got time to…?"

"No!" Martim barked. "Don't be stupid. This is business."

Paulos shut the door, nodded. "What now?"

Martim holstered his gun. "We load them onto the truck. Once Miguel and the others arrive, we'll set this shitty hotel alight and drive the women to Barbosa's seaport. Castellano gets his shipment, the boss gets paid in cash and product, we get a nice bonus. Who knows, there may be time for you to enjoy yourself before we deliver to the Mexicans. Either way – mission accomplished."

"Yes, brother." Paulos grinned. "Mission accomplished."

53

A cacophony of sounds swirled in Beckett's consciousness, stirring him sluggishly from the void. He clung to the darkness for a moment, but the insistent throbbing in his head could not be ignored. Something was wrong.

Something was very wrong.

Shit!

He opened his eyes and everything snapped into focus, an explosion of bright light sending spikes of fresh pain shooting through his skull. He saw the pool table, the pile of weapons; he saw the man standing over him with an assault rifle aimed at his head. It all came crashing back. The ambush, the sadistic comments from Silva, then a final burst of white-hot pain before oblivion took hold.

"Hey, man, you okay?"

He looked to his left to see Armando and Humberto. Like him, they were sitting with their backs to the wall but had not been tied up. Presumably, Silva didn't think it was necessary, seeing as there were three AK-47s pointed at them. Beckett reached up and touched the back of his head. He was still bleeding but the wound wasn't deep.

Humberto gave him a resigned smile. "I was worried for a moment there…"

"No. The old brain box is a bit sore," Beckett whispered, "but I've had worse beatings. I'll live."

"Yeah, but for how long?" Armando said, the bitterness in his voice unmistakeable.

As Beckett's awareness spread, he saw the Silvas on the other side of the room. Emilio was seated on a workout bench, his posture loose but his face taut as he fiddled with a dark tuft at the front of his hairline. Raul stood over him, his hands on his hips. They looked to be in deep discussion. Beckett was unable to hear what was being said, but the older man kept lifting his watch and showing it to his son. They were preparing to leave.

Which was the worst thing that could happen.

That meant the deal was about to go down. If that truck left São Lourenço with the captive women on board, their chances of getting them back were zero. They would be gone, doomed to a life of misery and pain. He could not – *would not* – allow that to happen.

A diversion was required, a few seconds of chaos he could exploit to shift the odds back in their favour. And it needed to happen soon.

"Mike, we're running out of time," Humberto hissed. "What do we do?"

"Give me a second," Beckett replied. "I'm thinking."

Armando's voice trembled with desperation. "I can't let them take Lina. I can't lose her."

As Beckett was considering his next move, Rodrigo Silva entered the room. Spotting Beckett slumped on the floor, and seeing who he was with, his eyes flashed with malevolence. He swaggered over to them, a cruel smirk curling his lips.

"Shit. It appears things have gone bad for you guys, huh?" He leaned over to examine the wound on Beckett's head and stuck out his bottom lip in an over-the-top show of compassion. The way a parent might do to a small child. "That looks painful. Damn!"

"It's just a scratch," Beckett replied. "I've had worse."

"You'll get worse," Rodrigo spat, turning his attention to the others. "You'll all get worse." He ruffled Beckett's hair before pulling a gun from behind his back and pointing it between his eyes. "You three sons of bitches are going to regret ever hearing the name Silva. You'll regret ever standing up to the might of my family." His cocky expression turned sour as he ground the muzzle of his pistol into the skin on Beckett's forehead.

Beckett remained poker-faced. He wasn't going to give this lowlife the satisfaction of seeing him in pain.

Rodrigo dug the hard metal into his skull for a few seconds longer before letting the gun drop. Laughing, he looked around for his father and brother. "I see you've been having fun without me." He strode over to them, returning the pistol to his waistband as he did. "We need to get going."

The elder Silva turned to look at him. "It's all good?"

"Oh yes, Father. The delivery driver rang me when he was twenty minutes away from Eagle House. He should be arriving about now. We need to get over there and start loading up the shipment."

Beckett braced himself as Silva's laughter filled the room.

"My word, what a day. I am so proud of my two sons. You know this? You have both outdone yourselves."

Rodrigo and Raul exchanged triumphant smiles.

"Thank you, Father," Rodrigo said. "But what are the extra men doing here – shouldn't they be at Eagle?"

Silva, still laughing, glanced at him. "What do you mean?"

"As I was arriving I saw two cars driving up to the property. I assumed you'd called in extra muscle, no?"

"What are you talking about?" Raul asked. "Where are these cars?"

"Outside. In the driveway," Rodrigo said, pointing through the glass doors as impatience raised his voice. "They've just pulled up and…" He trailed off as the realisation hit him.

"Fuck!" Silva yelled. "Barbosa…!"

Everyone twisted instinctively towards the windows as a barrage of automatic gunfire tore through the room, shredding the glass doors inwards with an ear-splitting crash. For an instant, shock paralysed the room. Then as more gunshots erupted, Silva leapt at Raul, pushing him in front of him. Two of the armed guards raised their assault rifles and returned fire, shards of glass and spent cartridges spraying across the tiled floors.

The man guarding Beckett and his friends was still in position but with his attention now seized by a much bigger threat. Seeing an opportunity, Beckett was on his feet in a second. As a hail of bullets pockmarked the back wall he lunged forward, colliding with the burly man and using his momentum to knock the rifle aside. They crashed into the pool table and grappled briefly before Beckett landed a solid elbow to the underside of the man's jaw, knocking him unconscious.

"Move!" he yelled, diving for cover behind the pool table alongside Armando and Humberto as bullets continued to rattle the room. One of Silva's men was caught in the onslaught, his body convulsing as the hot lead ripped through his chest and belly. Reaching up, Beckett grabbed one of the assault rifles from the pool table, clocking the large black SUV that had skidded to a stop on the back lawn and the five armed men advancing on the property.

He returned to his cover behind the pool table, holding the rifle to him, the cool metal against his cheek like the embrace of an old friend. This was it. The kingdom really was coming down around them. Barbosa's men were here to wipe out the Silva organisation and wouldn't care who Beckett and his allies were. They were here to clean up. To leave no witnesses.

Beckett grabbed Armando's shoulder. They had to move. Because if they stayed in this room a moment longer, they were dead men.

54

Bullets tore through the room from every direction. Deafening cracks merged with shattering glass and splintering wood.

Staying low, Beckett reached up and grabbed more weapons off the pool table, pocketing one of the Berettas and distributing the rest to Armando and Humberto. They didn't speak, they didn't have to. Each man knew what was expected of him. And what they needed to do.

The air was thick with dust, making it hard to tell who was who and which side they were on. But that wasn't a problem for Beckett. They were all the enemy.

Raising himself, he squeezed off controlled pairs, dropping two of Barbosa's men storming in from outside. Glancing around he saw Raul and Rodrigo huddled behind the gym equipment returning fire; Emilio crouched behind the bar counter doing the same. But more men were appearing from the darkness, a seemingly endless supply of armed thugs.

Two cars, Rodrigo had said.

Ten men, at least.

But it wasn't just Barbosa's men they had to worry about.

Through the gloom, Beckett spotted Rodrigo looking his way, weapon raised, ready to take him out. *Shit.* He wasn't going to get a clear shot in time. He twisted around, going for it anyway, before a loud crack muted his hearing and Rodrigo's head snapped back, a perfect 'O' right between the eyes.

Beckett looked back, saw Armando's gun raised, saw the determination in his eyes. "Thanks," he told him.

"Believe me, it was my pleasure. Now let's move."

Staying close to the ground, they made their way through the perforated walls of the games room into a hallway littered with debris. Beckett led the way towards the front of the house. But nearing the entrance they heard the unmistakable roar of an engine, and as they burst through the door they were greeted by the sight of more gunmen piling out of a third SUV. Beckett snapped off shots, firing as he moved, taking out two of the thugs while he leapt for cover around the side of the house. Humberto hustled in behind him. Armando followed, but not before the ex-soldier had emptied the magazine of his AK-47, spraying bullets indiscriminately into the throng as he screamed into the sky.

Humberto's car was parked two hundred metres away over the hillside. To reach it they'd have to expose themselves and to go now would be suicide. But if they didn't go soon, the truck would be gone and with it any chance of saving the women. While everyone grasped the gravity of their situation, Beckett was also concerned with ensuring Armando's desperation didn't lead to recklessness.

"This is bad," Humberto yelled, before leaning around and firing off a few shots. "There's too many of them."

As Beckett racked his brain for an escape strategy, he heard footsteps behind him. Swinging around, rifle in hand, he saw Raul Silva running towards them. Somehow he'd escaped the carnage in the games room and was no doubt sneaking down the side of the property to safety. He saw Beckett and the others but didn't stop running.

"You motherfuckers," he snarled. "This is all your fault."

Beckett's first instinct was to eliminate this new threat, but he paused. Could they exploit Raul's presence somehow? He was on edge, not thinking straight. That could work in their favour. Yet as Raul got closer, the extent of his despair became evident. Emitting a guttural cry, he launched himself at Armando, forcing him out into the open and using him as both a human shield and a distraction.

Beckett twisted on his heels, raising his rifle to react, but he was a fraction of a second too late. Before he could intervene, a bullet ripped through his friend's chest.

No!

Driven by cold rage, Beckett stepped out from the side of the house and unleashed a hail of bullets, taking out two of the assailants in quick succession. Raul, still hiding behind Armando, discharged his weapon into the final gunman before shoving Armando's limp body aside and sprinting away.

"*Bastardo!*" Humberto yelled, firing after him. But he was already gone.

Pushing Humberto back to the relative safety of the house, Beckett waited. He could hear the distant rattle of gunfire from the games room, but out here it was quiet. Testing the waters, he fired off a couple of rounds. He got nothing back. He waited a second more. Good enough.

Breaking cover, he rushed over to where Armando lay sprawled on the driveway. A deep crimson stain had spread across his shirt.

"Armando. Can you hear me?" Beckett's voice was raspy as he knelt beside him.

"I'm okay," he gasped. "I'm alive."

Beckett offered him a stern smile. Yes, he was alive. But for how long? He pulled back his friend's shirt to examine the wound.

Bugger.

It was bad.

"We need to get him to a hospital," he told Humberto. But Armando grabbed his wrist.

"No, Mike. The women... Lina... You have to get to them!"

Conflicted, Beckett hesitated. But then he heard it. The sound of a car engine revving up. He locked eyes with Humberto. "Stay with him," he instructed taking the old man's hand and placing it over the wound. "Do what you can. I'll be back in one minute."

Cautiously Beckett moved along the perimeter of the estate until he had eyes on the rear of the house. Both SUVs were still parked, one with its engine running, and there were dead bodies sprawled over the patio and on the floor of the games room. Just three men were left standing, now combing through the wreckage and casually putting down their dying foes as if it was a mere inconvenience. From the looks of it, they were Barbosa's men.

Beckett crouched in the shadows, straining his neck to locate Silva and Rodrigo amongst the chaos of fallen bodies. The sound of a door creaking open caught his attention and, looking round, he saw a man emerge from the rear of one of the vehicles. At least, his face was that of a man – he had the receding hairline and weathered skin – but he had the body of a pre-teen boy. He must have been only five feet tall, if that, with slack shoulders and next to no muscle. But despite his diminutive stature, the man's eyes shone with predatory menace as he surveyed the scene.

Salvador Barbosa.

Beckett watched from his vantage point as the notorious crime lord entered what remained of Silva's games room and walked up to a body lying on the floor. Leaning out as far as his cover allowed, Beckett saw it was Emilio Silva. Somehow, despite the horrific barrage he'd sustained, he was still clinging stubbornly to life. His clothes were torn, one shoe was missing, and his face was smeared with streaks of red, yet his eyes remained lucid, filled with animal panic as Barbosa stepped over him.

Barbosa lolled his head to one side, surveying the fallen man quizzically as if pondering a strange new life form. He appeared vaguely amused by Silva's persistence as the fallen man waved his hand in the air, begging for mercy. But he was talking to the wrong man.

In one fluid movement, Barbosa reached into his jacket, pulled out a chrome pistol and shot Silva in the face, sending a burst of bright crimson splattering up the wall behind him. Then, brushing the flecks of blood and brain matter from his sleeve, Barbosa casually strolled back to his waiting vehicle.

Retreating into the shadows, Beckett ran a quick assessment. Just three men left. Four including Barbosa. He preferred those odds. Now if he could just… Wait.

His heart dropped into his belly. Barbosa's men, the ones already in town who he'd seen at the stash house yesterday evening – they weren't here.

They never had been.

Shit!

They were already at the stash house. Probably loading the women onto the truck at this very moment.

Rushing back to where Humberto was waiting, he found Armando now barely conscious. If he was to survive, he needed proper medical attention, and fast.

"Help me," Beckett told Humberto, grabbing Armando's arm and hoisting him upright. He was a big man, and heavy, but Beckett gritted his teeth against the strain. Together they lifted him to his feet, and with an arm over each of their shoulders, made their way down the driveway towards the road. It would take them five minutes to reach Humberto's car. From there it was another ten minutes to the stash house. Once there, Beckett planned on instructing Humberto to take Armando to the hospital while he took on Barbosa's goons alone. He knew Humberto wasn't going to like that idea. And he didn't like it too much, either. But it was the only option they had.

They moved steadily through the grounds and down towards the open road. In the distance Beckett heard the roar of an engine, and glancing back he saw Barbosa's vehicle leaving the Silva estate via the dirt track they'd used to get here. If they kept going that way for another fifteen minutes it would bring them out by the stash house.

It was going to be close.

Too close.

Beside him Armando groaned weakly. His eyes stayed closed, but he managed to whisper faintly, "Save… Lina… the others…"

"Don't worry," Beckett told him. "She'll be fine. So will you."

As the three men stumbled out onto the roadside, car headlights cut through the darkness. Hand on his Beretta, Beckett braced himself as the vehicle skidded to a halt in front of them. He raised the pistol as the window rolled down to reveal the driver.

"Maria!" he gasped, dropping his aim. "What the hell are you doing here?"

"It looks like I'm saving your asses," she replied. "Now get in! Quickly!"

55

Beckett waited until the Silva estate was out of sight before shifting around in the passenger seat to face Maria. The muscles around her eyes and jawline were rigid with concentration and she was gripping the steering wheel as if her life depended on it.

"What are you doing, coming back here?" Beckett asked, checking both wing mirrors for any signs of a tail. But the road behind was dark and empty. "You were supposed to be picking Antonia up and getting out of town."

Maria kept her gaze fixed firmly ahead. "Lucky for you I came back though, huh?" Streetlights flared past in a blur, casting fleeting, contrasting patterns on her face. Her eyes were wide and unblinking.

"But my Antonia?" Humberto piped up from the back seat. "She is safe?"

"Yes. I went to her house like we discussed," Maria continued, as Humberto squeezed his hands together in prayer and thanked her. "She's a stubborn one but I finally convinced her to leave. We were driving out of town, heading to a hotel over in Luzimar. But on the way we passed three large SUVs with blacked-out windows coming the other way, heading for São Lourenço. They looked so out of place on that quiet road, I knew it was trouble. I couldn't get them out of my head. So I dropped Antonia off at the hotel and doubled back. I had to see for myself what was going on."

"It was Barbosa," Beckett told her. "Him and his men."

Maria's eyes clouded for a second. "My father…?" She shot Beckett a look. But she knew. He didn't need to say. "And my brothers?"

"Rodrigo is dead. Raul, though… he escaped. I don't where he is."

Maria nodded and returned her attention to the road. "And what were you doing there?"

"We were supposed to be over at the stash house as planned," Humberto chipped in. "But my darling son-in-law ambushed us. If Barbosa hadn't turned up when he did, we'd be dead as well. In a way, the vicious bastard did us a favour."

"Yes, well, let's not get too friendly with him," Beckett said, twisting around in his seat and regarding Armando. "How's he doing?"

Humberto shook his head. "Not good. He needs proper medical attention."

Maria puffed out a breath, her face a kaleidoscope of emotions as Beckett turned to face the road.

"I drove past the old hotel on the way here," she said, her voice strained with tension. "The truck has arrived and I saw two men standing outside. I didn't recognise them. They don't work for my father."

Beckett nodded grimly. "Barbosa's men. They're taking over the shipment and wiping the slate clean, eliminating any sign of your family's involvement."

They drove on in silence along the coastal road that wound up into the hills. Every minute that passed felt like an hour.

Finally, the stash house came into view down below, the bone-white moon above casting it in an eerie glow.

Maria cut the lights and rolled the car to a stop beneath a large cork tree that offered decent cover. In the valley below, parked in front of the stash house entrance and with its loading ramp already down, was the delivery truck. One of the men, the one with glasses who looked more like a bank manager than a killer, was standing at the rear of the vehicle, waving his gun at the line of women shuffling out of the building, gesturing for them to get on the truck. From this distance it was hard to make out faces, but the women looked exhausted and broken as if they hadn't eaten properly in days. The sluggish way some of them were walking made Beckett wonder if they'd been given some kind of sedative. It would make sense. Compliance made the bastards' job easier.

"Bastards," Maria whispered, echoing his thoughts.. "Treating those poor women like cattle."

Beckett nodded. But it wasn't the time for histrionics – only action.

"Maria, I need you to drive Armando to the nearest hospital," he whispered, tearing his gaze from the truck to address her. "He's bleeding out and he needs a doctor." Maria looked as if she was about to protest, but he continued before she had a chance. "Most likely they'll want to call the police when they see it's a gunshot wound, so let them. Tell them Salvador Barbosa is in town and has a beef with your family. Tell them Armando was out walking and got caught in the crossfire."

"But what about me?" she asked. "Remember who I am."

"You'll be fine. You've never been part of your father's business affairs, yes?" He gave her a hard look, and she nodded. "So you'll walk. There'll be questions to answer but you can manage that. I'm almost certain the police won't show up in time to help, but if we do walk away from this tonight, this creates a believable narrative. One that keeps us all out of trouble. Understood?"

Maria's eyes flared with determination. "But I want to fight. I can hold my own, you know."

"I don't doubt it," Beckett replied. "But right now Armando needs you."

He turned his attention back to the truck. No change. The women were still filing out of the building. He had hoped when he'd heard it was a military truck that it might be armoured, maybe bulletproof. But no such luck. Regardless, once all the women were loaded on, that would be his cue to move. He checked the mag on the assault rifle between his legs. It was a standard box magazine with a thirty capacity. He had about ten rounds left. Plus another ten in the Beretta. Enough. But if Barbosa and the rest of his men were on their way, he had to make each bullet count.

"Humberto, you go with Maria," he said. "I've got this."

Humberto scoffed. "No way. I'm coming with you!" Carefully he leaned Armando against the door.

"No, you're not," Beckett told him. "You've got Antonia to think of. She'll need her father now more than ever."

But the old man's face was set, his determination clear. "How can I look my daughter in the eye after this if I don't do all I can to protect my town and those poor innocent women? No. I've been living in fear for too long. It ends tonight."

The two men locked eyes for a moment. Then Beckett nodded. "Alright. We'll double back along the track and approach the hotel from the rear. That way we've half a chance of taking out the two hostiles without putting the women at risk."

"And if Barbosa shows up?" Maria asks.

"Then we'll deal with him too," Beckett replied, giving Humberto a reassuring wink. "The trees will provide good cover. But we've got to move. Now."

Humberto shunted over to the door. "Let's go."

As Beckett opened the car door, Maria reached out and gripped his arm. "Come back," she whispered.

Beckett smiled, giving her hand a reassuring squeeze. "We'll certainly try."

He followed Humberto out into the cool night air. Down below, the sounds from the stash house grew louder and off in the distance was the sound of a car engine. The situation was undeniably stacked against them. But giving up wasn't in John Beckett's DNA.

He met Humberto's firm gaze and was reminded suddenly of his father. "You ready, soldier?" he asked.

"More than ever," Humberto replied, setting off towards the house. "Let's finish this."

56

Moonlight bathed the mountainside as Beckett and Humberto negotiated their way over the rugged terrain towards the rear of the stash house. The chirping of cicadas filled the air, a rhythmic counterpoint to the unsettling sounds coming from the front of the building – shouts, sobs, the shuffle of movement, the truck creaking as the women were herded onto the canvas-covered flatbed. Beckett pushed on, sliding down a rocky incline and grabbing hold of an exposed root to steady himself. As long as the truck was stationary, they had a chance. They had time.

Reaching the base of the mountain, they took cover behind a thick line of shrubs that provided them with a strategic view of the south side of the hotel and the truck parked out front. Still standing next to the truck was the tall man with the spectacles. The one Beckett had surmised to be the senior enforcer. Gesturing for Humberto to follow him, Beckett circled round to the rear of the building, evaluating the situation moment to moment as he went, the possible outcomes, the known threats. He knew there were at least two of Barbosa's men onsite. The one by the truck and likely one more inside. But going in guns blazing wasn't an option; the risks to the captured women were too high. If they were to pull this off, it had to be a stealth mission.

He turned to Humberto crouched beside him, his old eyes sharp in the pale moonlight. "I'll gain entry through the rear of the building and take down any hostiles inside," Beckett whispered. "You return to the tree cover and circle around to the front, but wait for my signal before engaging the guy there. First I'm going to try to draw him into the building, away from the truck."

Humberto nodded. Beckett waited until he'd melted away into the darkness before breaking cover and approaching the stash house. There he found a sash window with an old frame that was full of termites, easy enough to force open with a little effort. Gritting his teeth he pushed the frame upwards, wincing at the sound of splintering wood. Raising the assault rifle strapped over his shoulder, he waited. Ready. No one came.

He flung the rifle back over his shoulder and hoisted himself through the window into the darkened room beyond. The musty space was empty except for a single bed, unmade. He touched the back of his hand to the mattress, to the pillow. Both were warm. Someone had lain here recently.

Pulling the Beretta from his waistband, he eased open the door and moved silently down the corridor, senses alert for any sign of danger. Deserted rooms lay in a line down one side. Most of the doors were hanging open, revealing more unmade beds and items of clothing strewn on the floor. By now most of the women were on the truck, but as he crept along the corridor he heard the sound of voices and shuffling footsteps from upstairs.

Flattening himself against the wall, Beckett made his way towards the end of the corridor, which opened out into a reception area. As he got closer, footsteps clattered above his head, as if heading across a landing. He counted six pairs of feet, moving slowly, dragging their heels as they went. Then a seventh pair, heavy and blundering. A man. A large man.

Squatting in a dark alcove, Beckett watched as the six women descended the stairs in a single line and funnelled out through the old hotel's main entrance. Up close, the poor women looked even more dishevelled, walking like zombies on a death march, their hair unwashed, their clothes torn. There wasn't one of them that didn't have bruises on her arms and legs. Pushing down his rage, Beckett held his ground. As the last woman left the reception area, the door swung shut behind her, but there was no sign of Barbosa's man. Beckett held his breath. And waited.

Moments later the shaven-headed man with facial tattoos appeared from the stairwell. He strode into the centre of the foyer and stopped, glancing around, perhaps listening for signs of any stragglers. He was bigger than Beckett had remembered. Much bigger. The muscles across his shoulders and neck bulged out the back of a black sleeveless top, and strapped across this was a leather shoulder holster complete with gun.

Beckett gripped the handle of the Beretta.

Damn it.

It would be so easy to take the bastard out with a carefully placed headshot. But that would alert his friend outside and that person was an unknown variable. Beckett couldn't risk him hurting the women or using them as leverage.

This had to be done as quietly as possible.

And it had to be done now.

He lifted the AK-47 off his shoulder and leaned it, silently, against the wall. Then he slipped the Beretta back into his waistband.

Hands free. Now he was ready.

He left the alcove and stalked closer, intent on taking the man down from behind. A disabling kick to the knee, an arm around the neck as he yanked the pistol from its holster. Then squeeze. Ten seconds, the guy would be out for the count. Twenty more and he'd be dead. Holding his breath, Beckett advanced until…

Shit!

He was almost there when a floorboard creaked beneath him.

The man spun around. "*Você!*" he yelled, fumbling for his gun. But Beckett was already moving.

He lunged at him, leading with a vicious elbow to the man's throat, which incapacitated him enough for Beckett to snatch the gun from its holster and toss it down the corridor. Ready to finish this as quickly as possible, he darted behind him, trying for a chokehold, but the gasping brute suddenly reared up, staggering backwards and slamming Beckett against the wall hard enough to crack plaster. He tasted blood. His vision blurred. He lost his grip.

Suddenly on the defensive, Beckett moved with the blow of a vicious right hook, but couldn't lessen the impact entirely and it sent him staggering, his brain rattled. Shifting down the corridor, putting distance between the two of them, he was able to recover and then exploded into action, retaliating with a punch to the man's gut as he came for him. It was a solid punch, with his whole shoulder behind it, but the big bastard didn't budge. In fact, his momentum seemed to build as he drove hammering fists into Beckett's ribs. Twisting away, Beckett landed a punishing counterblow into the man's kidneys. Except the brute seemed immune to pain, consumed by animal rage.

A headbutt sent stars flashing across Beckett's consciousness and for a moment he faltered. He stumbled away down the corridor, the air now thick with the stench of sweat and blood as the tattooed man bared his teeth in a smug grin.

He thought he had him.

He almost did.

But in that split second of arrogance, Beckett channelled his remaining strength. On a roar he leapt forward and smashed the heel of his fist into the man's nose with a sickening crunch. Howling, the goon blindly charged forward, and seizing his moment, Beckett stepped aside and redirected the thug's momentum, sending him crashing into the back wall of the corridor. His huge skull hit the unyielding surface with a crack, and as he staggered back, Beckett grabbed him around the neck.

He hoped that was it.

It should have been.

But the man's strength was immense. Every sinew in Beckett's body screamed in protest as he tightened his grip around the behemoth's thick neck. They struggled, both gnashing their teeth and red-faced, locked in mutual fury.

The world seemed to slow as Beckett's grip tightened, the man's windpipe constricting against his forearm. The thorns and vines on the man's face turned a dark shade of purple.

"Come on, you bastard," Beckett growled in his ear. "Die!"

Every muscle in his body was on fire. He held on, squeezing harder, all his strength and energy focused on this one action.

There was a final moment of desperate thrashing before he felt something give and the man's body went limp. Gasping, Beckett rode the man's huge frame to the floor, still constricting the blood flow to his brain. He counted to ten, twenty, thirty. He released and let him slump the rest of the way to the floor.

Breathing hard, Beckett got to his feet. His bruised ribs throbbed and his face was numb, but there was no time to rest. Flinging the assault rifle back over his shoulder, he approached the hotel entrance, peering through the narrow gap between the double doors. The spectacled man was nowhere in sight. Beckett shifted his position, trying to get eyes on Humberto, but from inside it was impossible. Where was he?

The women were now all on the back of the truck, with the loading ramp up and the awning buckled tight. If the second man was now in the driving seat, Beckett had seconds to stop him.

Sliding the Beretta from his waistband, he slipped through the double doors to the outside, and once there he stopped. He listened. The growl of an engine could be heard over to the north, but the truck's engine was silent. Raising his gun, he sidestepped over to the edge of the porch, ready to move down the steps to the ground below.

"Hey, Paulos," a voice rang out. "What's taking you—"

Beckett froze as the man in glasses appeared from around the side of the truck, an impatient frown distorting his features. They saw each other in the same moment. The man reached for his weapon. Beckett took aim. But with the proximity of the truck… the women… If he didn't pull the trigger he was a dead man, but—

Suddenly a shot rang out and the man's head jerked forward, his glasses flying off as a cloud of red mist burst out of his skull. Beckett refocused to see Humberto standing several feet behind where the dead man now lay. His gun was raised and he wore a look of grim satisfaction.

Beckett ran down the steps and over to him as Humberto stepped over the fallen man. "Good work," he told him. "That's both hostiles eliminated. Now we need to drive these women to safety."

But before they could move, the distinct sound of a revving engine was heard and headlights sliced through the darkness on the edge of the property.

It was a black SUV, approaching fast. Too fast for them to get to the truck and drive it away in time.

"Barbosa!"

Beckett glanced at Humberto, his grip tightening on the Beretta. "This is going to get messy," he said. "Are you ready?"

Humberto nodded. "Ready as I'll ever be, soldier."

Good enough, thought Beckett.

One way or another, this would end tonight.

57

Barbosa's black SUV screeched to a halt thirty metres away, and as the doors flew open, three remaining gunmen erupted from the vehicle. Seeing their dead comrade sprawled on the ground, they instantly opened fire at Beckett and Humberto as they ran for cover down the side of the hotel.

"We need to get inside, draw them away from the truck!" Beckett yelled over the gunfire, nudging Humberto toward the hotel entrance. They sprinted up the steps, Beckett returning fire as he went, holding them back.

Shards of wood and plasterboard exploded around them as Beckett and Humberto hurled themselves through the damaged door, narrowly escaping the hail of bullets chewing through the building's decaying facade. An old chaise longue was blasted into confetti in their wake, and as they made their way across the dimly lit reception area, a bullet brought a chandelier crashing down in a shower of glass and sparking wires.

Taking cover behind two sturdy pillars on either side of the room, Beckett and Humberto prepared to retaliate. The three gunmen had now spread out and were approaching the building steadily, firing as they went. When the first stepped across the entrance, Beckett fired three rounds into his chest cavity, sending him into a macabre death dance before he hit the ground.

One down. Two to go.

But the bullet whizzing past Beckett's ear, so close he could feel it, told him the conflict was far from over.

He leapt for cover behind his pillar as a blistering return of fire punctured the back wall of the room, sending dust and debris flying.

"How are you doing?" he called over to Humberto, who was giving as good as he got, a pistol in both hands.

"Running low," came the reply.

Didn't Beckett know it.

Leaning his back against the pillar, he checked the magazine on the Beretta. Three rounds left. That was it. Across the room, one of Humberto's guns clicked empty. The situation was dire. Neither had enough firepower to win the standoff.

As Beckett watched, Humberto crouched and sighted along his pistol, taking out a second man with a headshot. Excellent shooting from the old soldier.

Two down. One to go. Two if you included Barbosa. Which Beckett very much did. And with so little ammo they had to be clever about this.

"We need to back off, make these last rounds count," he called out to Humberto. "If we pull them in deeper we can get out through the rear window and circle back, take them by surprise. It's not ideal but it's our only chance."

But Humberto had stepped out from his cover to better hear him, and before he could respond he was caught in a fusillade of bullets, his body jerking violently before dropping to the floor.

"Humberto!"

Beckett rushed to his side. Blood was already pooling beneath the older man as he quickly determined his injuries. He'd taken a bullet in the leg, above the knee and two more in the stomach. None of the shots were visibly fatal, but the resilient old soldier was down, maybe for good. Beckett dragged him away from the door and propped him up behind one of the pillars.

Grimacing in pain, he looked up at Beckett and shook his head. "Go…" he gasped. "Do what you have to do… Save the women…"

Beckett's gaze flicked to the open doorway. Barbosa was there now also, he and his remaining henchman approaching the hotel, weapons drawn and ready. Ten seconds and they'd be here.

Beckett turned back to Humberto, the loyalty within him wrestling with his strategic mind. If he left Humberto, Barbosa would surely kill him the second he stepped through the door.

"Wait," he said. "I've got an idea."

He grabbed the tattooed man he'd taken out earlier and dragged his lifeless body in front of the pillar obscuring Humberto from view. He then stealthily shifted over to the second pillar and lay down behind it.

As the gunshots ceased and chaos receded, a tense stillness settled in, the dusty air thick with tension and uncertainty. Beckett could now hear Barbosa and his man outside and sensed their unease.

He glanced over at Humberto, who had slumped forward but was still, thankfully, concealed behind the dead man. Beckett steadied himself, the only pressure now coming from his finger on the trigger of his gun. Three rounds left. He waited. A second ticked by. And another. In times like this it felt as if time had stopped, but to give in to impatience was like signing your own death warrant. He heard the wooden steps outside creaking with applied weight. He heard a self-assured chuckle. That was a good sign. Complacency.

He adjusted his grip on the Beretta.

Another second ticked by.

From his position behind the pillar, he sensed rather than saw the two men as they entered the hotel. One of them – Barbosa most likely – let out a cry.

"Ah, Paulos. Gone like your brother." He sounded almost nostalgic. "Such a shame."

Time seemed to warp, to stretch. Hyperaware, Beckett could discern the shuffle of footsteps and the intake of Barbosa's breath. But the moment had to be perfect. Attuned to the subtle nuances in the room, he heard the men getting closer, the same floorboards that had given him away earlier now his allies.

In one fluid movement he emerged from behind the pillar and dispatched both men with lethal headshots. Two rounds. Two kills. He still had it. Not leaving anything to chance, he sent his last bullet tearing through Barbosa's heart, the vile pig stumbling over on top of his fallen henchman.

Catching his breath, Beckett took a moment before jumping to his feet and hurrying to Humberto.

"It's over," he said, assessing his friend's injuries in more depth. Despite the fact he was bleeding profusely, there were three exit wounds and that was a good sign.

"I'm going to check on the women," Beckett told him. "Then I'll come back and get you. Can you hold on?"

"Sure. I'll be okay," he rasped. "Make sure this wasn't all in vain."

Standing, Beckett stepped over Barbosa's body and sprinted for the truck still loaded with the captive women. As he jumped up onto the back bumper, a collective gasp echoed from under the canvas awning, followed by movement as the women recoiled in fright.

"Hey, it's alright, you're safe now," Beckett called out in Portuguese, holding up his hands to placate the chorus of frightened whispers. "I'm here to help. I am a friend of Armando Lopes."

The panicked cries slowly died down as the women studied him with wide, fearful eyes. After a tense moment, one of the women edged forward, her entire body trembling.

"You are the Englishman?" she asked.

"Yes. That's right." Beckett gave a reassuring nod. "You're Lina? Don't worry. Everything is going to be okay."

Tears of relief flooded the woman's eyes. "Is Armando with you?"

"No. But he's safe," he said, not wanting to add more uncertainty to the pot. He'd explain soon enough, but now wasn't the time to bring up Armando's condition.

"Please try to remain calm," he urged the frightened group in a gentle tone. "I'll return in just a moment with my friend. Then we'll get you away from here and back to your families."

Having delivered his assurances, Beckett jumped down from the truck and headed for the stash house to fetch Humberto. A sharp pain speared into his side, and as the adrenaline subsided, he suspected at least one of his ribs was cracked. For now he shrugged it off. He'd dealt with worse. But he'd not yet reached the steps of the stash house when a figure staggered out from the shadows. Beckett stopped in his tracks, recognising who it was even in the pale moonlight.

Raul Silva.

"You motherfucker!" Raul spat, every word dripping with venom. "You son of a whore, you piece of shit!"

A freely bleeding arm dangled by his side, but in his other hand he brandished a gun which he pointed at Beckett. His eyes were wild with demented rage.

"This is all your fault." He waved his gun in the air. "This was my time to shine. I was going to finally step out from my father's shadow and leave this pathetic town. Then you came along. You ruined it all…"

Beckett remained still, his muscles tense, ready to react in a microsecond. He gauged the distance between the two of them. He noted Raul's uneven breathing, the way his trigger finger twitched, the slight sway to his stance indicating waning strength. But the man was unpredictable and had nothing left to lose. One wrong move and Beckett was dead.

"You took everything from me," Raul snarled. "Everything! And now it's time I return the favour. Starting with your life!"

Beckett braced himself. He had no gun and no immediate cover, but an opportunity nonetheless. Raul's fatigue and blood loss would have weakened his aim. Beckett's only chance now was that he'd fire and miss or the shot wouldn't be fatal. He readied himself to charge. If he heard the shot, it meant he was still alive. If he heard the shot, he'd have to reach him before he fired again.

"Time to die, English!" Raul sneered, raising the trembling gun with both hands.

Beckett inhaled sharply. Time to move.

With a roar he went at Raul, anticipating the deafening shot, the pain, the blackness.

Then it came. A loud crack that muted his ears. But he'd heard it. He was still moving. He felt wetness on his face as he propelled himself forward, ready to seize his one chance…

Except then he stopped, his boots skidding in the dirt as he saw the exit wound between Raul's eyes. He stared at Beckett for a moment, then crumpled face-first into the dirt.

Beckett wiped Raul's blood from his cheek and looked up to see Humberto propped against the doorway, one hand clutching his stomach, the other holding Barbosa's gun, aimed where Raul had stood. He met Beckett's eye.

"You know what, soldier?" he wheezed. "I damn well

enjoyed that." A grim smile spread across his lips before he collapsed, unconscious, onto the porch.

Beckett stepped over Raul's corpse. He felt nothing. He never did. He'd had a job to do and if people got in his way that was on them.

And this bastard deserved everything he got.

In the distance, sirens wailed through the darkness – help was on its way. He'd have to get his story straight, they all would, but with two organised crime groups wiped out this evening, he didn't think the authorities would be picking at their stories too deeply.

Gritting his teeth through the pain in his side, he scooped up Humberto and carried him to the cab of the truck.

It was over. It was done.

58

Beckett stood alone in the corner of Maria Silva's spacious front room, cradling a glass of red wine. Shafts of late evening sunshine streamed in through the windows, reflecting off the large gilded mirror above the hearth and bathing the space in a warm golden glow.

Laughter bubbled up from the other side of the room, where Antonia and Humberto were talking, the old man's face alight with joy as he regarded his darling daughter. As Beckett had thought, the bullets he'd taken weren't fatal, and after a few hours in theatre the doctors had given him the all-clear. They'd discharged him a day later. Confined to a wheelchair until he healed, he wouldn't be running marathons anytime soon, but he was a tough old soldier. He was alive, he was happy, and he had his daughter back.

Antonia, too, was like a different person to the timid soul Beckett had met up on the hillside a few days earlier. Today she seemed lighter, breezier, freer. Probably because she was. The trauma of her life with Raul Silva would still be there to deal with, of course, as would all that came with being his widow, but for now she looked as if she didn't have a care in the world. And she had her father back.

Watching the two of them talking and laughing together, Beckett felt a fleeting pang of envy, but he quickly shook it off. He was a tough old soldier too.

Maria caught his eye and smiled as she entered the room carrying a fresh bottle of wine. Once Beckett had spoken to the police, and the medics had attended to his injuries – cuts and bruises, mainly, plus a hairline fracture in one of his lower left ribs that would heal itself in time – Maria had driven him back here, where he'd slept for twelve hours straight in her guest bedroom. He'd told her it was one of Barbosa's men who had killed Raul, rather than Humberto, and didn't feel any qualms about the lie. Maria hated her family but these were good people, and if they were going to work together to turn the town around, it was best she didn't look at Humberto as the person who killed her brother.

Three days had passed since the assault on the stash house, but it already felt like a lifetime ago for Beckett. Having never planned on staying in São Lourenço longer than a night or two, he was already getting itchy feet. Although he'd thought of leaving immediately after learning the captured women were all safe and well, he owed these people a proper farewell, and today was the first time everyone was able to get together after the bloody events of that night. Armando had been discharged from hospital only that morning – after surgery on a punctured lung and a blood transfusion – and was well on the mend. Another tough soldier. He and Lina were expected at the house any time now.

Beckett sipped his wine. He wasn't sure what grape it was but it tasted nice enough, full of blackberries and spice. Maria caught his eye again and waved the fresh bottle at him, but he turned the offer down with a smile and a shake of his head. He didn't want to get drunk. He was leaving once the party was over.

Having contacts that were high-ranking officials meant Humberto had been able to smooth things over with the intelligence agencies, and they'd accepted the version of events he'd provided. As far as they were concerned, the rescue of the women was carried out solely by Humberto and everyone who died did so at the hands of the rival gang members. Whether they fully bought that story, Beckett was unsure, but they'd let them all go, and they weren't asking any more questions. That was good enough for him. Humberto would continue to monitor the situation, but it sounded as if the reports were already written up and the case closed.

A knock on the door and a flurry of activity across the room marked the arrival of Armando and Lina. As Maria led them into the room, warm embraces, words of gratitude, and shared laughter filled the air. Beckett remained where he was, clutching the glass of wine in front of him like a shield. He didn't go in for outward displays of emotion. Though he was glad to see the two of them looking so well.

Armando's torso was bandaged and he refused all hugs, but he let out a hearty laugh as Humberto lifted himself from his wheelchair to shake his hand. Beckett smiled as he watched the two of them so animated, filled with infectious joy at their survival and reunion.

Beside Armando, Lina held back, a protective hand over her stomach; but she too was glowing, and once more Beckett was reminded of the deep resilience of people.

She'd be fine.

So would the baby.

Indeed, her swollen belly was the next focus of attention, with Antonia and Maria cooing in excitement and rubbing it affectionately.

In the midst of all this, Beckett caught Armando's eye and

the two men shared a silent salute of mutual respect. Humberto waved for Beckett to join them, but he remained where he was, placating the older man with a grin and a raise of his glass. This was their moment, their celebration. It was their town. Not his.

He placed his glass down and wandered through the kitchen and out onto the expansive patio overlooking the mountain range beyond. The vivid scenery under the soft glow of early evening was spectacular – a green and gold valley cradled between mighty slopes of rugged terrain. Beckett breathed it all in, the fresh night air invigorating his battered soul.

São Lourenço. It was now a different place entirely, no longer held in his mind as the town he and his father had visited together. Due to this, he had been worried he might lose a part of his father's memory, but he needn't have worried. He would be reminded of General Hugo Andres Beckett every time he looked in the mirror, every time he acted on his instincts and did the right thing regardless of personal cost.

So, yes.

His time in São Lourenço would keep his father in mind after all.

He closed his eyes and offered up a silent heartfelt prayer of gratitude to the man who had gifted him so much wisdom and inner resilience, and who continued to sustain and guide him even from beyond the grave.

Hearing footsteps behind him, he turned to see Maria stepping out onto the patio. Despite him staying in her guest bedroom for the last few nights, she'd been occupied sorting out her family's estate and all the upheaval that came with it, so they'd not seen much of each other. There was a lot still unsaid. But Beckett preferred it that way.

"I thought I'd find you here," she said. "Avoiding the party?"

"I just wanted some air."

She turned to the view and smiled. "It's beautiful, isn't it?"

"It certainly is."

"How are you feeling?" she asked, turning to look at him.

An uncertain tension fizzed in the air between them.

"Never better," Beckett replied, holding her gaze. "But I think I should be—"

"Oh, wait!" She held up her hand to cut him off. "I have something for you."

She ducked back inside for a moment, returning with his faded holdall. "I found it at the house, in my father's safe. I managed to retrieve it before the police got to it. I checked; your passport is still inside. Not much else though," she added with a playful smirk.

Beckett shrugged. "I like to travel light." Which was an understatement. There was a toothbrush, a change of clothes, his father's watch. That was it. "May I?" he asked, holding out his hand to retrieve the bag.

But Maria held it to her chest playfully, refusing to relinquish it. Her dusky eyes lingered on his. "If I give you this, does that mean you're leaving?"

"I have to."

She kept hold of the bag. "No, you don't."

"I do. There's a bus leaving town in two hours. I plan to be on it."

Maria stuck out her bottom lip. "You're going tonight? No…"

"It's best this way. Believe me."

She lowered her head, looking up at him through her thick eyelashes. "Can't you stay just one more night?"

A lifetime passed between them. It was only a second.

Beckett sighed. "Fine," he conceded. "Maybe one more night."

Maria's full lips blossomed into an enigmatic smile. "Good. I'll leave you to the view. Don't be too long."

She ducked back inside, leaving Beckett alone once more. He rolled his shoulders back, drinking in the fresh air, feeling a rare moment of contentment wash over him.

One more night.

But come sunrise he would move on. He was too restless a creature now to settle anywhere, or with anyone, for long. There was a whole world out there for him to explore.

São Lourenço would endure and hopefully flourish again, not through his input but through the bonds formed between these good people. He could leave, satisfied its light would continue to shine the way his father's memory shone inside of him, guiding him every step of the way.

Wherever the road took him next, that path took him, whatever adventures or challenges lay around the corner, John Beckett would face them as he always had done – with courage, honour, and an unyielding instinct to combat injustice wherever he found it.

After all, some wars, once begun, lasted a lifetime.

THE END

WANT MORE?

READ 'THE BECKETT FILES'

To show my appreciation to you for buying this book I want to offer you a transcript of Beckett's top secret interview prior to him joining S-Unit.

You'll also get access to my VIP Newsletter plus an exclusive John Beckett novella (coming soon)

To sign up and get 'The Beckett Files' go here:

https://www.matthewhattersley.com/jb/

GET BECKETT BOOK 3:

THE CITY OF SUN AND VIOLENCE

In the jungles of Venezuela a deadly force is on the rise…

Get your copy by clicking here

CAN YOU HELP?

Enjoyed this book? You can make a big difference

Honest reviews of my books help bring them to the attention of other readers. If you've enjoyed this book I would be very grateful if you could spend just five minutes leaving a review (it can be as short as you like) on the book's Amazon page.

ALSO BY MATTHEW HATTERSLEY

Have you read them all?

———

The Acid Vanilla series

Acid Vanilla

Acid Vanilla is an elite assassin, struggling with her mental health. Spook Horowitz is a mild-mannered hacker who saw something she shouldn't. Acid needs a holiday. Spook needs Acid Vanilla to NOT be coming to kill her. But life rarely works out the way we want it to.

BUY IT HERE

Seven Bullets

Acid Vanilla was the deadliest assassin at Annihilation Pest Control. That was until she was tragically betrayed by her former colleagues. Now, fuelled by an insatiable desire for vengeance, Acid travels the globe to carry out her bloody retribution. After all, a girl needs a hobby...

BUY IT HERE

Making a Killer

How it all began. Discover Acid Vanilla's past, her meeting with Caesar and how she became the deadliest female assassin in the world.

FREE TO DOWNLOAD HERE

———

Stand-alone novels

Double Bad Things

All undertaker Mikey wants is a quiet life and to write his comics. But then he's conned into hiding murders in closed-casket burials by a gang who are also trafficking young girls. Can a gentle giant whose only friends are a cosplay-obsessed teen and an imaginary alien really take down the gang and avoid arrest himself?

Double Bad Things is a dark and quirky crime thriller - for fans of Dexter and Six Feet Under.

BUY IT HERE

Cookies

Will Miles find love again after the worst six months of his life? The fortune cookies say yes. But they also say commit arson and murder, so maybe it's time to stop believing in them? If only he could…

"If you life Fight Club, you'll love Cookies." - TL Dyer, Author

BUY IT HERE

ABOUT THE AUTHOR

Over the last twenty years Matthew Hattersley has toured Europe in rock n roll bands, trained as a professional actor and founded a theatre and media company. He's also had a lot of dead end jobs…

Now he writes high-octane pulp action thrillers and crime fiction.

He lives with his wife and daughter in Derbyshire, UK and doesn't feel that comfortable writing about himself in the third person.

COPYRIGHT

A Boom Boom Press ebook

First published in Great Britain in April 2023 by Boom Boom Press.

Ebook first published in 2023 by Boom Boom Press.

Copyright © Boom Boom Press 2015 - 2023

The moral right of Matthew Hattersley to be identified as the author of this work has been asserted by him in accordance with the copyright, Designs and Patents Act 1988.

All the characters in this book are fictitious, and any resemblance to actual persons living or dead is purely coincidental.

All rights reserved. No part of this publication may be reproduced, stored in a retrieval system or transmitted in any form or by any means, without the prior permission in writing of the publisher, nor to be otherwise circulated in any form of binding or cover other than that in which it is published without a similar condition, including this condition, being imposed on the subsequent purchaser.

Printed in Great Britain
by Amazon